TARA'S TRUCE

Kavita Kané is a former journalist and a bestselling author of seven books. She is considered a revolutionary force in Indian writing because she has brought in feminism where it is most needed—mythology. Her seven novels are all based on women in Indian mythology.

Her journey began as a journalist, with twin post-graduation degrees in English literature as well as mass communication and journalism from the University of Pune. With a career spanning over two decades, working with Magna Publishing and *DNA*, she eventually quit her job as an assistant editor at the *Times of India* to devote herself to writing full-time. Passionate about theatre, cinema and the arts, she is also a columnist, screenplay writer and a motivational speaker.

She currently lives in Pune with her husband, two daughters, two dogs and an uncurious cat.

Also by the author

Karna's Wife
Sita's Sister
Menaka's Choice
Lanka's Princess
The Fisher Queen's Dynasty
Ahalya's Awakening
Sarasvati's Gift

Kavita Kané

Published by
Rupa Publications India Pvt. Ltd 2023
7/16, Ansari Road, Daryaganj
New Delhi 110002

Sales centres:
Bengaluru Chennai
Hyderabad Jaipur Kathmandu
Kolkata Mumbai Prayagraj

Copyright © Kavita Kané 2023

This is a work of fiction. Names, characters, places and incidents are either the product of the author's imagination or are used fictitiously and any resemblance to any actual person, living or dead, events or locales is entirely coincidental.

All rights reserved.
No part of this publication may be reproduced, transmitted, or stored in a retrieval system, in any form or by any means, electronic, mechanical, photocopying, recording or otherwise, without the prior permission of the publisher.

P-ISBN: 978-93-5702-768-7
E-ISBN: 978-93-5702-846-2

Second impression 2024

10 9 8 7 6 5 4 3 2

The moral right of the author has been asserted.

Printed in India

This book is sold subject to the condition that it shall not, by way of trade or otherwise, be lent, resold, hired out, or otherwise circulated, without the publisher's prior consent, in any form of binding or cover other than that in which it is published.

My Aai

The strongest, most stubborn person I was blessed with was my mother, who actuated me to take to writing—a novel, specifically. And who inspired me till her very end, as I finished the edits of this book, while she quilted another piece—our last moments together.

CONTENTS

Prologue: The Two Taras	ix
1. The Brothers	1
2. The Vanaras	16
3. Kishkindh	37
4. The Quartet	50
5. Conditions and Confrontations	65
6. Turmoil	80
7. Sugriv and Ruma	94
8. Vali and Ravan	105
9. Nuptials	115
10. Matrimony	125
11. The Two Couples	140
12. The Curse	153
13. Combat and Conflict	168

14. Waiting	176
15. Love and Loyalty	185
16. Reappearance	200
17. In Exile	217
18. Retribution	229
19. Death and Disillusionment	241
20. The New King	255
21. The Saviour	269
22. War and Peace	284
Epilogue: Tara's Curse	296

Prologue
THE TWO TARAS

Do I wear white for a widow or red for a bride? Tara held the soft red silk in her hand and let it slip through her stiff fingers.

Was she a widow or a bride? The sorrow in her heart was crushing her. It was her wedding day today—just a week after her husband had been killed. And she was to wed the man who had been responsible for her husband's death. She was to marry her husband's brother. Sugriv. Vali's brother. Vali's killer.

As she sat on her bed in her palace chamber, she couldn't bear looking at the jewellery that was laid out for her. The gems in the jewellery blinked at her, mocking her inability to chart the course of her own fate. Her face was pale. Her amber eyes were dry, already spent from mourning over the future that lay ahead and reminiscing about the life that had been.

How did it end up like this?

Vali, she murmured, the man whom she had loved and lost but who was alive in her weeping mind.

Clouded with memories, she breathed heavily and lifted her eyelids to look over at the window. Her heart, which was left pierced with a tearing ache, found some solace in the patch of the Kishkindh horizon visible from her bed.

Leaving the ornaments behind, Tara got up and came to the window. She could now see the river, gleaming like a mirror, as the moon shone radiantly behind the hills. She stood looking out at the night. There had never been so many stars in the sky, shimmering like a sequined shawl, each glinting mysteriously—glimmering glows in pervasive darkness. One beckoned her. Tara knew who it was.

'Tara, the Star Goddess!' she murmured, calling out to her namesake. 'We meet at last.'

The woman before her looked very different—she was tall and slender. With a fair face bathed in moonlight, she appeared ethereal, as if sheathed in silver gossamer. The woman smiled a slow, serene smile. 'We meet at last. This meeting was due but one must wait for the right time for everything.'

Tara folded her palms and offered her salutations. 'What brings you here, Goddess?' she asked.

'Your pain, your dilemma echoed. We are alike, Tara. And we share more than our name.'

'What else do we share? Who are you to me? I have dreamt about you and your story, over and over again. What is that we have in common besides our name?'

Tara stared at the woman with whom she had this strange connection. She supposed there were some grounds of commonality. Both of them had a tragic love story. Tara, the Star Goddess, while married to Rishi Brihaspati, the guru of the Devas, fell in love with Chandra, the Moon God. They eloped, much to the chagrin of the husband, who, supported by the Devas, declared war against the couple backed by the Asuras. To end the interminable, internecine war, Tara finally decided to return to her husband, forcing herself to live a life without Chandra, without love.

This was the story of the woman standing in front of Tara; this was the Goddess's truce. But what was *her* own story? What was *her* future? That she was to wed a man she despised? Was that to be her truce?

The fair woman nodded her, her dark hair shimmering in a twinkling glow. 'We are both Tara. We have suffered similar tragedies of love and loss, revenge and retribution,' she paused momentarily, 'making both of us women of chance and circumstance.'

'And war!' interceded Tara hotly. 'You are the divine Star Goddess and I am a mere mortal from Kishkindh. We are not victors but victims of war,' she blazed with anger. 'We were both used as weapons in wars or, worse, as trophies for the victor!'

'But in that war, we *are* peace,' exclaimed the Goddess. 'Because of us, there will be harmony after disquiet; hope after destruction. With the future resting on our shoulders, are we really mere trophies?'

The divine woman gave a small, knowing smile as she continued, 'I was married to Rishi Brihaspati but loved Chandra. I married two men and gave up the one I loved. It was the only way to save the world from annihilation. It was not fair to me, but sometimes, for the sake of those you love, you have to make a tough choice.'

'Compromise, you mean. But why? I have loved only one man. I pledged my soul to him for the rest of my life when I married him,' cried Tara in anguish. 'He was everything to me and he was taken from me forever,' she choked, her voice ending in a strangled cry. 'What reason do I have to compromise?'

'That is undeniable,' agreed the divine woman stoically. 'But you won peace for all.'

'Does peace count for any manner of victory when I have lost the reason to want peace? No!' Tara cried. 'In a war fuelled by jealousy, ego and hatred, what did I win? Nothing! I am only left with a life of despair.'

'Remember your son, Tara,' smiled the goddess beatifically, 'and remember mine. Our sons from the men we loved are symbols of a bright future we envisioned for the world. My Chandra's Buddh and your Vali's Angad. Don't they mean anything?'

A bitter smile outlined Tara's trembling lips. Her face calmed a little. She held on to the thought of Angad, using it as an anchor to keep her from spiralling.

'Do *we* mean anything?' Tara questioned hopelessly. 'Are our desires, our dreams relevant to the course of destiny at all?'

'That's apparent from our very name, Tara,' smiled the fair goddess, '*We* are our purpose.' The smile slowly slipped away from her porcelain face and she assumed an expression of grimness. 'We are guiding *stars*, leading lost souls to *their* purpose.'

She took a pause to gauge Tara's expressions, and continued, 'You guided Vali. And look what you both built together.' The Goddess noticed a hint of pride flicker in Tara's eyes. 'Now, as the queen of your kingdom, you must guide your people, you must guide Sugriv. You have to chart a course for the prosperity for your kingdom. Was that not your dream, your desire?' When Tara didn't respond immediately, the Goddess knew she had to become her beacon. Her voice took on a slow pace; she was making a promise. 'You do not have to do this alone. I am here to guide you, to help you walk this path.'

It seemed like an age had passed before Tara reacted. With a bitter laugh, she said, 'We have been warriors who fought for love with all our passion. We also fought battles along the way with compassion.' She paused and continued with a protest in her voice, 'And we ended up being the very first victims of the war we are accused of being the reason of.'

The Goddess held her in an immobile gaze. 'Tara, you and I embraced our passions. We are the quintessence of sacrifice and self-love; of duty and desire. As a price, we have to force our pain and humiliation aside, pledge away our broken promises so that others can have a life of harmony in a violent world. Tara, making this truce *is* our purpose.'

The divine woman paused and waited patiently for Tara to take in her words. She then continued, 'Our womanhood is tangled with our sacrifice. We must be women first, even before being a daughter, a lover, a wife, a mother or a queen. We have to make this compromise because that is how we find ourselves powerful.'

Tara stood still, pondering. The heavy eyelids gradually seemed to lose some of their weight. For the first time in weeks, she could see things the way they were meant to be seen.

She turned away from the window and glanced towards her bed. The jewellery was still laid out for her, next to the red silk that was waiting for her. She thought to herself that if she had to find her place in here and now, if she had to bring peace to the kingdom she loved, to the son she birthed, if she had to fulfil the dream she and Vali had seen together, she would have to don this red. She would have to adorn herself in these jewels and come to terms with the fact that they were not mocking her—that they could help her redefine a woman's resilience, her strength and her capabilities. She was going to redraw the lines of what was meant by honour, valour, respect and dignity. She would do what needed to be done.

Slowly, she looked up to the goddess and said, 'I understand. You *are* me. I *am* you.'

The goddess gave a slow nod. 'Yes, we share more than just our past or our fate. We share the same *purpose*, Tara. We are the ones who will save this world.'

1

THE BROTHERS

Looking back, Tara could see that the seeds of her life had been sown years ago, when she had first met the two brothers in the woods of Kishkindh. Seeds that finally produced love, hate, jealousy, rivalry, murder...

Back then, the two brothers had seemed liked twins. And now, as they lay inert and sick in bed, they were still startlingly alike. Notwithstanding the darkness of the shuttered room, Tara saw their faces out of a sudden urge of curiosity. It had been more than ten years since she had last seen them.

Vali and Sugriv, the two brothers. As an impressionable child, for her, Vali was her protector and Sugriv, a friend. Vali was wild; Sugriv, mild. Vali, sullen; Sugriv, soft-spoken. Tara recalled Vali as the more dominant of the two, several inches taller than his younger brother. Sugriv had always stood a few steps behind him. It seemed to be his natural position.

Tara threw a quick look at them as she moved around the dark chamber with a jug of fresh goat milk. She looked from one to the other. Both were dark, lean and extremely exhausted, with an unhealthy pallor blanching their haggard faces.

'Appa told me to give you this,' she announced loud enough to wake up the sleeping boys.

The taller of the two boys quickly sat up as he became aware that a girl had come into the room. He looked up at her with wary, unfocussed eyes and raised eyebrows, his head tilted a little to one side. His vision soon cleared up, driving the last vestige of sleep from his tired eyes. Vali held his breath; he had been waiting for her... *Tara has come at last.*

Tara's heart lurched unreasonably on seeing Vali look at her. She noticed Vali had grown bigger than what he was in her imagination: more muscular, yet lean and wiry; with a hooked nose, swarthy complexion and intense, restless eyes; and, as expected, an unsmiling mouth. His lean, dark face peered suspiciously at her, and as she approached him, she could not hide her grin. He hadn't changed but for his height, the sullen scowl pasted firmly on his face like always. Powerfully built, with his craggy looks, he looked more like a war general than a student fresh out of Rishi Gautam's ashram.

'I am very glad that you got us our medicine, Tara ji,' said Vali politely, forcing a smile on his grave face. But his smile was surprisingly sweet, a difficult smile that made his face seem less stern. 'All this time that we've been sick, it's only Guru Sushen's face we've seen.'

She chuckled with wry enjoyment. 'He's a stern doctor, as you well may know by now. He wouldn't allow anyone else to nurse you—'

'But you,' interceded Sugriv, awe in his voice. 'You were there each time I opened my fevered eyes.'

She barely glanced at Sugriv. He remained in the shadow of Vali, a shrunken version, shorter and slightly stouter than his tall, lean brother.

Her attention was still on Vali. 'And I wish you wouldn't call me Tara ji!' she said, 'It sounds...too proper.'

It was worse than that—it sounded formal, almost impersonal. 'When we were kids, we used to call each other by our names, Vali,' she reminded with impish emphasis.

Vali blushed a little, and his modesty filled Tara with amusement.

'Yes, but now you are a doctor, not a girl who smacked me around.' he said, his full lips outlining a crooked smile. 'Either way, you knew how to give me my dose of medicine, so, I didn't dare call you informally.'

'Well, you may dare,' she said, laughing. 'I'd much sooner call you simply Vali.'

She did not add that the word seemed to her the most beautiful in all names that ever existed, or that in the past week, since he had arrived in Kishkindh, ill and feeble, she had already repeated it to herself a thousand times.

They had been gazing into each other's eyes, and suddenly, without any obvious reason, Vali flushed again. Tara noticed it. A strange thrill ran through her and she too reddened, her amber eyes sparkling even more brightly than before.

'It'll be like the old days,' Sugriv interposed weakly, detecting the looks that had been exchanged, 'with us together again.'

Tara had first met the two brothers at the age of three when, as tribesmates, they used to be placed side by side in school, for no more compelling a reason than that they were brothers, coming one after the other on the class roll call. But it was always Vali and Sugriv, never Sugriv and Vali. Like on the list of names in the class register, the younger brother followed his elder brother devotedly.

Though the youngest in class, Tara was quick to see that the brothers were also the best of friends. As they progressed through school, nothing could divide them and their camaraderie, not even the fact that they were half-brothers. Nonetheless, they were curiously different; Vali deliberately put on a more brutal and hot-tempered representation than the other.

Yet the one who was still held strong in her memory and her heart was Vali—that little boy who had saved her from a falling branch, the angry boy she had smacked hard on the face when he had thrashed his younger brother.

'You still look like twins!' she remarked, as she moved further into the room. 'Vali was the tallest, strongest and oldest,' she turned to the other boy. 'And he believed that gave him the right to bully us. Right, Sugriv?'

Always second, Sugriv sighed internally. She had, at last, turned her eyes towards him. His face was as earnest as his voice. 'Like all elder brothers often do,' he defended his brother. 'We are as alike as we are close—like entwined fingers held like this!' he emphasized, pulling both his hands in front of him and crossing his fingers in a tight clasp.

'Yes, I know,' she nodded brightly, her earrings twinkling against her slender brown neck. Though the brothers, on immediate impression, seemed strongly alike, Sugriv, she knew, was always more approachable with his open, convivial face and an almost shy demeanour.

As Tara handed Vali a tumbler of milk, their fingers

touched and Vali felt a tingle in his chest. Her touch was not a little girl's touch; her voice was not a little girl's voice. Hers was a woman's voice, pitched low with a little drawl in it, a voice calculated to grab attention. At any rate, it grabbed his.

Tara's breath caught in her throat. As Vali came nearer, she saw him as she had imagined him to be: a tall fellow, big boned, with long arms and legs and a magnificent breadth of chest, all vigorously masculine. Even his bare feet gave her a thrill of pleasure by their very size, their dimensions suggesting a certain firmness of character that was intensely reassuring.

Meanwhile, Vali was fascinated by the colour of her hair: a dark reddish brown mane, coiled loose in a casual bun. *That little, quiet girl with her soft eyes and flaming hair*, he recalled, his eyes becoming tender.

Tara smiled, her eyes not leaving his face. She could easily follow his gaze.

'Yes, you used to call me an incense stick!' she said, indignantly, with gleaming eyes. Her eyes that were set wide apart were now looking at him questioningly, hoping to read his thoughts, and as far as he could judge in the uncertain light, they appeared to be as amber as the setting sun.

Sugriv cackled. 'His name for you had stuck, and everyone in school used to call you an incense stick!'

'And you nicknamed me a monkey,' Vali returned with a mock growl, his dark face inscrutable. His voice had changed, a male voice that sent an immediate prickle up her spine. His voice fitted this tall, powerfully built man, sun-tanned and surly.

She dimpled deliciously. 'That you were! You went swinging from one tree to another with your long arms! It was not a mean nickname, it was—er—a detail.'

'And as far as I can recall, initially you were too snooty to mingle with us,' cut in Sugriv, feeling left out of the conversation. 'You thought us street urchins.'

Tara looked surprised. 'Oh, did I come across as such? I was just too worried about playing with a pair of boisterous boys; not to forget your friend Hanuman, the most mischievous monkey, joined in too!'

'The mouse and the monkeys!' cut in Vali, sardonically.

Sugriv gave a quick nod, making the most of the chance to converse with her. 'It was only when Ruma cajoled you that you deigned to join us.'

'Ruma was a brat as well!' she grinned. 'She didn't mind roughing it out with you rascals.'

'Where's Ruma, by the way?' asked Vali, casually. 'I thought you would come together. Both of you were inseparable.'

Tara felt an inexplicable frisson of annoyance. 'She should be coming over soon. I had told her to join us here,' she said shortly. 'I had assumed she would already be here before me.'

'No, Sushen prohibited anyone to meet us, because our fever was contagious,' said Vali. 'You are our first visitor and I guess that's because you are our nurse.'

'I am your doctor right now,' she said importantly, straightening her square shoulders. 'As I am your doctor's and my father's assistant, you better obey my orders—have your milk and medicines right away! Your Appa is a very worried man—'

'Amma, you mean,' Vali amended her statement quietly.

Tara coloured up as he corrected her.

She had always been struck by the fact that they called Vriksharaj 'Amma'. Vriksharaj was, indeed, their father *and* mother. Vriksharaj, as their name implied—the King of the

Trees—was the chieftain of the Vanara tribe. They were also transgender—born a man but really a woman. They, as Aruni, had sired these two sons: Vali from Indra, the King of Gods and Sugriv from Surya, the Sun God. But soon they reverted to being half man–half woman, as their position as the chief of the tribe demanded their masculinity. But now, they were getting old and weak. Fearing that their position was becoming shaky, they had probably called back their sons, thought Tara.

Sugriv felt distinctly neglected, as it had always been with him. Even as a boy, he used to watch them both in awe, his brother and this girl he was smitten with. But she seemed different now; she was no longer shy and quiet. Her sharply arranged hair, her gracious smile, her gait, her eyes and chin, they all held in them a sense of determination and a quiet efficiency, prompting an instinct in anyone who fell in her path to step aside and let her pass.

Regarding her with a sidelong glance, the weary ache quickly dissipated from Sugriv's body. Tara was the most beautiful girl in his besotted eyes. This small, slim, honey-skinned girl, he thought, was as lovely as before. She was slightly younger than him and inexpressibly endearing, he thought, still utterly bewitched. There was a general elegance in the way her lips twisted down at the corners when she smiled, in the almost passionate quality of her eyes and her passionate gaze.

But as usual, she was not looking at him.

'You mustn't have completed your studies; you look far too young,' Tara changed the topic hurriedly, a little flustered. She handed Vali his medicine. 'Why did you decide to leave Rishi Gautam's ashram?'

He grimaced as if her question tasted as bitter as the

ground herbs in his mouth. They had been travelling for months, and every bone and muscle in his body was sore from the ravaging fever both the brothers had caught on their journey. But that was not why he was scowling.

'I decided that I was too old; I wanted to do something else,' he said curtly. 'And your inquisitiveness is not very polite to guests,' he raised his brow again.

Tara looked unfazed; she had that smile again—radiant, blatantly unrepentant, convincing.

'I am curious. And you are not a guest, Vali,' she replied coolly. 'It's just that you have come back home to Kishkindh after a long time. So, what do you wish to do if not study further?'

Vali threw her a searching look, somewhat annoyed by her prying. She was younger than him, but she was destined to be breathtakingly beautiful and it showed, he thought with an inward sigh. Her spark was perceptible. She might have been quiet, almost taciturn, particularly when in a group, but now, there was a vitality born in her. It was utterly evident, shining through her slim frame in a sort of glow. At her gentlest, she reminded him of his foster-mother, Ahalya, with her pristine beauty and wise, brown eyes... He brushed away the idea quickly.

'Or is it that you find me inquisitive because you don't approve that I asked why you left the ashram abruptly?' Tara goaded, crossing her arms.

Now she was arguing with him as she used to as a child— persistent and persevering. Vali noticed this with grudging amusement.

'After Rishi Gautam abandoned his ashram, I thought we would be better off returning home,' Vali returned tersely.

'Everyone knows why Rishi Gautam left his ashram,' she

stated. 'He could not bear his wife's infidelity and wanted to escape from what he did. After all, he cursed his wife Ahalya in all his righteousness,' she said with a grim expression. 'He couldn't face his students, I suppose!' her full lips curled in contempt.

'Who are *you* to pass judgment?' Vali barked, his jaws clenched.

'I am wondering how such a learned man could behave like a patriarchal husband!' she lifted her slim shoulders, regarding him steadily, her chin up, her dark brown eyes serene and sensible as always.

'What do you know what went on between them?' demanded Vali, his face darkening, trying to control his temper. He wanted to make a good impression on this girl, and snarling at her wasn't the way to do it. She was the first person he had talked to since his return to Kishkindh, besides their physician Sushen, his mother and brother. She had come all the way from her house on the other side of the village to bring them the medicines for their fever, and he was behaving like an ungracious boor.

Vali watched her move to a low coir stool in the corner and settle herself down neatly as if readying herself for a long debate. Her movements were unhurried, graceful and calm. Tara had grown, and how! She was tall; her shoulders square; her thick auburn hair glossy. She was not what he would call conventionally 'pretty', but there was a compelling intelligent handsomeness in those big, liquid brown eyes, in the tiny nose and the wide, firm mouth. But all this wasn't what sent a shiver up his spine. This girl exuded a magnetic sensuality that was like a hungry flare, flimsily concealed. He could see it, just as Sugriv had observed it. And yet, by her calmness and by the way she was looking directly at them without any sign of self-consciousness, he couldn't be sure if she was aware of it or not. This intrigued him.

'Exactly! It was a very personal matter between Rishi Gautam and Ahalya,' she returned evenly, her hands folded on her lap. 'It was about them—husband and wife—but he turned it into a public show for the world to see, speak of and censor! And clearly, society readily condemned her to the fate of a promiscuous adulteress from that of a dutiful wife!'

Tara remained still, her eyes looking unwaveringly into his, as he looked away, his angry expression fading.

'She was like a mother to us,' muttered Vali, his voice low and hoarse. 'It was terrible what happened...' he exhaled sharply. 'The ashram lost its soul, and I reckon the rishi was too devastated and could not bear it any longer.'

Hearing the raw pain in his voice, Tara felt acutely contrite. She now wished she had not broached this unpleasant topic and that she had been more sensitive.

She knew why the boys had been sent to the ashram away from Kishkindh. Vriksharaj, as the chieftain and an ambitious parent, had hoped to provide their sons with the best education at Rishi Gautam's ashram where they could have been brought up by his wife Ahalya. But probably, because of the recent ugly turn of events at the ashram, things did not go as planned. Rishi Gautam had caught his wife with Indra, and in a fit of hurt and rage, had cursed both of them, abandoning his ashram to seek solace in the mountains. Vriksharaj must have been forced to bring his sons back to Kishkindh.

As Vali said nothing, maintaining a sullen silence, she found herself wordless out of sheer embarrassment. *Foot in the mouth*, she scolded herself silently, when all she had wanted to do was to chat with him longer.

In the thickening silence, Sugriv felt the atmosphere suddenly tighten. He moved uneasily.

Tara got up, smiled and glanced cautiously around, her eyes falling in transit on Vali for an instant.

Then she said to Sugriv, handing him a tray, 'I guess if you are feeling a lot better with Appa's medicines, I shall get your buddy Ruma next time? She's a better conversationalist.'

Sugriv nodded wordlessly, gulping down the mud-coloured paste with the tumbler of fresh milk. He struggled to keep his face straight, smiling wanly instead, gazing at her.

Suddenly, startled by himself, he blurted, 'Oh, don't say that. Ruma is a fine talker, but *you* are the charmer! Why, you made us feel much better now, more than this horrid medicine!'

'Oh!' For a moment this baffled her, but she swiftly recovered, shifting her weight on her right and then left foot. 'That's kind of you to say, Sugriv, you are too sweet! And yes, I shall convey your message to Ruma,' she added pointedly with a sly look. 'She is all agog to meet you!'

Tara gave him her soft, teasing smile that sent heat searing through him. After all, he was being personally addressed by her. Not only that, he was also being treated to that exhilarating smile, the memory of which he would carry for at least the next few weeks. He stood perfectly still, his mouth slightly ajar. He knew that if he moved forward by even a step, his gaze would be in her line of vision; if he moved backwards, he would lose the full view of her face.

Tara turned and took back the tumbler from Vali. The touch of his big, firm fingers made her tremble. His hand was massive and hard as if it were made of stone. She looked up at him and smiled.

'The medicine?' she asked, hoping her voice was not

shaking as much as she was from inside. Convention and a strange awkwardness were barring her from uttering anything but the most commonplace of words.

'It's awful!' he grimaced with an exaggerated expression. 'As bad as the wordy doses you used to preach, Miss Prim and Proper!' he chuckled softly.

Her head snapped instantly at him. 'That medicine was punishment for boorish behaviour,' she said primly.

'You forget that this boor once saved you from a mad dog,' he said with feigned injury in his voice.

'I still carry the scars,' she stretched out her left arm, 'and all those memories...of us...' It came out all wrong. She heard her heart beating at an absurd rate.

Vali's tanned skin turned red and he seemed to have some difficulty in finding a reply; his confusion and his ingenuous air were new enchantments to Tara.

She let out a little sigh and the silence between them was swift and strained. *If only he knew how I adored him!* She thought to herself, but she couldn't have told him in so many words.

'You left out the part where I, too, had rushed to your rescue, Tara,' Sugriv grumbled in an aggrieved tone. 'But Vali has always had a way of grabbing all the accolades!'

Tara looked across at Sugriv, her eyes gliding over him, unseeing. Sugriv wasn't sure if she was listening to what he had been saying before. Vali burst into a loud laugh. 'You recall that, Sugriv? I thought you would be traumatized by how the dog turned on you instead.... Poor Sugriv couldn't move for days without yelping in pain!'

Sugriv flushed, slightly annoyed but more astonished that Vali had lost all his sullenness of the last few days and was seeming perfectly cheerful in their new company. Tara, too, took a long look at him. Now that Vali had smiled, it had wiped the sullen mask off his face, changing it completely. His intense eyes now twinkled in recalled amusement.

'I do recall,' she shrugged. 'And I thank you for saving me too, Sugriv.' She continued, 'But I agree, Vali was a bully! And we were both so scared of him.' When she said this without any heat, Sugriv was quick to notice the look exchanged between Tara and Vali.

'And who was I afraid of? Your father, Sushen!' grinned Vali. 'His medicines were more bitter than his rebukes!'

'Deservedly so!' Tara chirped saucily. Her spirits had suddenly gone up and she was feeling extraordinarily happy. Vali had to merely raise one thick brow, making her feeling warm and pink all over again.

'Vali still is a bully,' Sugriv stated. 'He beat me black and blue just before we left the ashram because I was unwilling to come away with him. But then, I didn't have you, Tara, who was the only one to stand up to him. Once, in my defence, you even slapped him back!' It was Sugriv's turn to chortle.

Tara gave a self-conscious laugh. 'This brother of yours made me violent as well!'

'We both seem to provoke the beast in the other,' said Vali. Again, his brow that rose mockingly made her heart flutter. It was impossible to determine whether this statement was ingenuous or malicious, but his insinuations seem to be having an odd effect on her.

Her glance fell casually on each of them—she then scanned the room for her tray of herbs and milk. 'I should be going.'

As she collected the emptied tumblers and arranged them on the tray, Sugriv was again aware of a disconcerting strain hanging heavy in the tiny room. He covertly regarded the girl who stood before him. She seemed flustered for some odd reason, running a nervous hand down her hips. He noticed she wore a rough, white half sari that rimmed her neck, her right shoulder bare and her honey skin accentuated. The expressive exaggeration that had made her passionate eyes and downturned mouth seem endearing when she was a child was still present; only now, it was sensuous. The colour in her cheeks because of the outside heat—or was it something else?—had a fluctuating, feverish warmth, yet was so shadowy that it added to her enigma. This heightened colour and the mobility of her words gave an impression of flux, of intense life, of passionate vitality, moderately balanced by the serenity of her eyes.

Unaware of his gaze, Tara went about clearing the room with quick, efficient movements. She looked up at the boys, her eyes lingering longer at the brooding brother. With a quick, sincere smile and a careless statement—'Ruma should be here sometime later in the day. Get rest!'—she set off at a flowing pace, slipping into the daylight, leaving Vali to follow her with his eyes.

Sugriv expelled a slow, long breath. 'That Tara!' he breathed, his eyes too set on the departing figure.

'That Tara who used to rebuke you each time you teased her pets, and whom you followed like a lamb!' snorted Vali. 'And yet all you recall is me beating you up and she nursing you!'

'And how she scolded you for beating me up,' Sugriv gave a triumphant grin. 'That was the first time I saw that quiet girl roar,' he chortled with undisguised glee. 'She lashed you with her words instead—'

'And her tiny hand, deceptively soft,' recalled Vali, wryly. He lifted his massive shoulders under his shawl. Well, they had started on a quarrel—as before. Not a great start, he told himself. He could have done better. He shook his head. He caught the way his brother was looking at him strangely. He forced a weak smile.

'It's good to be back home.'

But both the brothers knew different. *It was good to see Tara again.*

2

THE VANARAS

Tara sat with her smooth, brown elbows resting against the bamboo balustrade of her house, waiting for Vali to turn up. The brothers had recovered swiftly, and that had given her fewer opportunities to see Vali. She wondered what he had been doing. During lunch with her father, she had hardly spoken to him, listlessly playing with the rice in her plate. In the night, she could not sleep and glanced at the horizon a dozen times, waiting for the sun to rise, and got absurdly startled when the rooster crowed the hour.

It was a blistering day, as usual, and the distant temple bell clanged for the noon prayers. Tara was about to give up when she spied the tall, lanky frame heading towards their courtyard.

Vali! Her heart skipped a beat. The morning sun fell on the thick gold necklace Vali wore, and the flaming blue gem at the centre winked at her.

He was the very picture of health; the harsh winds of Kishkindh were like summer breezes to him and his face glowed with the pleasant heat. His cheeks were flushed and his eyes glistened. His vitality was intense, shining upon others with an almost tangible warmth.

Watching Vali's figure loom closer, Tara thought about the mysterious sparks that fly sometimes when two people meet. Some call it love at first sight. Whatever it was, it was a sudden reaction, and it had now happened in her. At her first sight of Vali, she had known that he was the man she really wanted. Fate, destiny—call it what you may—had brought them back together. She wondered if he felt the sparks too. This was something she had to find out.

Standing on the steps of her hut, watching Vali amble closer, she turned her face at him, taking in his lithe frame. His pallor clearly showed how recently he had emerged from his illness. To her, he was like a magnificent beast that chased its prey. As for him? He was like a lone lion walking in a crowd.

The men that thronged Vali's path, temple wards and village girls on the street dressed in brilliant flowers—none aroused Vali's interest. His dark eyes were only on Tara—steady and measured.

Tara returned his stare with the same unrushed look. She glanced at him while he let his warm, liquid eyes melt her. With a pang, she found him breathlessly exciting, her skin prickling. As he came closer, she fell in step with him. She moved forward fluidly, feeling the heat of his body as they walked closely. In the jostling crowd with the giggling girls, Vali had felt an acute loneliness. But the presence of the special girl made him feel warm again, especially when her hip touched his, the spark between them ravaging him from the inside.

'You have been watching me all the way I was heading here,' he remarked quickly, hoping to even out his accelerated breathing.

'You did the same,' she smiled and stopped. 'Frankly, it was your new necklace that caught my eye. Where did you get such a flashy piece?'

He gave an awkward grin. 'Amma gave it to me yesterday, on my eighteenth birthday,' he responded, embarrassed. He traced the necklace lightly with his fingers, the act hypnotizing her. 'It was my father's gift for me when I was born, to be worn when I was ready to handle it. It is said to be very powerful.'

'When did a proud son of the forest, a Vanara, start believing in magic?' she asked dryly.

He looked at her and found her eyes trusting him. 'This necklace is said to have a boon, such that, in any duel, my opponent would lose half his strength to me.'

'Which makes you invincible,' she said, raking the necklace with her clear, clever eyes. 'You believe all this? In the "powers of the Gods"? Don't we Vanaras rather believe solely in ourselves? The only friend we have is the jungle.'

He met her steady gaze, frowning. 'When did you become a cynic, Tara? Even in the worst of times you had the gift of seeing the best.'

'You're right,' she riposted with a faint smile. 'Maybe that's why I can't believe that you believe in this necklace and not your own powers. What are you afraid of? Living in fear of the future extracts the joy out of the present. The only comfort is that almost none of your fears have come true,' she said quietly. 'Have they?'

'Actually, it is the past that I am scared of—of what it will do to me now.'

She laughed. 'Your past—what is that but a privileged one, where the son of a chieftain is sent to a prestigious ashram to study?' Her smile died noticing his shuttered look.

'You are a cynic,' he repeated, scrutinizing her with a solemn look. 'You've changed so much in these years,' he said, 'I can't fathom you.'

'You have changed too, Vali. We are no longer some silly kids.'

His eyes blatantly raked her. 'That I am well aware of,' he said dryly.

'It's nice you notice things beside yourself!' She lifted her shoulders in an unconcerned shrug.

He crossed his arms, regarding her quizzically. 'But I like the change. You wear this fearless look now—quite unlike the frightened doe of afore. What made you change?'

'The jungle! We are jungle dwellers,' she said. 'We have to be alert and assertive.'

'Oh, you're a hunter? So, am I a predator or prey?' he asked, his voice soft, a soft purr, but the smile in his voice perceptible to her.

'Humans are the worst,' she said roundly. 'Worse than the wildest animals! Don't ever show your fear to them. Never lower your gaze, and they'll leave you alone.'

'You haven't shown fear or lowered your gaze, and yet I shan't leave you alone,' he stated lazily.

'Oh, you won't?' she raised an imperious brow. 'What will you do?'

'This—'

And before her bewildered eyes, he came swiftly to her and bent his handsome head; she found his lips on hers. The touch of his firm lips on her soft, yielding ones sent her heart racing. The kiss was so unexpected and brief she thought she had imagined it, but the phantom of the pleasurable pressure that still lingered proved otherwise.

Tara titlted her head to one side as she looked at him.

Her face was slightly flushed, her lips were parted and there was that look in her eyes that he had seen before. She looked the most devastating woman in the world.

'If not that, I can just look at you,' he added insolently.

She refused to be daunted. 'So then go on, look at me!' she commanded. 'I shall too. Let's see who breaks the gaze.'

She regarded him with her large, limpid eyes fixed on him. Not a muscle on his face moved. She tightened her jaw and widened her eyes. He did not flinch either. She could feel the heat of his gaze.

A burst of giggles snapped their concentration. A group of girls were now pointing at them, laughing loudly.

Vali glanced around self-consciously. The girls were openly grinning at him with unrestrained amusement. Tara seemed unaffected, more amused at his discomfort as she waved at them sportingly, joining in their laughter.

'For all your bravado, you are quite the shy guy,' she teased him, amused.

He shrugged, his face sheepish. 'I am comfortable only with you.'

Even if he had not said charming things to her, his eyes, warm with admiration, would have betrayed him. His ease was delightful. He was not self-conscious when he was with her. Tara found that she was unusually comfortable with him. She was amused by the way in which, amid their banter, he would insinuate more than casual flirting. Like the last time when they had met, while leaving, he had pressed her hand in a way that she could not mistake for anything else but his feelings for her.

'So, what do you plan to do now that you are back on your feet?' she asked casually.

'Spread my wings,' he smiled.

'You mean be the chief of our tribe as you will inevitably be some day?'

'No. I mean, I want to be a king, have a kingdom.'

'These are dreams, not plans,' she said, crossing her arms, regarding him with her big, brown eyes.

'No. I have plans to make my dreams come real. I shall do it—with the help of this necklace,' he smiled again at her, his crooked, private smile. 'But as soon as the pressure is off, I want to get married.'

She raised her brows. 'Any particular girl?'

'I might have found one, but I'm not sure yet,' he teased.

She regarded him, then looked away. Her lips curled into a little smile. Vali had the idea that she had received the message.

*

On either side of where Vali and Tara were standing were thatched roofs, sloping in parallel with the slope of the hillock they were standing on. The hay over the roofs suddenly rustled as a vulture alighted on the ground next to them.

It was Jatayu. His brown plumes were as regal as his eyes that held everyone in their hard, steady gaze. His brown, wise eyes spoke volumes. He rarely smiled, but when he did, he cackled, often laughing at his own words. He must have witnessed them together. *Did he see the kiss too*, Tara wondered, and was amazed that it did not bother her much. He must have, she fathomed from the formidable scowl on his face.

'How come you are this side of the hill, Vali?' Jatayu asked pleasantly. But both Vali and Tara were quick to note the curtness in his voice.

'To restock our medicine from our valued physician,' Vali replied smoothly, stroking his very young moustache. Tara hid a grin; he was a glib liar. 'What are you doing here, sir?' Vali asked politely but he was curious to know what the old vulture who was fond of roaming the skies and forests was doing in Kishkindh.

'I came here to meet Vriksharaj,' he returned unperturbed. 'Going back to the ashram soon?'

'No! Never!' returned Vali strongly. 'I am done there; I need to stay home and look after things.'

'You are the chief's son, you will be a chief soon,' commented Tara. 'Natural law of inheritance, natural law of the forest.'

'Especially when our society is founded on the matrilineal kinship,' Vali retorted, stung by her sarcasm. 'And as you rightly claimed, the natural law of the forest runs on the survival of the fittest,' he added gruffly.

'And that's you, of course.'

He nodded. 'Yet you have to fight it out.'

She raised a brow. 'Your only contender will be Sugriv. Are you going to fight your brother?'

'Yes, *if* he challenges me,' Vali lifted his heavy shoulders, the act immediately drawing her eyes to his burly physique again. 'Or anyone else for that matter!'

'You thrive on challenge?' she pestered, her burnished brown eyes, openly laughing at him. 'Or is it your bloodlust itching for a fight?'

'Whatever,' he shrugged his broad shoulders again. 'The outcome is the same—I win.'

Jatayu appraised the young man with his hard, alert eyes. 'Even in jest, don't take this lightly. I had a brother once. I lost him. So, cherish what you have, Vali. Brothers are for revelry, not rivalry. That's why you are born in one family, connected by blood.'

Tara hid her astonishment. This was the first time she had heard Jatayu mention a brother. 'What was his name?' she couldn't resist asking.

'Sampati,' he smiled sadly. 'As kids, we used to compete who could fly higher. In that attempt, Sampati flew so high that he ended up close to the sun. His wings got scorched and he fell to his death,' he explained, his voice toneless. 'So, Vali, value what you have: a brother, a father—'

'Mother,' corrected Vali, his dark eyes narrowing. 'For all of you, Vriksharaj is the chief of the tribe; for me, she is my mother.'

Jatayu's eyes softened. 'Oh, you are not as arrogant as you want us to believe.'

Unlike his milder brother, Vali was a rogue and a rebel, but Jatayu felt kindly for him. Jatayu respected fighters, and Vali had a lot of fight in him. Add to that a roguish charm that few could resist—even this sceptic—intrigued by the recklessness in Vali in which he squandered the priceless treasure of discipline, yet managed to lead the pack.

For all his fire and fury, Vali was a reticent man. He was a Vanara at heart, proud and untamed. But what he had done at the ashram and why he had left the ashram—Jayatu had no idea. However, rumours claimed that Rishi Gautam had thrown him out. Jatayu could not ever quite tell to what class Vali belonged either. When Vali would be in his coarse loincloth, his hair long and shaggy over his broad shoulders, talking to his native villagers and fisher folk, he would seem as rough, boisterous and unlettered as most of them. But if his handwriting was any indication, he was a man with high education and a sharp mind. On occasion, when one got him alone, if he had a few drinks but was not yet drunk, he would talk of matters that neither a local tribesman nor a fisherman would know anything about. And for Tara, he was a suave suitor.

His face inscrutable, Vali said shortly, 'Being Vriksharaj's son is not a privilege, it's a responsibility—to me and to my people. If she earned her place as a chief, so shall I. I wish for no entitlement. I shall prove my worth,' he bowed his head in mock respect. 'You or any elder can test me.'

'But a match of strength challenges only the brawn, not the brain,' maintained Tara. 'We need a chief who is wise, not just strong,' she said, her eyes saucily travelling from his handsome head, down his lean length to his bare feet.

'You will need the wisdom and knowledge you have gleaned at the rishi's ashram,' said Jatayu. 'That was the training Vriksharaj sent you boys for.'

'Yes, I have received it, and it's time to give back,' agreed Vali spryly.

Jatayu had a certain sensitivity and he realized that Vali spoke to him neither as a superior would to an inferior, nor as the young to an elderly but as an equal. That's how Vali gained respect and gave respect, Jatayu realized.

'Where's your brother?' he asked, curious to meet the other offspring of Vriksharaj.

Vali gave a shrug. 'He must be with Hanuman. They are thick as thieves.'

'Not surprising,' croaked Jatayu with a throaty chuckle. 'They are the fire and the wind, being sons of Surya and Vayu.'

'With that logic, being the son of Indra, God of Rain and Thunder, I must be their adversary, dousing their friendship,' commented Vali flippantly.

Jatayu threw him a thoughtful glance, his eyes watchful. 'No, you are his elder brother.'

'I am,' said Vali mildly. 'I am older to them, and Hanuman and Sugriv are the same age, which is why they get along like a house on fire and not because of some mythical connections.'

Quick to observe that Vali was in a stubborn mood, Tara interceded, 'Hanuman veritably moves swiftly as the wind!' she remarked, aware of the sudden undercurrent. 'And yet he can be as gentle as a breeze. He is the mildest person I know—kind, grave and caring. Who can believe he was once a brat everyone dreaded?' she laughed, recalling the naughty boy for what he was and what he had now become—a boy of a slender, athletic build with solemn eyes and a serious, unsmiling face. Yet, it was an earnest face, warm and anxious to help. Sugriv and Hanuman had promptly renewed their old childhood friendship, with the former constantly seeking the latter's counsel.

'How did he lose all that fire?' Vali asked curiously. 'He seems very tame now.'

'Wisened up over time,' she said. 'I guess he is slowly realizing his potential.'

'Hanuman is the son of the brave warrior Kesari and Anjana. He will inherently be a fierce combatant,' maintained Vali.

'That's why there are so many stories around him. And there are stories around you too, Vali.'

'Let's not believe in all this romanticized glorification,' he scoffed, drumming his fingers.

'If you can have faith in the power of your boon-giving necklace, so can the simple folks believe in their ballads about their heroes. It is their way free themselves from the yoke of discrimination and disdain.' Tara sounded sardonic. 'This glorification makes them feel proud of themselves. It boosts the sagging morale of a collective.'

Vali's face was now set, and his black eyes gleamed. 'Are you mocking me?'

'Alerting you,' she said, the smile vacating her face. 'If you want to be a leader, you first need to know your people well. For one, we like tall stories around us. We are proud folks, proud of our history, our heroes. We are the original people of the forest, the Vanaras, the "nar" of the "van"! And these little stories make us feel big.'

'But we aren't!'

'But "vaa" also means "other" in Sanskrit and "nar" is "human". "Vanara" can also mean "other human" or "super human", Vali!' she added with asperity. 'And these tales glorify just that!'

There was a long pause of silence while Vali studied Tara, a slight frown crumpling his forehead, his eyes now wary. Jatayu, sensing the throbbing energy, looked around him. *They can diffuse it themselves*, he thought with some amusement.

Around the corner, in front of the old cotton tree, stood a Shiva temple. Glancing in that direction, Jatayu thought that he spotted Vriksharaj heading their way. 'I have to go,' he said unceremoniously, and with a strong beat of his great wings, took a magnificent flight.

As they strolled along the winding path, Vali felt a strange sense of contentment. He had been home for a while, but only when he was around this gril did he feel he was truly home. She made the life of the forest pleasant and easy. As he enjoyed the long walk down the path, straggling along the edge of the lagoon, he realized that he had never known freedom or leisure like he felt with her in that moment. He was intoxicated by the sunshine. As he walked beside her, his head reeled at the beauty next to him and that surrounded him. The woods, unlike the hilly terrain of the nearby villages, were indescribably fertile. In parts, the forest was still virgin—a tangle of strange trees, luxuriant undergrowth and vines, it made a mysterious and troubling impression on him.

'What is that you wish to give back and to whom?' Tara questioned curiously, savouring the sensation of his rough hand in her soft palms.

Vali threw her an amused look. 'We are back to me now, aren't we? Yes, I want to give back all that I have learnt to my people here,' he said, picking a coil of thick rope from the ground. 'The democratic spirit, for instance, or egalitarianism. The ashram was home to one and all. Rishi Gautam did not discriminate among any of his students.'

'As we do here?' she asked astutely, helping him prepare the rope to to climb the tall tree and move through the branches, from one tree to another.

'Aren't we discriminated against, though?' he countered. 'You just spoke about it.'

'You insist on the need to prove that you are a Vanara,' she remarked, tightening knot of the rope at her waist. 'You won't make the other person forget that.'

'True, that's probably why I picked quite a few fights at the ashram,' he grinned unabashedly, taking the other end of the rope and expertly twisting it into a firm knot around his own waist. I am a Vanara. However, we are not seen as a community of people living in this forest but as savages. They shame us by calling us monkeys!' he scowled. 'But few know—forget that—few respect us and the art of swinging on trees that we have long mastered.'

'And in the ashram, were you treated to your expectations and given that due recognition?'

'It took time and tolerance, but I managed to gain the

respect we seem to have lost in collective ridicule,' muttered Vali, his lips drawn back in a grimace, pulling himself up, and swinging high. 'I may swing like a monkey now but we are not apes! We are Vanaras—Men of the Forests—the original dwellers of the forests now taken over by marauding invaders and greedy kings! If they had their way, we would be slaves!' he roared, the rope shaking violently.

Tara lifted her eyebrows and gave him a steady stare. 'We can never be slaves, Vali; we are too proud a tribe. The world may reduce "Vanara" to mean "monkey" over the years, but that's probably because they see us leaping on and off trees, with our distinctive, thick mane and, of course, these ropes at the waist that they call tails!' she smiled, tugging at the rope that bit into her waist as she swung smoothly from one tree to another. It felt incredibly exhilarating—free and wild like the other birds and beasts in the forest.

'That's how they perceive us and have painted us, even in their art and literature!' growled Vali.

Tara eyed him as he lowered himself to the ground. She did the same, detecting the simmering rage ready to boil over. His education seemed to have made him wiser on the question of his identity, of who he was and, more importantly, what he wanted to become and how the world perceived him. His ambition, she quickly surmised, stemmed from this uncertainty of acknowledgement and appreciation. People mistook him to be a wild bully, but she saw in his intimidation a restlessness to rule and conquer, not just the land of Kishkindh but his own fears.

It was a miracle how Vali kept body and soul together. He roamed the forest, climbed the highest peaks, trailed the treetops. He was an incorrigible adventurer, a wanderer. He knew the various dialects spoken in the region and how to make the solemn locals laugh. As a result, he was never at a loss for a meal or a mat to sleep on. They admired him, even feared him a little for his enormous physical strength, but they liked his company. As did she.

'We have the cultured dignity like other humans,' Tara insisted, in her customary calm voice. 'And if others find our language, clothing, habitations, customs unusual, it's their outlook,' she gave a slight shrug. 'Have you considered that they think us odd possibly because of our supernatural abilities of climbing, jumping and scaling trees and heights?' she asked quietly. 'We are also called the Vidyadharas, and since the flag of our clan bears monkeys as an emblem, people have assumed us as those.'

Vali gave a derisive grunt. 'Next you will start believing all those fancy stories of gods turning us into some mythological beings! Of how Brahma, the Creator, created us from his tears as Vanaras, a noble clan of warriors on some noble mission!' Vali expostulated with a deep exhale.

'How do you know that they're just fancy stories? We might face something like them someday...' she cryptically remarked.

He was not sure if she was jesting or was being ironic. 'So, I am the son of Indra; Sugriv, the son of Surya; Nila is the son of the celestial architect Vishwakarma; and even your father, Sushen, is the son of Varun, the God of the Seas, they say.'

'Well, not to split hairs, but my father should have been the son of Dhanvantari, the God of Medicine, considering Appa is a physician! Anyway, they also say that I am an *apsara*, a nymph,' she laughed, her eyes twinkling, hoping to calm the irate young man.

Vali glanced at her. 'Yes, you look like one,' he blurted. 'Beautiful, born from the waters of this river, a kindred spirit out to save lives—and the world—which is true,' Vali smiled back, easing the tension. 'The last I heard, you had a flair of talking to birds and beasts of the forest and collecting herbs for the wonder cure,' he teased.

His teasing tone made her surprisingly churlish. Mimicking his tone, she said, 'And the last I heard, you and the other Vanaras were thrown out of Rishi Gautam's ashram after being called a bunch of monkeys.'

The colour drained from Vali's face and he stood dangerously still, like a tree about to collapse. She felt like he made a move to strike her but saw him controlling himself. His slit of a mouth pursed and he squinted his deep-set eyes that were like granite.

His hand snaked out, closing on her arm, the big thick fingers pressing into her muscle, making her squirm.

'Mind what you say, Tara,' he growled through gritted teeth, holding her chin roughly with his other hand. He raised her face; they looked at each other. She saw the snarling anger in his eyes and flinched away, but his giant fingers crushed her chin.

'Is it not true?' she lashed back, belligerently glaring up into his dark, liquid eyes. Her cheeks were flaming, and bruised pique dispelled her usual diffidence.

'Oh, the mouse has become a lioness,' he gave a chuckle, the fury rapidly draining from his face. Smiling dangerously, he lowered his great face down and crushed his lips over hers. He held her like that, his mouth softening and his clasp on her chin turning gentle.

She leaned towards him. The desire she felt for him was scorching. A thrill of excitement passed through her, and at the same time, so did a faint sensation of indignation at his audacity.

A light flush on her face and she pulled away. 'You *are* a brute ape!' she said shakily but she was not sure if it was anger or desire that was making the blood pound. 'That's why it rankles you when you are called a Vanara!'

His eyes hardened. 'I am one! But no one dares say that to me disparagingly now.'

'But Rishi Gautam did, when he found out that you had seen his wife with Indra—'

'Stop it, Tara!' he barked. 'It doesn't suit you to indulge in dirty gossip!'

Tara felt a sliver of shame; had she gone too far? Was there more to his flare of anger? Tension tautened the silence, the imprint of her kiss as livid on his face as the weight of her careless words.

'I had seen Indra talking with Ahalya Ma near the river,' he admitted, his tone flat, drained of anger. 'Like a fool I divulged this to Rishi Gautam when he returned to the ashram. Distraught, he threw both of us out,' he exhaled a ragged breath. 'Were it not for my loose tongue...'

Vali closed his eyes. He suddenly was back in the ashram again on that dreadful day.

'You can't blame yourself for what happened,' Tara said, placing a hand on his arm.

Feeling oddly assured by her gesture, he gave a grimace. 'It's more than that...'

'That your faith in love and relationship was shaken?' she said perceptively.

Vali gave a wretched look. 'I can't believe what happened... They were perfect for each other. Yet...'

'Imperfections, not perfections, make for perfect love,' she said.

He scrutinized her, a flare of admiration in his eyes. 'You seem to know it all; you have grown up, Tara,' he gave a wry smile.

'In every way,' she agreed, lightly licking her swollen lips.

He stared, fascinated.

'Great lovers often hurt those they love,' he said. 'I read it somewhere, so it must be true.'

He absently peered down at the wayside bush and began to caress the petals of a wild rose. For such a large man, he touched the flower with instinctive tenderness.

Tara was suddenly aware of a new tension between them, quite enjoying it. There was a long, heavy silence. Tara watched Vali closely. He was still frowning.

'Even now having returned, I don't know where to start, how to begin or do what I want to do.'

'Do what? Be the next chief?' The words came out of Tara's mouth almost like a smirk.

His jaw clenched. 'No, be a conqueror.'

'Aberrant ambition!'

Vali gave a voluble stare. 'What is wrong in being ambitious in taking back all what we have lost?'

'Conquering is expansion; ruling is consolidation,' she cautioned. 'You can't do both.'

Again, he was struck by her inherent intelligence. While he was looking at her and thinking she had the brightest mind and the largest eyes he had ever seen, curtained by long, willowy eyelashes, she was staring back at him with questions. In the few second of silence that followed, they sized each other up with frank curiosity.

'I hope to do both,' he said vehemently.

'How?'

'With you.' His response was spontaneous.

She coloured up deliciously, feeling a thrill warm her neck.

'And, of course, with Sugriv,' he hurriedly added. 'He can rule while I win new lands.'

A smile flickered on Tara's lips. Vali, noticing it, gave his customary shrug. 'Victors win respect; losers lose it. We won't be ruled anymore by Ravan or anyone else!'

Tara gave a quick snort of a laugh. 'Vali, you intend to challenge Ravan, the new emperor of Lanka, who has taken over the mainland and this part of our forest?' There was amused incredulity in her voice.

'Yes, one day.'

'He is invincible!' she countered. 'Besides, he has a huge army, and all you might be able to manage is a bunch of jungle folks and a gang of Vanaras. All untrained—and worse—disunited.'

'I shall train them; I shall unite them.'

Vali, standing against the cliff, stared down over the straggly roofs of the village, his eyes drawn towards the river Pampa streaming down the rocky hills. 'We all go the wrong way, that's why we are treated wrongly. I see it now more clearly since I have come back home...' He lowered his voice and said with passion lacing his breath, 'I hate what we have done to ourselves! I hate what we have done to this place. I hate what we have done to our people. I hate what Vanaras mean to the world—monkeys! How dare they call us that...' he stopped abruptly to look around him. 'But look at us, look at that silly boy down there with a feather propped on his head. He should be practicing how to shoot arrows and poison darts. But our capabilities are being underestimated.

We are wasting time, wasting ourselves. We are still collecting firewood and sticks from the forest. We don't value the worth and wealth of the forest and our land. We would rather be food gatherers, led by the Asuras ruling this forest… I'll drive them away one day!'

'You hope to fight the Asuras?' Tara asked sceptically, her voice thick with doubt. 'Under Ravan, they have taken over the whole region of this dense Dandak Forest, right from the Vindhya mountains in the north, down the peninsula, to the south.'

'I intend to make all that into my kingdom,' Vali said softly. '*Our* kingdom, of our people,' he corrected himself, quickly observing the change of expression on her face. 'Our very own Kishkindh of the Vanaras.'

He has an answer for everything. Tara hadn't the heart to burst his buoyant optimism. His determination lifted her too. Yet they were starkly different. She was convinced that the world was good and not evil—unlike what Vali stoutly believed—and the people not as vicious as he insisted. They were two strong, opposing individuals who, unsurprisingly, were going to be at loggerheads.

She eyed his tall, bulky frame. Her large, doe eyes were thoughtful. 'Frankly, I believe you have a better chance of winning if you challenge him personally to a duel. Even if defeated, it would be a small ignominy—an emperor beating an upstart. But if you win, it would be a victory, bigger than the triumph of conquering lands. It would be the conquest of a conqueror. Not a drop of blood of Vanaras will be spilled, who would likely be massacred by his gigantic army if ever we were to fight on a battlefield.'

Vali gave her a wordless stare, mulling over her words.

'I didn't know you are savvy about warfare too,' he said.

'You are full of surprises...' He threw her a piercing look. 'Tara, *who* are you?'

'My father's daughter. A healer,' she lifted her slight shoulders.

'Why?'

'What do you mean "why"?' she retorted.

'Why are you a healer?' he asked mildly, his eyes serious. 'It's an unusual choice. There must be a reason for it.'

The gentleness in his voice overwhelmed her. 'You followed your parent, and identify as a warrior. So did I; I became a physician,' she said airily.

'But why?' he persisted, pausing to bestow on her his rare smile. There was an interminable pause as his warm eyes fixed on hers.

'Because my mother died while giving birth to my brother, and then, so did he,' she said tightly, her words pressed under the burden of recalled grief. 'I was about four, but I can hear her screams, the blood, the sheer violence of giving birth...the bloody, pointless death of two people,' she exhaled, her breath shaking. 'It's not different from a battlefield, is it? But there's no glory, no heroism in such a death. It's so usual, just data and digits, and life goes on as usually as death...'

She blinked, her eyes dulled with reminisced pain. 'We talk about heroes dying on the battlefield. What about so many women battling their death during childbirth? Are they not brave? Don't they face a certain death? Yet they are not hailed as heroes, just a vague casualty in the scheme of things.'

The silence grew heavy and Vali could not take his eyes off the raw pain on the young girl's face. His face softened. Tara had grown from a withdrawn, quiet girl to a woman, wise and ripe beyond her years. Nothing in her appearance would have prepared anyone for such determination as she had shown and proved so often when she treated her father's patients. She was a fierce optimist with a ruthless fortitude to look upon the bright side of things—even death and disease, which she stoically handled every day.

Vali took her hand in his, turning it gently to tie a delicate red bead-and-shell bracelet on her slim, strong wrist. Tara was taken by surprise and was too elated to utter a word, making her forget all her pain momentarily.

'I made it for you,' he said softly, gently kissing her wrist, his lips warm on her cool skin.

She felt a rush of blood in her veins.

'Is this my fee for nursing you back to health?' she asked, a stilted laugh in her voice.

'No, it's *our* band, representing our hopes, our dreams... It's clear both of us have our battles to fight, wars to win,' he smiled, pulling her closer. 'This is a reminder that we can do our little bit as Vanaras for Vanaras. Together.'

3

KISHKINDH

Kishkindh was dying. Mass invasions, along with the kingdom's primitive methods of self-production, had not been able to compete with the brutality of the attacks from the Asuras or their military camps that had sprung up overnight in the neighbouring districts.

In the past, it had been the most populous territory of the Vanaras, a prosperous little pocket in the forest kingdom. Its two large village industries, specializing in making ropes and wood logging, had been a lucrative source of wealth. But it was no longer so.

The new kingdom of the Asuras in the Dandak Forest, Janasthan, had almost destroyed Kishkindh. Janasthan was a rapidly expanding forest outpost of Ravan's kingdom. It was a mushroom town, a town for the younger generation with brightly painted shops; neat, cheap little houses, not forest huts; swift chariots; and a young, vigorous beating heart of commerce that had been slowly strangling Kishkindh—the people, the industry, the city.

Kishkindh was tired. She could see it in the shabby huts, in the open shops—mostly empty—along the narrow and tortuous streets, with their sparse wares displayed indifferently. She could see it in the dignified dilapidation of the small colony of veteran warriors who had seen and survived several wars, who had seen glory in the golden age and were content to live out their days in this sad, stagnating jungle heartland. And she could particularly see it in the rising numbers of the bored and the young who gathered at street corners, idle, indifferent and apathetic or, worse, addicted.

Still, everything was done with a great deal of bustle—the unloading of the boats, the examination of the fish brought ashore—and everyone seemed to smile at each other. Howsoever hot it was, their smiles and the colours of the countryside dazzled.

Kishkindh was still visually spectacular. The rock-strewn landscape marked by smooth, huge boulders hanging precariously atop each other, as if defying nature with its very existence of bare, barren beauty.

'As brutal as it is to rhapsodize, the actual reason for the rock formations is far more scientific,' remarked Vali dryly. 'Turns out, these rocks are some of the oldest exposed surfaces on earth. At one point in time, these very boulders had been part of a giant monolith, but centuries of exposure to elements like rain, rivers and wind has eroded them into what they are today. Are they not majestic?' he asked in open wonderment, his deep-set eyes flashing with a strange fire.

It was this flare of faith she recognized in his eyes that was spreading in the remotest corners of the kingdom. Was Vali meant to be their saviour, she wondered as she stood by his side, standing close together, surveying the rocky wasteland on one side and the dense woods on the other, with the dust settled and the Pampas River bubbling to the brim, the fresh greenery blending with the ruins; there was hope in their hopelessness. Vali seemed to have infused a new spirit in all of them through his vision of making Kishkindh the kingdom he wished to eventually form and rule.

'It's beautiful, isn't it?' he said, his eyes fixed on the craggy silhouetted horizon. 'The kingdom perfectly quiet and I suppose we know better how to cope with the climate and even the unrest... I missed Kishkindh, I missed my land,' he added, feeling at home in this forest, their new learning ground, their new school. Both Sugriv and he had proceeded to live the life of two young branches of a tree, for that is undoubtedly how they saw themselves. But neither could escape the real world any longer.

Tara rested her head on his shoulder, sighing. 'It's so quiet, so still. Yet, when I am alone here, I never feel lonely,' she confessed, fingering the bracelet he had given to her.

Vali could not help but keep gazing at her. Tara looked very crisp and fresh in her coarse linen drape. The heat did not distress her.

She felt his arms go slack around her. 'Do you want to run down to the river?' he asked suddenly, lifting his head. 'Like we did as kids? Then we can go boating.'

She nodded, thinking of the time when they used to play as children. Over time, the topography changed as rapidly as their flying feet. The sombre hillscape gave way to the silent, impenetrable jungle with its great, cheerful river, which was unlike its ominous self in the lashing rains.

As they moved into the boat, she realized that, with Vali by her side, she was able to rediscover their land through his worshipping eyes. The beauty of the scene took her breath away—it was awe-inspiring.

'It's as if this forest where we meet is the only one to know our secret,' he sighed, his bronzed arms rippling as he moved the oars smoothly. 'This is our land. I shall have it all one day, with you as my queen,' he vowed, leaning forward, his breath fanning her face. She was not sure if it was the warmth of his breath or the heat of his words that made her flush, colour flowing into her cheeks.

'Are you proposing to me or planning your ambitions?' she said raising an eyebrow in mock indignation.

'Both,' he grinned. 'I also know that the answer for both is yes.'

She laughed. 'I don't know what I see in you.'

But, of course, she knew perfectly well. He was a serious, determined, hungry man who took everything very solemnly but he was constantly charmed, eyeing the world with a sceptic amusement and boundless optimism. He made her laugh frequently, breaking her usual demeanour of solemnity.

Vali looked at her as he rowed the boat. 'I would have persuaded you otherwise, were it not for the oars,' he assured her with his melting smile. She laughed, her heartiness warming his heart and making him laugh too. She was the only person with whom he found life a pleasing affair rather than serious business. She climbed over to him, the boat bobbing gently as she sat on her knees, and took his face in her hand, his bracelet at her wrist jingling against his cheek, and said, 'You are an ugly hulk of a man, Vali, but you've got charm.'

'And I can't help loving you,' he replied huskily, halting his rowing, his hands on her shoulders. Her only answer was to throw her arms round his neck and kiss him wildly.

'You will overturn the boat! Don't make it harder for me, Tara, you got me helpless!' he laughed.

'Do you think I can let you go now? I love you.'

His dark eyes turned swiftly serious.

'But your father will never let you marry me. I have nothing to my name but dreams,' he said, doubting his own proposal.

'You are to be the next chief, so you are eligible enough!' She lifted her shoulders in explanation.

'But I want to be a king—an emperor!' There was a grim tone in his voice. 'I hope to give my all for Kishkindh. What if I don't get time for you?'

She shook her head. 'Will I be a distraction? You just said that we'll take care of everything together—our dreams, our desires.'

He told her his plans. He had to make Kishkindh glorious once again. Jatayu, the old friend of his family, and Jambavan, Vriksharaj's minister, had offered to take him under their wing and have him meet all the important clans and tribes scattered across the forest. If he had to unite and lead all of them, he needed an army, a band of foot soldiers. He would have to train them all. Jatayu was powerful and his reach was spread across many territories. He had suggested that Vali should scour the entire Kishkindh for the next few months, where, under his mentorship, Vali could learn the details of that varied trade called diplomacy and politics. Towards the end, Jambavan promised, the young man would become a leader all would dread—

'And respect,' she interrupted.

Vali smiled. 'It is a wonderful opportunity.'

A wave of emotion swept over her, and her eyes filled with sudden tears. She saw his face contorted for a moment with the intensity of his feeling. His voice was a little shaky when he said, 'For this, I need you by my side.'

She did not need to say anything; she did not want to hear anything else either. Her heart was filled with an undecipherable joy as her eyes rested on the man she loved with a grateful, assured affection.

'I was on my way to your house. I must drop the medicines for your mother,' she said as they came to a stop at the gravelly shore. 'Is she feeling better?'

'Quite. I just gave her breakfast and came here. And I have to meet Sugriv and Jatayu,' he said, helping her out of the boat. 'I shall try to meet you again later in the night.'

No further words were necessary but just an eloquent look and a knowing smile.

*

The moment Tara entered the hut, Vriksharaj noticed the high colour on the young girl's dusky face. She wordlessly handed the medicines in their leathery palms, and they tucked it at the waist in the fold of their nine-yard sari.

'Can you help me with the stew?' Vriksharaj requested. 'I can't stir it for long with my stiff fingers.'

Tara nodded and obediently took the ladle from their hand.

Until very recently, Tara had seen Vriksharaj as a man—the chief of their tribe. But being with Vali had made her see them in the same light as their sons—as a woman, their mother, dressed in feminine robes, somewhere in her late middle age. In their fraternity, age did not matter; achievements did. And as the chief of the clan, they had contributed to its very existence. Some ten years ago, when Kishkindh was fairly prosperous, Vriksharaj had decided that they would provide the best grooming and education for their sons and had, accordingly, sent them to Rishi Gautam's ashram. Little did they know that they would be the heirs to a kingdom that was lost and defeated when the children were away. But they still endeavoured to influence the citizens of Kishkindh with their political views, their ethics and their decisions.

Yet Tara recognized the angry sadness and disillusionment simmering in Vriksharaj. Their tired, cynical eyes could see the cracks not only in the topography of the land but also in the makeup of his people. 'The people are as lost and defeated as the kingdom,' they sighed, watching Tara stir the pot of stew. 'But Vali will change all that!' they beamed.

Tara knew that their eyes were on her, taking stock of her. They were good-natured but shrewd and ruthless, she very well knew.

'The elders of the village would have undoubtedly withdrawn their support for me because of my gender if not for your father,' they confessed, shrugging their thin shoulders, a gesture their older son seemed to have inherited—a gesture as voluble as their vehement words. 'I reverted to being a man only for them, lest someone snatched my power and position.'

'But aren't we a matrilineal clan?'

'If that is so, it makes it easier for my sons, not me. I had clawed my way up... I didn't give up even when I was pregnant with my two boys!' they guffawed loudly, taking the ladle from her hands and mixing the stew vigorously. 'And I don't intend to vacate my position easily either,' they added, their tone grim. 'I have groomed my boys, they are the best, they are my worthy sons!'

'You keep saying "they", but there will come a time when one of them becomes king,' interposed Tara, in her soft, firm voice. 'Who will it be—Vali or Sugriv?'

'Vali, of course,' Vriksharaj replied without a moment's hesitation. 'He will do it!' they exulted with renewed vigour, their gruff voice excited.

'Because he is older?'

'No, because he is a born leader! Besides, he has earned it,' the old woman shook their hoary head. 'Moreover, Vali is stronger—in every sense of the word... Sugriv is a good boy, but he's no trailblazer. Some lead, others follow. It is best if he shadows his older brother,' they paused, stopping the stirring. 'Why? Why are you so keen to know?' they asked shrewdly, glancing up as she reached for the ladle. Their small, rubbery face split into an uneasy scowl, as they neatly assessed the girl sitting beside them.

They had known her since she was born, their friend's daughter who had lost her mother when she was just four. With her innate cleverness and self-possession declaring her astonishing efficiency, Tara had proved herself to be a capable healer herself. She had smoothly taken over her father's profession and people's hearts with her sharp intellect and kindly ways. *Even the hearts of my sons*, they wildly suspected with a sudden spurt of worry.

Sushen's daughter mystified Vriksharaj. Sushen was as worthy a doctor and a father. His daughter was like him—or even better, they acknowledged grudgingly. Where the good doctor was doing his duty conscientiously with an obvious conviction that everything in the world was hopeless and incurable, his daughter, Tara, was resolutely cheerful.

'Vali and Sugriv are so close,' remarked Tara. 'I wonder who will give up what for the other.'

The old chief drew in a sharp breath. 'They will decide comfortably by themselves. They need no one else. And no one is to come between them,' they tersely added.

Tara detected the stern tone of reprimand in their voice. She glanced at the old woman in surprise.

'They need each other; they are dependent. You have

seen to it,' observed Tara.

They tightened their jaw at her statement, which, Tara realized, must have come across as criticism. 'They only have each other. One needs to defend the other,' Vriksharaj said fiercely, 'though it's often Vali who is the self-proclaimed protector. They were not quite welcomed at the ashram, seen as savages of the jungle who needed to be tamed—'

'Yet you sent them there,' quipped Tara in between.

'Because it's true! If they had remained at Kishkindh, they would have become barbaric brutes—or worse, lazy idlers as most in the village are!' snorted Vriksharaj. 'My sons are proud Vanaras and I want them to make all the Vanaras be proud of themselves too. For that they need a mission, and Vali has one. He knows the most prized possession of a human being is his identity—his selfhood, his roots and his destination!'

Tara was quick to detect the pride in their voice.

Vriksharaj's crafty eyes gleamed. 'But there's lots to be done here. Both are trying to cajole and liaise with other tribes. Right now, Vali is trying to unite all the clans of Kishkindh. Only he can do it. Over the years, the clans have lost their unity, either because of greedy self-interest or for fear of Ravan. He has come over to the mainland from that tiny island kingdom of his and struck terror into the minds of everyone in the Dandak. The first task for Vali is to go and talk with each tribe and create a unified alliance against a common foe. If the Asuras and Rakshasas are our enemies, Vali will rope in all the other Vanaras, the Yakshas and the Kinnaras on his side.'

Tara stared thoughtfully at the old chief. 'More importantly, they share another trait,' Vriksharaj continued, 'all are closely connected with nature and the forest. And that's the fundamental law of the jungle the Rakshasas have broken. Like us, the Kinnaras and the Yakshas have a common motto to live by—save the jungles.

'Oh, they can be sly too!' they chuckled. 'They are powerful magicians and shape-shifters also, mind you. Ravan's maternal grandmother Taraka incidentally was a Yaksha princess, and her two sons Subahu and Maricha are as canny as her. If Subahu is a murderous brute, Maricha is a master magician like his mother. They are going to side with Ravan. He is family after all.'

Tara looked at Vriksharaj, an astonished expression on her face, and said, 'Oh, are they? But for these too, I am sure the other Yakshas and other tribes like the Kimpurushas, Salabhas and the staunch Sun followers, Valikhilyas, might agree to team up with Vali against Ravan.'

Vriksharaj paused, their eyes wary and watchful. 'You know our tribes as well as the herbs you study and gather!'

Tara looked at them, surprised at the oblique commendation. She hesitated, her delicate brows creased in concern. 'Ravan *is* a formidable opponent.'

'Adversaries are always formidable,' they retorted. 'It is the arrogant who underestimates his rival.'

'Which I think Ravan is and is going to commit that mistake,' she observed thoughtfully.

'Fortunately, Ravan hasn't even heard of Vali or he would have attacked Kishkindh by now!' said Vriksharaj in vicious glee. 'Vali can catch him unprepared.'

'Surely not!' exclaimed Tara. 'Vali is getting famous for his super deeds and, yes, his magnificent necklace!'

Something in her voice made Vriksharaj look sharply at her.

'You talk of Vali with a certain familiar possessiveness,'

they remarked, their hawk eyes trailing to her slim wrist. 'Like that bracelet that you keep brandishing before my eyes!'

Tara bit her lower lip, instinctively touching the bracelet.

'For a person who is not too fond of jewellery, the bracelet seems new, Tara. Who gave it to you?' demanded Vriksharaj, their eyes fixed on the trinket she was covering self-consciously with her hand.

'I got it from the local fair,' she said warily, wondering why she was lying. She disliked deception.

Not convinced, they threw her a suspicious glare. 'I know you too well, young lady. I have seen you grow from a girl to a lady—and I am sure your father will want you to marry some doctor, teacher or scholar!' Vriksharaj said not too subtly, unsteadily getting on their feet. They rose to their full height.

'I don't want you mixing with my sons!' they warned her quietly but she could detect the passion in their voice. 'You think I haven't noticed? You seem to have some hold over both of them. You are no longer kids playing a game. I don't want you hurting them or coming in their way! If you are his well-wisher, you will know what's good for him!'

Tara met their furious gaze with her steady one. She was not surprised by the suddenness of this attack; she remained motionless, staring at the older woman. All her puzzled mind could comprehend was Vriksharaj had mentioned *both* their sons. What did Sugriv have to do with her, she wondered perplexed.

'I think you are overreacting,' Tara said quietly but the firmness in her voice was hard. 'We are all childhood friends as you well know, your sons, Ruma and I.'

The chief snorted. Their leathery complexion turned a dark red. 'You, Vali, Sugriv and Ruma,' they exploded. 'I don't want either of you girls coming between my sons! The boys are one—like this,' they shook their fist at her, meant to be seen as a symbol of strength and unity between the brothers but cleverly cloaked as a threatening gesture.

Tara felt a hot flush of mortification climb up her neck. 'Should you not discuss this with your sons instead of me or Ruma?' she added pointedly.

Vriksharaj was quick to discern the quiet acerbity in the young girl's voice as she threw his own words at them. Their tone hardened. 'One day, Vali will be king and he needs to marry someone of strategic importance.'

'Some princess for a political alliance, you mean.'

Again, they caught something in Tara's voice. Vriksharaj nodded their hoary head violently, ignoring the jibe. 'It would prove good for all, wouldn't it?' they snapped, surprised at the girl's cool response.

Tara seemed untroubled, calmly stirring the pot, giving a slow nod making her auburn hair glow red in the sunshine. Tara knew that the dread of losing control over their sons had turned Vriksharaj into this shrill fury, venting their rage-stricken fear on her.

Tara smiled, pleasantly. 'True, Vali will be most sought after,' she said lightly, hoping to pacify the agitated chief. 'Let's leave it to him, shall we?'

Vriksharaj discerned the quiet threat in her voice. 'I shall leave nothing to chance,' they said haughtily. 'Vali is currently basking in fresh praise from all over. He's popular. There are songs made about him. Stories about how invincibly powerful he is, with his strength equalling that of thousands of elephants; about no one being able to defeat him in a battle, do good!'

'Or that Vali is favoured by the gods themselves,' said Tara to put the old chief in a good mood. 'That he helped the gods to churn the oceans, and that, to thank Vali, the gods gave him a boon where all of his challengers would immediately lose half of their strength to him. So which story is true? This one, of Brahma's boon or the power of Indra's necklace?'

Vriksharaj's raddled face twisted in a tight grimace. 'Vali is gaining favour because he is Indra's son, not because he is mine,' they said unhappily.

'You mustn't talk like that,' Tara said quietly. 'It's quite untrue. You know you mean the world to your sons. Such grandiose, larger-than-life tales are always sung about heroes. As Vali rightly says, you are both—the mother *and* father.'

The chief lifted their frail shoulders but there was a certain forlornness in his shrug. 'But for how long?' they said wistfully. 'I wish to retire, handing all my responsibilities to Vali and then I can die in peace,' they sighed. 'But I do know that the future of Kishkindh lies in the future of both my sons.'

4

THE QUARTET

Vali picked up his lifestyle before the ashram very quickly. Besides his political acumen and suave diplomacy, he knew how to be the people's man. Sometimes, he would go fishing with the fishermen and bring home a basket full of coloured fish. Sometimes, at night, he would go out with them with a lantern to catch lobsters.

Meanwhile, during the day, Tara would pick plantains off the trees around her hut and roast them for her evening meal. She knew how to make delicious concoctions from coconuts and the breadfruit tree by the side of the creek that gave them its fruit.

However, some things had changed for Tara since Vali's return to the village. Who would have thought that within six months, they would be so close, Tara wondered as she absently threaded her fingers through his thick hair, his head cradled on her lap. He, too, had got used to lying like this for hours while Tara chatted with that slow smile on her face as she weaved ropes and grass mats with deft fingers.

'You are good at this too,' he grumbled.

'It's almost like stitching up a person or an injured animal,' she shrugged.

'You nurse animals too?' he said with astonishment. 'Most would fear going near a wounded animal.'

Tara gave a nonchalant shrug. 'Animals are part of the jungle family. We have to live in the forest together as fellow beings. Should we not protect them since man claims he is the higher animal?' she said quizzically. 'Though, of course, "higher" does not necessarily indicate nobility.'

'So, you clearly disapprove of hunting?'

'As a man-made pleasure, definitely yes; try facing an animal without a weapon and see what happens!' she flamed, her brown eyes glittering. 'To kill an animal for entertainment is cowardice—it is simply vile!'

'Try telling the mighty kings and their herd of hunters,' he drawled.

He was greeted by an angry snort from Tara, and he could not stop smiling; he liked ruffling her righteous feathers.

✳

Now that Tara knew what love was, she had begun to feel sympathy for the love Ruma nursed for Sugriv. Vriksharaj's worry about Ruma had not been unfounded. She could sense that he did not seem to return her ardour. Tara would playfully tease Sugriv about it. It amused her to see the slow smile with which he received her banter.

But little did she know that Sugriv was uncomfortable. She had mistaken his reticence for shyness while he wished she would stop her incessant teasing. He loved *her*, not Ruma, he screamed inside. Since the time they had returned to the village, he had repeated to himself the words he meant to say. Doubts assailed him; fear haunted him. His conscience, always very delicate, was not at ease.

He was sure no one guessed he was in love with Tara. It was something he couldn't help and wouldn't change. Mercifully, Tara didn't realize his feelings, and for that he was grateful.

Confusion was gradually brewing in him. A kind of vexation was stirring the depths of his being and, preventing him from concentrating on what he had to do. They were friends, but he wanted more. They chatted endlessly, but he could not get himself to voice his feelings for her. Was that why he kept waiting for Tara, to walk past the street to catch a momentary glimpse of her?

The answer came swiftly and viciously to him one day. Tara spotted him hovering inside the window.

'Come out!' she called. 'We are going to the pool.'

'We?' he asked, with a sinking feeling. He had hoped she would wait and chat with him.

'I am meeting Ruma round the corner.'

His heart sank further. *Ruma*, he sighed, feeling that he had no desire to talk. They barely walked for two minutes when Ruma joined them. Ignoring her addition and excitement, he nevertheless asked, 'What pool?'

'At the end of the forest, there's a pond, higher up, off the river bank,' Ruma interjected with a delighted squeal. 'And where Tara and Vali meet every day,' she added slyly.

His heart froze. So, what he had suspected was true. *Vali and Tara*. He felt a burning sensation in his chest, which seemed to be, concentrated rage. He found himself boiling over with uncontrollable anger. This impertinent girl had suddenly given him a reason to despise her by confirming his long-lingering doubt. 'I can't join in, I am busy!'

Seeing Tara shrug in hurt—she did not seem to care much whether he joined them or not. But he noticed how Ruma's face fell.

'Come Sugriv, don't say no! We were planning to have a swim there,' Ruma pleaded, regarding him with a hopeful glance. 'It's too hot here.'

He flushed and firmly shook his head.

'Oh come on, Vali may join us too,' said Tara with her small smile.

'Was it decided already?' he asked shortly.

'Vaguely,' she nodded. 'Yesterday, when we met up.'

Again, a sliver of pain pierced his heart.

'So, why am *I* intruding?' he asked peevishly.

Tara looked puzzled. 'You aren't intruding, Sugriv! Ruma's here too. It'll be good fun—all of us together, like old times!' she laughed, pulling at his arm.

Sugriv felt himself melt under the heat of her touch.

He gave a brief grin and allowed himself to be dragged by his arm, his hand in hers. Suddenly, he caught sight of the bracelet tinkling at her hand.

'Where did you get that?' he asked without thinking.

'Vali's gift to her!' informed Ruma with undisguised glee.

Sugriv dropped her hand, as if it was scorching hot but Tara barely noticed as she strolled ahead, bending over to peer at the wayside wildflowers.

Tara looked back to notice Ruma linking her hand with Sugriv's. She smiled fondly at them. They looked good together. Ruma had grasped his arm and Sugriv was looking stiff and stoic as always, as Tara watched them in deep conversation interspersed with Ruma's frequent hearty laughs.

That's how they are spending these idyllic days, Tara

thought as they climbed into the round boat. The ripples in the river seemed to dimple around them.

*

Downstream, under the shade of a tree, sprawled Vali. Lying on his stomach, his head resting on his hands, he gazed fixedly at the winding river.

This was his haven with Tara...

Screwing up his eyes on account of the glaring reflection of the river, Vali, thinking about meeting Tara, grunted with pleasure and contentment. She would arrive soon. A few minutes more and she would be there, with her soft, serene smile. She would throw her arms around him and kiss him, and would give him the news of what was going on yonder in her soft, sonorous voice. They would go for a quick swim in the pool, make love. That is how they spent every afternoon together. And at sunset, he would row her back over the river against the sharp evening air.

He had opened his eyes and noticed that, in the distance, a black spot danced on the river. The boat. Tara was here.

As he watched the little black spot grow larger, it seemed to him that Tara was not alone in the boat. Could Ruma have come along with her? Vali grimaced, moving heavily on the sand. He sat up, shading his eyes with his hands, and with a show of ill humour began to strain his eyes to see who was coming. No, the person rowing was not Ruma; she rowed strong but clumsily. It was Sugriv. *Damn*, he swore silently. Just when he wanted some stolen time with Tara...

'Hey there!' cried Vali impatiently.

'Vali! You reached before me!' a voice came back from the boat. It was Tara's, crystal clear over the river breeze.

'Row faster!' commanded Tara, and Sugriv obeyed.

His stroke was so vigorous that the boat was carried up the beach on a wave. It fell over on one side and then righted itself while the wave rolled back laughing into the river. Sugriv jumped out on the beach and, going up to Vali, asked insolently:

'How are you, brother?'

'Sugriv, I thought you were to go to the hills with Amma!' cried Vali, pretending to look pleased. 'This is a surprise.'

They embraced. Vali's surprise became mingled with both relief and unease. He ran impatient fingers through his thick hair with one hand and with the other gesticulated, 'I knew something was up; trust Tara to plan a nice get together!'

Vali would have liked to look at Tara, but his brother's quiet eyes were upon him and he did not dare. The love he felt for Tara, so strong and lovely, struggled in him against the embarrassment caused by the presence of Sugriv. For the first time, he had a secret, something he had not shared with his brother. He shuffled about and kept asking Sugriv one question after another, often without waiting for a reply. His head felt awhirl, and he felt particularly uneasy when he heard Ruma say in a mocking tone, 'We caught your hideout, didn't we?'

One brother examined the other from head to toe. On the latter's lips hovered that sneer Vali knew so well.

Tara turned her amber eyes from one brother to the other, while Ruma, linked her arms through Sugriv's. Sugriv smiled and, for a few seconds that were excruciating for Vali, all four remained silent.

'Well, we girls brought you brothers together with us, didn't we?' said Ruma, brushing up against Sugriv's robust frame.

Sugriv gave a shrug of ill humour and replied, 'We

brothers don't need you to bring us together, do we?' he said gruffly.

Tara widened her eyes in surprise at his curt words. Ruma laughed louder to hide her hurt.

Her laugh displeased Sugriv. He paid no attention to Ruma and noticed Tara's rising blush.

'And here's how you catch quick fish!' cried Tara, dipping into the river and coming up with a wriggling fish, grappling it with both her hands, aware of the thickening tension among the quartet.

Vali had not got over his apprehension but had succeeded in dissimulating it deep within him. Now he looked at his unexpected guests with a certain resigned good humour; only his manner was more agitated than usual.

'I'll make a fire in a minute, and we'll talk. Sugriv, help me with the firewood,' he announced, immediately taking over the tense situation.

Ruma continued gazing familiarly at Sugriv, her eyes stormy. He tried not to meet her eyes or Tara's, although he would have liked to. Then, intimidated by the silence, he said aloud, 'Give me a minute. Ruma, you have my knife.'

'It's in the boat,' she said stiltedly.

'Where?' Show me?' he said with a tight smile.

Ruma rose leisurely and Sugriv followed her down to the boat. Vali waited till they disappeared. Then he bent down towards Tara and snapped at her with anger, 'What did you want to bring him for? What shall I tell him about you?'

'What's that to me? Am I afraid of him? Or of you?' demanded Tara, her golden brown eyes widening with disdain. 'Besides I am sure he has guessed about us!' Then she gave a short laugh, 'How you went on when you saw him. It was so funny!'

'Funny?! I am—'

The sand crunched under Sugriv's steps and they had to suspend their conversation. Sugriv had a sharp knife. He cast a hostile look at Vali.

'I am going for the firewood. Meanwhile, you catch more fish. With Tara,' Sugriv testily added. 'She seems to be decidedly good at it.'

Tara made no attempt to reply, sensing his antagonism. She frowned, perplexed—more so because he would not meet her gaze.

'No, let's collect the wood,' said Vali, his tone hard. 'The girls can catch fish.'

Without further ado, he strode out and Sugriv followed him, watching his brother's stiff, muscled back. They walked together in stony silence and started gathering firewood.

'Where did you meet Tara?' asked Vali, finally.

'On the way,' said Sugriv, vaguely, blinking his eyes, 'as Tara was coming to meet you here,' he added cuttingly.

'So now you know about us,' Vali exhaled sharply. He threw his brother an anxious look. 'And... What do you think of...us?'

'What's it to me?' said Sugriv. 'It's your affair. I'm not your judge.'

'You are my brother,' said Vali. 'Your opinion is important to me.'

'Why are you suddenly asking me this now?' Sugriv said furiously, his temper getting the better of him. 'I've known Tara a damn sight longer than you—'

Vali was taken aback at the savageness of his tone, his impassive eyes flaring in surprise. He pursed his lips into a hard line. 'You are a fine one to talk. Until you barged in, we've never had any trouble.'

'Take it easy,' Sugriv returned, with a hard little smile. 'I didn't ask to barge in, you know. She invited me over. Just treat her right, will you, and tell her I've been called away. I am leaving.'

Vali said hastily, 'Now look, Sugriv, I'm sorry for what I said. I was just rattled with you and your unreasonable behaviour. Sit down and forget it.'

Sugriv looked sufficiently mollified. 'You should have told me before,' he groused, his tone distinctly surly.

'I am telling you now,' Vali replied. His eyes narrowed. 'You don't look too happy about it.'

Sugriv restrained himself with an effort. 'I *am* happy. Happy for you. For Tara. Congratulations,' he said shortly. 'It's just that you didn't confide in me earlier, unlike you always do. We have never held secrets, have we?' He raised one brow, sighed and spoke in a beseeching tone, yet he wanted to speak brutally to his brother. 'You love her. She loves you. Great. Let's return to the girls. They must be waiting.'

Vali stopped him, placing a restraining arm on his brother's shoulder. 'Sugriv,' he said with warmth, and Sugriv, turned around, guilt and fury tearing at his heart. The world would have said Vali had reasons for hate, not him. *Has it never occurred to Vali that I too might love Tara?* But Vali was blind, the blinkers of trust still firmly on, the fact that Vali could not see his treacherous heart. Both Tara and Vali trusted him; he was the loyal brother, the trusted friend. *They are too trusting...*

'Sugriv, I wished to tell you before but something kept turning up and I kept pushing it—' Vali threw up his hands in a helpless gesture.

Sugriv cut him short, 'As long as Tara is happy too.'

'Happy?' Vali looked up at him as though his inflection of the word sounded strange. 'Why wouldn't she be?'

'Yes, happy. That is important. To be happy. When you are miserable, you envy other people's happiness.'

Vali's face transformed. 'Why would you say that? Are you miserable?'

Sugriv gave a quick shake of the head. It wasn't what he had wanted to say. But there, in that phrase, his bitterness leaked out of his heart.

He forced a short laugh. 'I meant generally, not specific to me. I meant there might be some opposition to this,' he said tactfully. 'Are *you* happy?'

'But of course!'

'Are you sure?'

'Very. And so is she.'

'That's all that matters,' Sugriv responded sourly, clenching his fists. 'We have enough wood for the meal. Let's go.'

Jealousy existed only with possessiveness, or so he had believed. Today, he was experiencing it. Tara was his friend first. He had made friends with her first when he had tentatively approached the quiet, withdrawn girl sitting in the last row of the classroom. Vali had got to know her much later. Yet, she had become closer to Vali than to him. On their return from the ashram, it had been he who had been with her almost all of the time. Yet, it was Vali she had fallen in love with... He felt crushed under the weight of heavy hopelessness. *Why couldn't Tara love me instead*?

Vali followed his brother as he heaved the pile of twigs and branches on his broad shoulders. He felt faintly uneasy, the feeling mounting every passing moment. Something was not right. He had expected a warmer, heartier reaction from Sugriv. As Vali made his way back to where everyone else was, he noticed that Sugriv had already lit a flame with a flint stick and dried leaves. He hurried over to add the twigs and branches he held to get the fire going. While placing the pot on the fire, he brooded over Sugriv's reaction. Henceforth, he thought, his life would be less agreeable, less free. Sugriv strangely had not taken kindly to the news. *Why?* Sugriv must have surely guessed what Tara was to him, although he had not confided in him. So what was his anger for?

Vali regarded his brother quizzically. Sugriv was sitting close to Ruma, who was trying to tease his brother with her bold eyes. Vali looked at them with shuttered eyes; they looked good together. If he had Tara, Sugriv had Ruma, who was clearly madly in love with him.

Yet why did it not feel right?

Having already collected enough fish, Tara now returned with the plantain leaves, and they sat down for lunch. They ate without talking, relishing their meal and spitting fish bones out on the sand. Sugriv literally devoured his food, which seemed to please Ruma vastly. Vali was not hungry. He tried, however, to appear absorbed in the meal to be able to watch Tara and Sugriv with more aware, alert eyes.

After a while, when Sugriv had eaten his fill, he announced he was sleepy.

'Let's lie down here,' suggested Ruma. 'Tara will wake us up.'

'Willingly,' he agreed, sinking down on the soft sand, watching Tara walk up to Vali to sit near him. He felt a burning stab of resentment. 'And what will *you* do?' he questioned, turning to Vali with a fake smile.

Vali's face darkened, but he restrained himself as Tara slipped her hand in his and pressed it in a gesture of warning. Sugriv watched this with mixed feelings. Then he said without thinking, 'That's smooth, Tara. You call us over under the pretext of meeting my brother?'

Vali's face flared and darkened even further. The embarrassment due to his brother's mockery took over him, causing him to turn on his heel and walk away, leaving behind an uneasy silence.

Sugriv pursed his lips. Again, that sudden feeling of jealousy swamped his better judgement. 'Oh, rot!' he said, angrily. 'I was fooling around, just teasing my brother for his romance,' he sneered. 'Do I need your permission to do that? But you two needn't look so damned guilty about it.' He gave Tara a sharp look. 'What are you blushing for, anyway?'

Tara threw him an icy glare and walked away, gathering control over her temper and frustration.

Sugriv's eyes followed her bleakly.

'You were caught flat footed there,' Ruma said quietly, toying with a stray tendril.

Sugriv ran his fingers through his hair. 'What's the matter with Tara? I've never seen her like that before.' He looked at Ruma, anger in his eyes. 'I think I've made a mistake coming here...'

Ruma gave an impatient sigh and pulled him down, next to her. 'Oh, leave them be,' she said unperturbed. 'Tara is tired; it's a new romance. She's anxious and doesn't want you brothers quarrelling. Why are you fighting, anyway?' she asked, her eyes narrowing in sudden thought.

'Nothing. Just wished he'd told me himself, as a brother should.'

'But now he's a lover too, Sugriv, and the brother in him had to take a step back,' Ruma said lazily.

She saw his mouth tighten. She placed a finger on his pursed lips. 'You are mighty possessive! Look after me instead, can't you? You've got someone worthwhile.'

Sugriv turned over and pretended to sleep. Through half-closed eyes, he looked at Ruma. Squatting on the sand, with her long legs drawn up to her chin, Ruma balanced herself gently to and fro, idly gazing with her raven eyes over the dazzling joyous river, and she smiled with triumph as women do when they understand the power of their beauty. But he did not like her raven, cynical eyes. He shut his eyes and it was the image of Tara that emerged immediately; her soft, brown eyes; her soft, serene smile; her soft, gentle touch... But she must be with Vali now, lying with him, arms entwined... He shut his eyes in blind rage.

*

Vali had fixed three stakes in the sand and, with a piece of matting, had rigged a shelter for some shade. Then he lay down flat on his back and contemplated the sky. When Tara laid down on the sand by his side, he turned towards her with vexation plainly written on his face.

'Well,' she said, twisting the bracelet with her right forefinger. 'You don't seem pleased to see your brother. Nor he, you.'

'He mocks me. And, why? Because of you,' replied Vali testily.

'Oh, I am sorry. So what are we to do? Stop meeting? Stop coming here? Stop loving you?' Her tone was scornful.

He saw she was annoyed and, with a visible effort, controlled his foul mood. She was turning the bracelet agitatedly with her other hand, and the sight of it melted away his displeasure. He pulled her towards him, the bracelet tinkling. 'A siren that you are! Ah, Tara! He sneers at me, and now you too—and yet you know you are dearest to me.'

He moved close to her, but she sat stiff, straight-backed and silent.

'Why don't you speak?' asked Vali, outlining her compressed lips with his finger.

'I am angry, and I am thinking,' she said slowly. Then after a pause she added, 'I thought we would have this picnic together—the four of us. But it did not work. We have split— we here, those two there...'

'You were to meet me in private,' he corrected her, again annoyed. '*You* got them here.'

'Is that why you are sulking?' she enquired, with a small smile.

Vali did not return her smile.

She puckered her brows in consternation. 'Sugriv's usually a gentle fellow, but he seems angry today. And I was rude to him too.'

'What's that to you?' cried Vali. 'Brothers fight.'

'Needlessly. He is your brother; he is my friend. I would have thought he would be a lot amiable about this,' she observed, frowning.

Vali glanced at her sneakily. 'He's upset I didn't tell him before,' he sighed. 'But yes, his reaction is odd. I'm a patient man, though. I will wait for him to come around.'

He ground his teeth and clenched his fist.

'What if he doesn't, Vali?' she asked worriedly, without looking up at him.

'Well, there's nothing to worry about. We are close and...' he exhaled in quiet resignation. 'I guess, he isn't too happy about sharing me with you,' he teased, his eyes twinkling.

'Stop joking.'

She shook her head with concern, playing impatiently with her bracelet.

'At this rate, you are sure to break that bracelet!'

Alarmed, she stopped fiddling. Her anxiety cooled Vali's humour. He had never seen her look so anxious and beautiful.

Tara gazed with apprehension at his smiling face.

'I'm not even your wife yet, and trouble seems to be brewing already,' she fretted. 'You have been accustomed to your brother all your life. You are brothers first. I have no wish to come between you and him.'

'That's not what this is about,' Vali stroked her cheek. 'It's just that he is very possessive and in time, he'll come around—'

'No, possessiveness is not reason enough for this. Moreover, I am free. I belong only to myself, and I am afraid of no one. But I am scared of being the reason for today's antagonism between the two of you. Why he was downright hostile to me? I, in turn, turned nasty myself. I don't like it, Vali. You are very close as brothers but, remember, all of us are also friends. I don't wish for any conflict among us.'

'You are making too much out of this. Sugriv has his odd moments; he throws tantrums. He's my younger brother after all. Today was one of them. It is just that you have never seen this side of him.'

Tara nodded slowly, 'And I thought I knew him better.'

✷

5

CONDITIONS AND CONFRONTATIONS

Tara slept badly; she was riddled with guilt and pique and uncertainty.

Vriksharaj had publicly announced Vali as their successor the previous morning at a meeting in the assembly hall, and proclaimed him as the new chief. It was clearly not a surprise and was hailed unanimously; no one challenged the decision; no one dared challenge Vali—not even Sugriv, the sole candidate of opposition. Tara had seen him applauding thunderously, his benign face animated with unbridled pride. The brothers seemed to have mended fences, she thought with relief. His eyes briefly met hers and the smile immediately drained from his face. *No, the problem is still festering*, Tara told herself with a sinking heart, waving her hands at Sugriv in a gesture of friendliness. It wasn't reciprocated.

She decided that she would have to settle this once and for all. Since the episode at the river a fortnight ago, she had been thinking of Vali and herself, of confronting Sugriv, of the questions she needed to ask, and for days, she had rehearsed for the conversation she could have with him. She was neither timid nor afraid to ask even the indiscreet. Some accused her of being too upfront. But right now, she was more hesitant than afraid. Was it wise to directly tackle Sugriv herself? He hadn't been too friendly with her—churlish and mostly taciturn, clearly trying to avoid her. She sighed. That was why she would have to face him, friend to friend. And then there was Vali to think of... Did she have the courage in her what she planned to tell him?

Occupied till late with her nursing chores, she hurried down the dusty track, quickening her pace, knowing she was going to be late that afternoon to meet Vali at the pool. With her mind as rushed as her steps, she kept thinking, worrying if what she was going to do was right.

Vali was sitting there. As she walked closer, he glanced around and noiselessly slid into the water. He vanished like a fish and she stood surprised, wondering where he had hidden himself. Vali and his little games, she gave an exasperated sigh as she spotted him again perched on a rock. She looked at him with uncurious eyes.

'Is this why you wanted me to come? To cavort with you?' she grumbled. Something in her voice made him look at her. She sounded uncharacteristically annoyed, and as she stood standing over him like a wild creature of the water and the woods, she looked more alluring than ever, with bare feet and hair loose and tousled, tumbling over her exposed, brown shoulders.

It looked as though an idea occurred to him, for he turned towards her with his charming smile and tone. 'I want to say something to you.'

She looked at him quickly and she saw that his eyes were filled with a suppressed excitement. His voice was eager. She knew the reason for his heightened sense of exhilaration. 'Now that I am the chief, let's get married!'

Tara didn't respond but shook back her hair and then let it spread over her shoulders in luxuriant curls. Inside, she was a little chilled.

'Are you proposing again?' she countered, her eyes oddly serious.

He grinned, 'Yes, of course. Now I am in a better position.'

'Oh, are you sure I will say yes?' she questioned with a mirthless smile.

She was glad to have an opportunity to laugh a little, for on that fine, sunny day, the air about them seemed a bit heavy with sudden foreboding.

He frowned, puzzled. 'What do you mean?'

'I mean, I say no. I don't want to marry you.'

Sitting close to him, she felt his arm muscles tense. He looked at her blankly. What she said was so unexpected that at the first moment he could hardly gather its sense.

'What on earth are you talking about?' he faltered, his eyes darkening.

'I can't marry you.'

She thought he would explode with rage. Instead, he said nothing more but rose majestically to his feet. He stood stock-still. His immobility was strangely terrifying. 'Why?' he asked finally.

'Because you are not what I thought you to be.'

His head jerked up, a dark, angry flush staining his face.

'For God's sake, just a few days ago, you were all willing and ready.'

'Things have changed,' she remarked tightly.

He frowned. 'What? My quarrel with Sugriv? Or yesterday's announcement?'

'*You* have changed,' she insisted quietly.

'Now that I am chief?' he asked incredulously. 'How does

it affect our plans to get married? In fact, my new status should improve matters for everyone. And now that I am no longer a vagabond, your father won't object anymore.'

'You were made chief through dynastic privilege, Vali. You have done nothing to earn it,' she corrected.

Vali flushed.

'Besides, it's I, and not my father, who have objections,' she reminded him.

He shrugged helplessly. 'I don't understand you, Tara. You allege I am a drifter, yet you resent me becoming a chief and have now made it an argument against our marriage. I know you love me and want to marry me. Or am I stupid?' He continued, 'I want to tell you that I love you more than anything in the world, but I find it so awfully difficult to say more...'

'You are anything but stupid, Vali, but you are getting smug and abundantly complacent. Have you accomplished even a single goal you had once discussed with me? You were to go with Jatayu and talk with the clans to unite them. You started it and left it midway. You still are a self-satisfied drifter, Vali, and I have no wish to marry a man with no sense of responsibility!'

Vali looked surprised; if anything, he had not expected these words from her. His face twisted in a scowl. There was a pause. But all at once he looked up, and a gleam of malicious amusement came into his eyes.

'Is this your idea of honesty?'

He spoke almost flippantly, and when she glanced at him, she was surprised to see in his eyes a tinge of mockery. She did not seem to be able to make Vali see how desperately grave the situation was. His airiness made her impatient. The surroundings, otherwise lovely, now intimidated her. Would it have been much easier to say what she had wanted in a more clinical ambience? Or could she have been in his arms, with hers around his neck, and persuaded him otherwise? Hers had to be harsh words, she thought to herself, understanding that her enticing pleas would not work anymore.

'Honesty is often harsh to hear.'

'What about your honesty?' he demanded. 'Are you not being stubborn? Wilful? Don't you realize this is desperately serious? We've come to the crossroads, and what we do now is going to affect our whole lives.'

'Believe me, I'm serious. And yes, I am stubborn to get what you promised me. Have you seen yourself these days, Vali?' she asked, but it wasn't a question. She was stating her observation. 'Now that you have won a handful of the tribesmen on your side, you think your work's done. You are doing nothing but spending time with me or playing the fool with your friends, drinking away the night. We are constantly together, and we could be spending the entire day in each other's arms were it not for my work, the patients and the clinic. But what about *you*, Vali? What about *your* work? *Your* ambitions? The ones you serenaded me with? I know you love me, but that is clearly not enough. I want more from you, like once you wanted more from yourself, for yourself. You are distracted, Vali. You have lost focus. And if I marry you now, I shall destroy you.'

'Which means?' he said dully, but his eyes were cold.

'Pull yourself together, Vali. Be the man of mission you had promised yourself to be. Love seems to have blunted all your drive and determination. All you have are empty dreams...'

'I am the chief now,' he said roughly.

'Of a barren wasteland,' she returned fiercely. 'Where

is that empire of Kishkindh you wished to eke out for the Vanaras? Has it been restored to its former glory?'

'I am the chief now,' he repeated. 'I shall do it.'

'You once were ambitious, a man of action. But what have you done till date?' she asked cruelly. 'Today, you are a foolish lover, gloating over his love and life, when I have the power to deprive you of both. And I am doing so. I can't marry you,' she stated with finality. 'I shan't marry you till you prove yourself.'

His brows shot up in disbelief. 'What exactly do you mean?' he said.

She looked at him quickly, for his voice was hoarse, and she saw that his face was a dull red. 'I shall marry you once you show that you are more than what you are now,' she declared without a moment's hesitation.

Vali expelled a deep breath, his heart sinking, hating the contempt lacing her silken voice.

It was dreadful that he should love her so devotedly and yet feel such bitterness towards her. It was not possible that she understood how much she meant to him.

'Oh, Tara, don't you know how I love you?'

'But we need more than love; we need a purpose. You really must be reasonable.'

Vali heaved a ragged sigh. 'How can I be reasonable? To me, our love is everything, and you are my whole life. It is not very pleasant to know that to you I am just a contest in which I have to win.' He paused, and continued, 'If you loved me, you wouldn't make me so unhappy.'

'I do love you,' she replied calmly. 'Regrettably, one can't do what one thinks is right without making someone unhappy.' She spread her hands with eloquent grace. 'I can't, Vali. It would be death for me. And, more importantly, death to you too, though you don't seem to realize it. It would be the betrayal of your soul. I don't want to be unkind and, Heaven knows, I don't want to hurt your feelings, but I must tell you the truth.'

'That I am a wastrel.'

'That you are no ordinary person. But you have to strive at being the extraordinary man. You have had it too easy—your position and the love of your life. You need to earn both. Go, Vali, seize your dreams. And then come to me, victorious, in all your glory.'

She suddenly grew conscious of the look in his eyes, tender as it always was when fixed on her, but troubled. She gave a self-conscious smile. 'You think I'm being unreasonable and demanding, don't you?'

'No, I don't so. I think what you say is very natural. Very wise,' he said bleakly. 'But I don't know how much I can do,' he rubbed his jaw thoughtfully, his tone dubious. 'Tara, don't you see you're asking something of me that I'm not fit for, that I'm not interested in anymore? You claim I have made a hash of my life. Is doing what you most want, to live under the conditions that please you, in peace with yourself, success? Or does success only mean being a mighty king with a beautiful queen? I suppose it depends on what meaning you attach to life. I no longer wish to be the ruler of an empire...'

'Exactly, you have lost your fire. I want you to be the Vali you once were,' she cut in decisively. 'And it's more than just you. You are now the leader. *You* had promised to lend the Vanaras the dignity, the independence they deserve.'

Vali stood staring down at the carpet of wild flowers, rubbing the back of his neck with his hand while his eyes brooded. Then, shrugging, he said, 'How often have I got to repeat to you that I'm just an ordinary man who wants to marry the woman he loves, have children with her? You want me to be king when I am content to be a chieftain. And as the head, I shall try to ameliorate the living standards herein this jungle—'

'But Vali,' she interrupted him desperately, 'you promised us an empire, not just a jungle! All this that you mention, you will have anyway. It is just trifling. It's not going to lead you anywhere. For your own sake, I beseech you to seek more. Be a fighter, Vali, and do a warrior's work. You have been blessed with sagacity, courage and brute strength. Vali, if you love me, you will merit these gifts... After all, you won't be giving me up for a reality but for fulfillment of a dream.'

He was standing with his back to the shimmering pond. She got up and went up to him so that they were face to face.

'Vali, if you hadn't a penny to your name and got the lowest job that fetched one meal a day, I'd marry you now without a minute's hesitation. But you are capable of so much more than what you are. Living like this means living in a sordid beastly way all our lives with nothing to look forward to. It means that I should be a drudge to the day of my death—'

'You would be my queen!'

'But you aren't a king yet! I would be living in disappointment and you in regret—'

'Never,' he cried passionately. 'I can never regret loving you, living with you.'

She smiled and took his arm. 'There's more to us than that,' she said quietly. 'Wasted, thwarted lives are to no purpose. It's a toss-up when you decide to leave the beaten track. Many have a calling, but few are chosen. You are now the successional head of a tribe and land, both fast crumbling.

You claimed to have ambitions, but you ought to work at it. That's how you are going to contribute to the welfare of the Vanaras, of our community, of our country. You promised to give us a better future—so give it.'

He looked at her, his deeply tanned face expressionless. 'Does that mean that unless I'm prepared to prove myself, you won't marry me?'

Something in his voice made Tara hesitate. She was afraid, but she had to risk it.

'Yes, Vali, that's just what it means.'

He looked up at the sunless sky. He was silent for what seemed an endless time. She stood as she had stood before, facing him. Her heart was beating madly and she was sick with apprehension. She would have given a lot to know exactly what Vali was feeling. But it was always difficult to know that; his smooth face with his dark eyes, were a mask that even she, who had known him for so many years, could not penetrate.

He turned at last. His eyes were still fixed on her and she could not lower hers. He paused for an instant, as though he were undecided. And then, abruptly and without looking or saying anything, he walked away from her with measured steps as her unhappy eyes followed him. She heard him go through the wooded banks. The impounding feeling of loneliness smothered her. But with no need for self-restraint anymore, she gave herself up to a passion of tears that had been fogging her eyes. She suddenly felt alien in *their* spot. Tara walked back home. *Have I been too extreme, too hasty? Have I pushed him away? Forever?* She had said what she wanted to say to Vali but she had not spoken in the tone she had intended.

✽

'Tara, have you seen Vali?'

The ordinariness of the question made her come to an abrupt stop, halting her step and her unshed tears. She blinked. It was Sugriv, his face anxious, his small eyes curious. He was the last person she wished to talk to right now and forcing a quick shake of her head, she picked up her pace.

'Tara,' he called, but she did not slow down. He rushed towards her with hurried footsteps. 'I wanted to apologize for that day's behaviour,' he said hastily. 'I... I have been angry... And hurt. And I guess... I guess, I vented it more on you than I had meant to.'

Tara sighed. It didn't matter anymore to her. Yet she could not hurt Sugriv because she was upset with herself. It disconcerted her to realize how emotional he really was right now, his face twisted in agonized apprehension.

'It's not you I am upset with, Sugriv,' she said, wearily.

Her manner was so dramatically unconcerned that only Sugriv's acute sensitivity could have discerned in her statement a very deep anxiety.

'I have been a little silly and I said a few things that I meant to say, but I am not sure if I can take the consequences of having said them.'

'You'll never utter a silly word,' Sugriv hastened to reassure her. 'And I am sure whatever the wise advice you gave will result in something good.' He halted, his voice unsure. 'Does it have something to do with Vali?'

She nodded without thinking and regretted it immediately. She blinked away the hot prick of tears behind her eyes. Either her face must have given her away or, as usual, he was quick to notice her mood. Instinctively, he seized her hand.

'Oh, Tara, don't, don't,' he said. 'I can't bear to see you so sad.'

She was so unstrung that she let her hand rest in his. He tried to console her. Sugriv saw an admirable fortitude in her.

'I don't want to know what it was that has so upset you now,' he hastily assured her, his voice still diffident. 'But I am there for you.'

To distract herself from her pain, she persisted, 'No, it's *you* who are still angry with me. And Vali. But why?'

Sugriv was silent for a moment, and his sensitive face darkened. *She deserves to know after my uncouth conduct*, he reprimanded himself mentally. 'I hardly know how to begin,' he said sheepishly.

There was a long silence before Sugriv spoke again, and for each of them it was filled with many thoughts. It would be a difficult story he had to divulge, for he was keen to reveal everything, yet he would have to omit the biggest truth—a voice warned him.

Sugriv had passed days of bitter, heart-aching moments, but he could not deny that Vali was worthy of his good fortune. Anxious that nothing should impair the friendship— more with Tara than his brother—he had agonizingly come to a decision he so greatly valued: he would take care to never, not even by a hint, disclose his own feelings.

Sugriv, standing there, knew his heart was not as pure as he wished it to be. He was not sure how steadfastly he would be able to endure the scrutiny of Tara's cool eyes if she were to learn the truth of his feelings for her. They were far-seeing and wise, and he trembled that someday, they would see what he was trying to hide. A pang seized him when he remembered what he had to tell her in explanation of his boorish behaviour.

'If it's about that incident, it is just that I was taken aback—and honestly very hurt—that Vali had not bothered to confide in me about...his feelings for you,' Sugriv cleared his throat. 'We are not just brothers, we are mates, we are friends. That something as special as this, he did not wish me to know, made me mad. And I expelled it on all of you that day—Vali, Ruma and you. I guess it was a tantrum of sorts.'

'That's what Vali said too,' she said thoughtfully. 'Did you talk and clear this with Vali?' she asked in her soft, clear voice.

'Yes,' he said, awkwardly. 'There and then, though not in the most courteous manner.'

'But have you patched up?' she persisted and there was an anxious tremor Sugriv detected in her voice.

'Of course, we did! We're brothers! We fight, we patch up!' he airily said.

She looked down at the bead bracelet on her right wrist that Vali had given her and touched it tenderly.

Sugriv did not miss the gesture. 'Is it Vali? Did he upset you?' he demanded with a resurging trace of anger.

She gave a thin smile. 'Rather I upset him. I have cut off our relationship because I thought it would be best for him— an incentive for him.' She again stroked the bracelet. Sugriv watched her with a heart beating so fast that he could hardly breathe. She was no longer with Vali. *I still have a chance...*

'I wanted to spur him from his stupor,' she said with a catch in her voice. 'I thought if anything could enable him to achieve success it was the thought that I loved him. I have done all I could, even broken off with him to make him see larger sense... It's hopeless. I don't even know if I did the right thing!'

'I think what you've done is right,' said Sugriv.

'Then why do I feel bad?'

'Do you?'

With a strained smile still on her lips, she nodded. 'I know that from every practical standpoint of worldly wisdom and common decency, I've done what I thought I ought to do. Yet, at the bottom of my heart, I've got an uneasy feeling that if I was better, if I was more supportive, less selfish, I'd marry Vali and let him lead his life.'

'You might put it the other way around. If he loved you enough, he wouldn't hesitate to do what you want.'

'I've said that to myself too. But it doesn't help. It's expected more from a woman as part of her nature to sacrifice herself than it is from a man.' He could see she had gone pale. 'I'm afraid of losing him,' she whispered, her tone anguished. 'Did I push him away?'

'Do you love him very much?' he asked at last, his heart contracting with jealous grief.

'Yes. Even though I'm impatient and exasperated with him, I keep longing for him.' Silence again fell upon them. Sugriv didn't know what to say; a sharp pain teared at his heart.

Sugriv moved closer to her and broke the silence. 'If that's so, it would only be weakness on your part not to recognize the facts. He can be exasperatingly stubborn and he is a very proud man. I am sure he'll soon see sense. You did your best, Tara. You are so selfless you're simply wonderful.'

He spoke quickly, the words tumbling one after the other in his excitement, and there was a sincere and affectionate emotion in his voice. Tara was touched but she felt so miserable that even Sugriv's kindness could not alleviate her bleak misery. 'You see, Sugriv, I thought when it came to a showdown, he would not knuckle under. I knew he was not weak.'

'Weak?' Sugriv cried. 'Of course, he's weak. What made you think otherwise? He's had everything too easy—power, success, even love. You are now making him earn all that. I suppose you'd call it your better nature.'

She gave a sad sigh. 'Then my better nature must face the consequences. In the future, I'll be more careful—that is, if we do have a future.'

'Are you sorry?' he asked tactlessly.

She swept him an impatient look. She knew and reminded herself that he was struggling to console her and that she should not allow herself to get annoyed.

She smiled, 'Dear Sugriv, you always think the best of me! How can I ever thank you for cheering me up with your compliments?' she said. 'You're being kind but I have to face the consequence of what I have done. And I know I could trust you.'

Guilt and shame grabbed his voice, making him speechless. He took her hand and held it, her bracelet dangling daintily between them. Tara had never looked more beautiful in his hopeful eyes.

'Oh, Tara, don't make me feel small,' he laughed in a shamefaced way. 'I would do so much more for you than that. You know that I only ask to be allowed to love and serve you.'

Tara froze, amazed at his words, robbing her of speech. There was tenderness in his deep-set eyes, which she had never seen before. But there was something beseeching in them, like a dying deer's life, which slightly unnerved her. Was Sugriv in love with her? She mentally shook her head, her thoughts dizzy. *No, I must be imagining things...*

She pulled her hand away and gave a short laugh. 'You're so loyal,' she said uneasily. 'It gives me such an assuring feeling of confidence. But don't be so serious, Sugriv. I am fine now. There's no need to feel so sad and sorry for me,' she gave a firm smile. 'I did it for Vali and I know he'll come back to me—in all the glory he's destined for.'

6

TURMOIL

The river was like a mirror against the radiantly setting sun, behind one of the craggy hills, for a few minutes changing Kishkindh into a mystic abode of the skies. Tara turned away from the bewitching sight. The gnawing unease of not having met or seen Vali for a week since their confrontation was swelling into a spiralling fear. *Where is he?*

No sooner had Tara neared his house on the way to the clinic was she assailed by a volley of furious words from a visibly belligerent Vriksharaj.

'You are happily roaming around while throwing out my poor son from your life, this village and this very home!' they shouted, livid.

Tara was so surprised by the suddenness of this attack that she froze, staring into Vriksharaj's incensed eyes.

'Who have you come for—Vali or Sugriv?' he shouted. 'Vali is gone! And Sugriv has gone away too in search of his brother!'

'Gone?' her whisper came out as a strangled cry.

'Yes. He informed me he can't accept his post as chief till he had done something worthwhile. Sugriv tells me you put that atrocious idea into his head!'

Bewildered, Tara hurried to clarify, but the crumpled, withered face and fury in their eyes made it impossible for her.

'When did he leave?' She met the older woman's eyes and flinched back from the look in their eyes that threatened to hit her. 'Did he say where?'

'Vali has left!' Vriksharaj repeated, his voice going shrill. 'That's what matters. You're the bane of our lives—pitting one brother against another, making them fight over you! They had a fearful row, and now Vali is gone!'

Their voice cracked; their raddled face seemed to fall to pieces. They dropped back against the step, hands across their eyes. The wrinkled column of their throat jerked spasmodically as they struggled with their tears.

'After everything that I dreamt for the boys, I am alone now,' they wailed, and tears began to run down their worn cheeks. 'Oh, Vali! Vali! How could you do it?' It was the anguished cry of a mother and it disturbed Tara. She put her hand gently on their shuddering shoulder, but they threw it off so violently that Tara stepped back, startled.

'*You*—all because of you and your silly selfish love!' Vriksharaj went on, their voice strident. Now, get out! Don't you ever dare come here again. I hate you!'

'You mustn't talk like that,' Tara said desperately. 'He will come back. I know—'

'Go away!' Vriksharaj leaned on the fence, gesticulating wildly. 'Stay out! And don't try to offer me any platitudes because I won't take them! Now, go!'

Shocked at their virulence, Tara fled into the street, aware of the curious eyes on her.

Bewilderment choked her thoughts. Vali had left. But

where to? What were his plans? When would he be back? Had he left *her*, she thought, a heavy knot of fear in her heart. Oh, why had she told him all that! She kept replaying the conversation in her mind. And why had Sugriv mentioned her name to make it worse for everyone? What row had the brothers had? *Sugriv*. It kept coming back to him. *Sugriv*. And she had trusted him...

Again, that sense of foreboding rose within her. Had the brothers fought out of jealousy and not over the explanation Sugriv had chosen to give? Was Sugriv also in love with her? The thought made her go cold. Being the sharp person Vriksharaj was, they had immediately deciphered the reason behind the tension between their sons. Tara forced herself to recall all their previous conversations and suddenly comprehended the reason for the hostility.

She covered her face with trembling fingers, recollecting all the small incidents with Sugriv. She did not know why he came to the clinic; he seemed to know little of herbs and medicine. She had never suspected that he was in love with her. She had given Sugriv just a little more of her attention than she had wanted to because he was Vali's brother and a childhood friend—she always thought him as so.

She remembered her father's reaction at Sugriv's frequent presence at the clinic.

'Did you ask him to come here?'

'No, he said he was passing by,' she had shrugged.

'Strange, he used to follow Vali. Now he follows you,' her father had given her a sceptical look. 'Is he in love with you?'

Tara had burst into a loud laugh. 'Upon my word, Appa, you think all the boys in town are in love with me. I am no apsara!'

'I should have thought you knew by now when a young

man was in love with you.'

'I wouldn't marry Sugriv even if he were,' Tara had told him lightly.

Sushen had not answered. His silence had been heavy with displeasure.

Walking slowly back home, Tara, with an impatient flick of her hand, decided she should not take either of them seriously—neither Sugriv nor Vriksharaj.

Vriksharaj was distraught now and would recover once Vali came back. They were known to be exceedingly proud and possessive about their sons. Moreover, they were a bitter person and had suffered much; not many had been kind to them, except Tara's father, probably because he was a doctor and their friend.

Sushen's compassionate demeanour towards Vriksharaj had largely altered the villagers' attitude and they had begun to look kindly towards their chief. Soon, with his exceptional administrative efficiency, Vriksharaj had been able to gather support and respect and continued as the head of the tribe and Kishkindh. And now, at long last, when they wanted to hand over the chieftainship to their son, Vali had left them—because of her.

She bit her lip.

'What's troubling you so much that you still are holding on to the medicines I told you to deliver?' Sushen's prosaic voice cut into her troubled thoughts.

Tara had no intention of mentioning her problems to her father, nor was she going to allow the incident to affect her further. She forced a smile, her voice loud and bright. 'I had gone to hand over Vriksharaj her medicines,' she returned lightly.

'Which you didn't,' her father reminded her gently. His

eyes narrowed. 'You too have started addressing them as "her". Is it because of Vali?' he asked astutely.

'That's what she likes to be known as, if the world permitted her,' Tara replied. 'Vriksharaj had once mentioned how she forced herself to be a man, rejecting her womanhood to be a chief, and how you are the only person who has always been strongly supportive of her.'

Sushen took his shawl off, picked up a pouch of seeds from a shelf and began to empty it in a mortar. 'They used to come to me for a cure,' he said quietly, grinding the seeds in the mortar. 'I dissuaded them and said they couldn't be "cured" because they weren't diseased in any way. It took a lot of persuasion on my part to make them see sense and accept themselves.'

Tara looked up at her father, her eyes suddenly trusting. 'You might have just saved them then.'

'It takes a lot of strength to come to terms with who you are,' said Sushen, with a sad shake of his head. 'Vriksharaj was miserable, figuring out how to view themselves and how they were viewed by the world. Trying to achieve their dreams in a land where people tend to mock more than understand, made their life even more cruel.'

The nurse in her looked at her father with her calm, kind eyes that had seen all the horror and pain of the world and yet remained serene. 'This basic need of being identified in a community one wants to be ascribed to is oblivious to everyone,' she made a helpless little movement. 'See, I see Vriksharaj as a woman, as do her sons. But everyone defines her as a man, possibly because she's the chief of our tribe, a "manly" position based on a certain social construct,' she scoffed. 'But as a doctor, all you saw was a person who you empathized with as a human being, and by doing so, you managed to enlighten the ignorant others.'

'That was the least I could do to break the cruel stigma. If our literature and grammar mention more than two genders, why can't we as individuals and society accommodate the same?' he sighed, stoking the fire for the pot that had lentils for lunch, 'You see this fire—this *agni*—and the two sticks you used to create this fire? The two sticks or *arani*s used in the ritual are referred to as feminine, perceived as parents of Agni, who is identified as a child of two mothers. There are several such mentions of deities changing gender, manifesting as different genders at different times or combining to form androgynous or hermaphroditic beings. God has never condemned them,' he added dryly. 'We have. In fact, many such interactions have occurred with the divine blessing. Why, even Gods change sex or manifest as an avatar of the opposite sex in order to challenge sexual convention! Lord Shiva in the form of Ardhnarishvara—half man and half woman—who we worship here in Kishkindh and all around the country. And then there's also the story of Buddh, the supposed illegitimate son of Tara and Chandra...'

Tara! Why does my namesake stir strange emotions in me?

'Parents are illegitimate, never the child,' interrupted Tara, forcefully. 'That's the righteous claim of a spurned Rishi Brihaspati who could not take that his wife Tara was in love with another man, and that she had chosen Chandra over him and even dared to have a child with the man she loved.'

Even as she recounted the doomed love story, Tara was filled again with a strong sense of presentiment: why did the story of the Star Goddess haunt her to mindless distraction?

'Both Chandra and Brihaspati claimed to be the father,' she continued. 'Tara kept silent. But as the debate raged and tension erupted, the unborn child cried out. He wanted to know who his father was. All those gathered there were amazed by the desire of the child to know the truth. The Gods declared that he is Buddh—the lord that rules the intellect. Eventually, the unborn child divulged the truth about his father from inside his mother's womb, revealing he was a love child, born of Chandra. A furious Brihaspati cursed the unborn Buddh to be born androgynous. And thus, Buddh is "mercurial", quickly changeable, both male and female.'

'This makes for another perspective,' contended Sushen, in his dry, clipped voice. 'Buddh is intellect, the mind, which is genderless. Buddh is the mercurial God, who is asexual, as against Chandra, his father, the Moon God—romantic and emotional. Brihaspati is associated with rationality but whose wife Tara, the Star Goddess, prefers heart over mind. In their own ways, these stories of the stars, planets and celestial bodies have been used to map the human mind.'

Tara had a thoughtful look, her eyes concerned. 'Buddh becomes an example of gender fluidity. Later, Buddh marries Ila, a prince cursed to be a man on full moon nights and a woman on new moon nights. Thus, like Buddh, Ila is gender-fluid and alternates between being a man and a woman every alternate month. The two lived together as man and wife only when Ila was a female. Soon, Ila gave birth to a son, after which the curse was lifted, with Shiva eventually restoring Ila's masculinity permanently.'

Sushen's expressionless eyes moved to her. 'Such stories of positive valuation of women and femininity in Buddh, Ila and Ardhnarishvara prove that fluidity in genders and sexualities has been an integral part of our philosophy.'

Tara looked unimpressed. 'But that's not what we see here, do we, Appa?' she derided. 'Most are only civil to

Vriksharaj because of her status as chief.'

'Vriksharaj has the knack of rubbing most people the wrong way,' chuckled Sushen.

'There's a reason why she is so prickly,' Tara quickly defended. 'Most, if not many, don't like being talked down at by a female chief, never mind if she has worked her own way up through the male dominant power ladder.'

'Vriksharaj has been receiving a lot of flak since the announcement of Vali as the next chief—and to add to their troubles, the boy has disappeared!' said Sushen, pounding the pestle to crush a herbal mix. 'But why are we discussing Vriksharaj here? Are they the reason for your bad mood?' her father asked, his eyes probing.

'Vriksharaj blames me for Vali leaving Kishkindh. Worse, Vali and Sugriv had a massive fight.'

'Over you?' Sushen asked sharply.

'Supposedly. Easy to blame the woman, isn't it?' Tara replied. 'Tara was blamed for the war between Brihaspati and Chandra. But don't the men bear any responsibility?'

'They should,' he gave his customary nod of the head. Scrutinizing his daughter's worried face, he said gently. 'And don't mind Vriksharaj. They are upset right now. They wished to hand over *their* responsibilities to Vali, and since Vali has disappeared, they are unsurprisingly angry. But it's time Vali took over!'

Noticing the colour on her pale cheeks at the mention of his name, he continued quietly, 'Vali is already showing signs of being an able leader—he suggests, guides, rarely commands, creating a sense of freedom and democratic discussion while taking decisions. He knows he is preparing a line of control and is dealing with his fellow tribesmen, not lesser subjects. Vali is compassionate and friendly with his people. That's a heartening indication, inevitably making him their chosen leader.'

Sushen noticed the consternation on his daughter's face. Misinterpreting it as shyness, a look of faint animation came over his thin face. Happily, he patted her on her shoulder. 'You've got something there, I know,' he said. 'The fellow's got brains. I've known him a long time.'

'It all depends on Vriksharaj—and the people,' she said quietly. 'And Vali.'

'They love him. As do you,' he said looking at Tara who was now blushing. 'I approve. With his qualities and qualifications, Vali will adeptly handle his future, which he's got all planned, mind you.' He paused to light a cheroot, and then went on, 'Tara, when you get to my position, it becomes fun to play God—'

'You play God each time you save your patient from a certain death,' she responded, her brows furrowed in her characteristic thoughtful frown.

'I earn good will,' he chuckled. 'I haven't yet made a mistake, and I don't think I'm going to make a mistake with Vali.'

'What do you mean?'

'I voted for Vali in the meeting to be our next chief and shall support him wholeheartedly. I hope to give you in marriage to him—as soon as he's back,' said Sushen, his shrewd eyes contemplating her. 'That will be good for both of you.'

'Yes, Appa.' Her heart was beginning to thump. 'You have it all chalked out.'

'I may have,' he conceded. 'But what I say or believe doesn't matter. The two of you, I know, have made up your mind. Vali is a good boy, but you are better.'

Tara gave a tight smile. 'Most fathers believe their daughters are the best.'

'And more importantly, that she deserves the best,' said her father quietly. 'Vali is like a wild horse. You, Tara, are the only one who can rein him in, not Sugriv or Vriksharaj. He listens only to you.'

And he did, she thought unhappily.

'You make it sound like a heavy burden,' she murmured disconsolately.

'It is,' said Sushen enigmatically. 'It is all on you.'

To stop thinking of Vali, she broached a matter that had troubled her since long.

'Why did you name me Tara, Appa?' she asked suddenly, the topic of the Star Goddess still fresh but uneasily lingering in her thoughts.

Sushen paused grinding the herbs, his back stiffening.

'What an odd question to ask at an odd time!' he remarked but his hoary brow wrinkled deeply. 'It's a pretty name, isn't it?'

Tara ignored his stretched smile, noticing his frown. 'Appa, you are a man of science and medicine who wouldn't bother with a pretty name,' she scoffed. 'Names have a reason, some definition. How did you come upon it?'

Sushen exhaled, prevaricating. *Had the time come to tell her?*

'Tara is a *graha*, the star; but Tara is also one of the Mahavidya, a group of ten great Wisdom Goddesses,' he started carefully. 'She is the spiritual essence, the highest evolution of consciousness. As you rightly said, a name has to have a definition. "Tara" is derived from the root word "tṛ", meaning to cross—Tara is the *shakti* or the energy that ferries us across the worldly ocean. This means the word

"Tara" can be translated as "rescuer" as well as "star".'

Rescuer, thought Tara wildly. Who would she be rescuing? She herself needed to be rescued—from herself!

'Tara, the Star Goddess,' she murmured. 'Chandra's Tara...'

'No, Rishi Brihaspati's wife,' her father corrected.

'Appa, everyone knows Tara and Chandra are almost synergetic—they are said in one breath. The Star and the Moon,' she maintained. 'The eternal lovers!'

'She was Brihaspati's wife,' repeated Sushen, his voice forceful. 'With the moon and the star in the sky, there's also the Brihaspati graha.'

'But you see Tara only when Chandra rises in the sky and then she shines for him the whole night...'

Sushen gave a snort. 'Now you are being a silly romantic!'

'Am I?' she said thoughtfully. 'There's a cosmic reason behind the fate of Chandra and Tara, just as there's this connection between that Tara and me.'

'Besides the name, nothing,' he insisted, but his taut shoulders and clenched jaw told her that there was more than she knew.

'That same lovely Tara was also the cause of the bloody Tarakamaya war between Devas and Asuras,' she persisted, breaking the strained pause. 'And coming back to my argument, it's usual to blame the woman for war,' Tara said with a reflective, grim look at her father. 'Frankly, Tara was the victim in this war, not the cause of it.'

'All should have ended there and then,' said Sushen abstractedly.

'But it didn't, did it? Tara did not get to make her choice, it was the warring men who decided eventually,' she derisively said. 'To avoid bloodshed, she returned to her husband, but pregnant with Chandra's child. When her son Buddh was born, she did not hide behind conventions or hesitate to reveal the truth. If that's the Tara you named me after, I am proud of it—and her!' she finished fiercely.

But even as she said it, she was flooded with a wave of foreboding, and a sudden realization tightened the twisted knot of dread. 'You think the same story will be repeated with me? That I shall be the reason for war between the two brothers?'

Even as she voiced it, she knew it was this dread that had been mounting each day into an indescribable fear.

Her father gave her shoulder a reassuring pat. 'No, that's not why you are Tara! Tara, as the star, is the one who guides and brings one back to their inner self, their home,' he smiled, but she was quick to notice that his smile was strained.

'But even as she shines brilliantly, Tara has been forever tainted by the stain of this decimating discord,' she reminded him bleakly. 'Is that why I am plagued with this unknown fear?' she cried, her voice strident.

'It is odd,' she began with unease and restlessness. 'I have these dreams.' She shook her head stubbornly, tapping her temples with a shaking finger. 'They started when Ma passed away, but have recurred recently.'

Sushen gave a start. 'What dreams? Why didn't you mention earlier?'

'I simply can't fathom them,' she mumbled. 'But they get stronger each day—more vivid, more meaningful,' she shrugged feebly.

She caught the anxious note in her voice. 'About Tara. And Chandra. And yes, sometimes Brihaspati too,' she added vaguely. 'But it's always Tara and Chandra.'

Fear gripped Sushen's mind. He restrained his alarm with

an effort. 'What are the dreams like? What do you dream about these people?'

'I see them as they lived and loved. And lost,' she returned, her eyes puzzled. 'Why? Why do I see them almost every night?' she cried urgently, her hands gripping his. 'I am Tara, your daughter. How does that Tara affect me?' she shook her head violently. 'And then, oddly again, there's Vali. And sometimes Sugriv too,' she said lifting her shoulders, lacing and unlacing her slim fingers.

Sushen could see she was desperately anxious to get to the root of things. He felt that she was possessed by some shapeless dread that robbed her of all self-control.

Tara sat down suddenly as if the strength had seeped out of her legs. Her face turned pale under her honey skin. 'Appa, what do these dreams really mean? I have to know, it's been plaguing me ever since Vali returned. And now he's gone again... Oh, I have to know!'

'By interpreting your dreams, you can discover things about yourself that you may not like. Or control,' her father said softly. It came as a warning, and she stared at him, perplexed.

'I want to know,' she breathed unsteadily.

'It is what your brain is trying to tell you about what you really want in life,' he said. 'It can also tell you what you're afraid of and what you truly desire...'

Tara shivered. 'I desire... What? Whom?' she stared at him. *Vali, nothing else.*

He could see at once that she believed him. Her little face seemed to fall to pieces. She dropped back against the chair, her hand across her eyes. The column of her throat jerked fitfully as she struggled with her emotions. 'There's more than you are telling me!'

He wanted to be honest and tell her what her dreams indicated: that the Star Goddess was her guardian and that their fates mirrored each other. But the innocence in her face and terror in her eyes made it impossible for him to do anything more than hint at what may have been happening.

'You might not have the power to change the unpleasant or the unknown, but you can choose how you respond to it with courage and grace,' he said as gently as he could.

She took an appreciable time to answer. Her tone was worried. 'I can endure the inevitable, but I can only hope I have a cure for what I can't,' she gave a wan smile. 'As you said, we are Tara, who lead and guide. We are the one who help people across...' Tara paused, her voice soft. 'We are the one who save. In whichever way I can, I shall save.'

7

SUGRIV AND RUMA

She never had a chance to bid him a proper farewell; she had driven him away from there, from her. They did not have a chance to separate with many protestations of devotion either, thought Tara wryly. Yet she was consoled by her certainty of Vali's passionate love. It was a strange feeling that she had. It hurt her to part from him and yet she was happy because he had gone for her sake.

Tara found work to be refreshing against her sagging spirit. She went to the clinic every morning soon after sunrise and did not return to the house till the westering sun had flooded the languid river with dusk-gold. Her father handed her a new responsibility—a school—which put into her care small children, most of them orphaned because of disease or war. Besides regular lessons of grammar, science and math, Tara hoped she could introduce something closer to her heart to these children. She had a practical sense of housekeeping and other crucial skills she spoke of lightly, often underestimating them.

The children thrived under her care. Every day she saw her bond with them getting stronger. Many of them were babies, and she personally took charge of them while keeping a vigilant eye on the sickly and the weak.

Tara felt that she had found her purpose and that was evolving as a person. The constant occupation distracted her mind, and the glimpses she had of others' lives and outlooks awakened her imagination. She began to regain her spirits; she felt better and stronger. It had seemed to her that she could do nothing now but brood. But to her surprise, and not a little to her confusion, she caught herself laughing at the smallest gestures of the children. She was devoted to them now. They would miss her if she went. In fact, she did not know what she would do without them.

'You seem to have created your own new world. I hardly get to see you,' said a familiar voice, the earthy heartiness brought a ready smile to her face. *Ruma.*

The classroom door was open and Ruma stood on the threshold. Tara, abashed, extricated herself from the clutches of a dozen little children who, with wild shrieks, had seized her.

'Is this how you keep them good and quiet?' asked Ruma, an anxious smile on her lips.

'We were playing a game, Ruma. They got excited!'

Ruma looked at Tara with a long, hard look. Tara was flushed and breathing quickly. Her liquid eyes were shining, and her lovely auburn hair, in all the struggling and the laughter, was disarranged in adorable chaos.

'How come you are here?' Tara asked as she led her friend outside, to the wide, low-roof verandah.

'I don't get to see you these days so I thought of coming to meet you myself,' shrugged Ruma in her usual, blunt manner. 'Are you avoiding us?'

'By us you mean whom?'

'Sugriv and I,' said Ruma. 'We barely meet you since Vali left. It is not Sugriv's fault, you know that, yet you blame him for it. Vali left because of...*you*!'

A flash of anger passed through Tara. She whirled around, her face pale.

'That's exactly the reason I am not keen on meeting up,' she stated tightly, in a flat, final tone. 'I have nothing to say on this.'

Ruma paused for a moment, hesitating, as though for reflection. 'Forgive Sugriv, he is feeling equally wretched, if not more. He regrets he had that quarrel with Vali, and it's tearing him apart that the brothers parted on such an angry note. Vriksharaj is furious with him too...'

Tara gave Ruma a glance and very nearly laughed. 'Oh no, Vriksharaj blames me for the brothers fighting,' her lips curled in bitter resentment.

An odd expression flit Ruma's vivacious eyes. 'And why would that be?' her tone turning frosty.

Tara faltered; she did not want to hurt Ruma.

Ruma bristled, misinterpreting her silence. Tara had the knack of making her feel small and inconsequential, although Ruma knew she was grander a beauty than her diminutive friend. But there was some other quality in Tara that Ruma always vaguely perceived but could not put a name to. It was something that, notwithstanding Tara's warmth, cordiality and the innate wisdom that made Ruma feel like an awkward schoolgirl, held her at a distance. But today, she was going to have none of it.

'Are you insinuating the brothers fought because of *you*?' she sneered. 'Sugriv loves me with all his heart and soul!' she burst out. 'He loves me as passionately as I love him. You've known this. He means everything in the world to me and I'll be glad when we can announce it to the world.'

'Did he tell you that in so many words or is that the impression you have gained from his manner?'

Tara's eyes shone with bitter mockery. They made Ruma a trifle uneasy. 'I don't think you know what love is!' snapped Ruma. 'Or you would not have sent Vali away for some wild, selfish ambition of yours! You have no conception how desperately in love Sugriv and I are with one another. It really is the only thing that matters and every sacrifice that our love calls for will be as easy as—'

'You stupid fool.'

Tara's tone was so contemptuous that Ruma flushed with anger. And perhaps her anger was greater because she had never before heard Tara say to her anything but sensible and kind things.

'Sugriv seems to have become the centre of your thoughts, reason and beliefs! He seems to be accustomed to have made you subservient to all his whims,' Tara said scornfully.

She wanted to scream loudly to her friend the truth that she was herself struggling to come to terms with. But Tara thought it wise to remain silent; Ruma, the pampered daughter of the powerful headsman Panas, accustomed to flattery all her life, would not be able to take the brutal truth.

Ruma blanched; jealous rage grabbed her throat. She had never heard such things said to her before. Blind wrath, driving out fear, arose in her heart.

'You are just being spiteful. You can't love, Tara, and you can't bear others being in love! You have ruined your relationship with Vali. With Sugriv. And now me! And here I had come to you as your friend, to make you feel better... You don't deserve us!'

She stormed out leaving behind a long, unpleasant silence

lingering in the verandah and in Tara's mind.

Sugriv, she thought with sudden anger. It was all because of him. Tara worked herself up into a towering rage. But she knew she was angrier with herself than with Sugriv.

Later in the day, as she was just about to head home, she heard a cart draw up to the gate of the school. It was Sugriv. Tara wondered why he had come. He could not have timed his visit more poorly. As she watched him climb the front steps, she had no inkling about what was in his mind. He did not reckon she knew his truth he had lied about. She supposed he was dedicated and diligent as everyone seemed to think he was, but she realized, her eyes hardening, she could not trust him any longer.

'May I come in?' He said nothing more and entered the room, coming into the darkness, for the long, low room was lit only by a shaded lamp. His voice had that constrained note—half fearful, half polite. He did not look at her; his eyes wandered restlessly.

Tara unclenched her fists; she felt fairly sure of herself now. She refused to start the conversation and make things easier for him.

'It is Vali...' he started undecidedly, but he knew he had grabbed her attention.

She flinched, giving him a fixed, wordless stare, absently touching the bracelet at her wrist.

'From hearsay, we can safely conclude that Vali must have gone south,' he cleared his throat. 'For a long time, he had wanted to visit all the pilgrimage spots in the country.'

His voice sounded strange to her. It was raised on the last word in order to give his remark a casual air, but it was forced. She wondered if he saw that she was frozen cold to him. He dropped his eyes. *When is she going to speak?*

'As you well know, Vali is an ardent worshipper of Lord Shiva. Thus, he has gone to the east to pay homage before taking on the mantle of the chief,' he continued weakly, hoping she would say something.

He finally sat down without speaking a word. There still was this stifling silence between them. Then he made a remark, and because it was so commonplace, it had a ridiculous air.

'It is so hot. I had assumed you would not be at the school today.'

She looked at him now and saw that his eyes were fixed on the floor. She still could not bring herself to respond to him, thickening the strained silence of those excruciating minutes.

Sugriv was afraid to make the smallest gesture or sound, wondering if he should simply leave. He sat quite still, and stared with those wide, immobile eyes of his at his own hands.

When she stood up suddenly, he got startled. 'If you have nothing more to say, I have some work,' she said in that quiet, toneless voice, her eyes averted. 'If you don't mind, I am closing up now.'

It was a clear rebuff.

Her steady, brown eyes were fixed on him and he could not lower his; they demanded his full attention now. He tried to read her expression, but he was nervous and could only discern a strange watchfulness.

'I also wanted to talk about Ruma,' he started again, in his usual earnestness. 'She came to me weeping about the quarrel you had this morning.'

'Ruma weeping?' Tara's lips outlined an ironic smile. 'When she left, she was raging mad at me. Did she not tell you why?'

She spoke almost flippantly and when he glanced at her he was surprised to see in her eyes a gleam of mockery. He could not understand.

'Why are you so upset with me...with all of us?' he blurted suddenly.

Tara would have taken a vicious pleasure of letting him know the truth. Instead, she checked her temper and decided to deal with the lesser castigation. 'I trusted you, Sugriv,' she said pleasantly, her tone accusing.

She had the pleasure of seeing him flush furiously.

'When I told you what happened between Vali and I, it was meant to be private. I confided in you, in my lowest hour, thinking you were my friend, that you had *our* best interest at heart,' she said, stressing on 'our' to make him sufficiently uncomfortable.

Though her face remained impassive, the shadow of disdain once more crossed her eyes.

He took a while to answer. A shudder passed through him. 'I didn't tell Amma anything. She must have guessed,' his voice shook with sudden emotion.

'How did Vriksharaj come to know that I had placed the condition on Vali?' she asked after a cold, deliberate pause.

He looked at her quickly. He thought he had heard amiss. Her large, brown eyes were fixed on him, without the usual warmth but cold and hard.

'Vriksharaj themselves told me so,' she said flatly. 'That you told him. They have has no need to lie; do you?'

Panic seized him.

'Amma assumed,' he said wildly. 'She was already furious about the quarrel we had—'

'What did you fight about with Vali?' she demanded, her eyes glinting.

His heart began to beat a little faster, his throat dry. It was more than uneasiness that he felt. It was, he desperately realized, fear—unadulterated fear.

'I was persuading him not to leave,' he said weakly. Even to his ears, his reply sounded false.

She shook her head. It was with sadness, not with anger any more. 'Your mother heard you clearly, Sugriv. And they told me everything,' she paused with great deliberation. 'Did you fight because you are in love with me?'

She could not have been clearer and straighter. Yet Sugriv could not bring it upon himself to admit the truth. He felt the knot grow stronger at the pit of his stomach, making breathing difficult.

'Yes, I love you, as a friend would!' he cried, protesting in a loud voice. 'So, yes, we were fighting over you!' His hands trembled and he clenched his fists. He could not tell the whole truth; it would be too humiliating. 'About how he could up and leave without a thought for you. I guess I defended you too strongly... Probably, I do feel overprotective about you.' He looked helplessly at her but she stood still, unmoved.

But the moment he said this he flushed, for he was ashamed of the half-truth he had just uttered.

The shadow of that same sardonic smile flickered on her lips. Tara would have liked to believe him. But she suddenly felt tired, weary of the emotional impediments. She sighed, giving him the opportunity to recover his nerves.

'I have much too great a regard for your welfare. I could never hurt you!' Sugriv insisted.

'Well, you did,' she said quietly. She wanted to shout at him but bit her lip instead. She found it strange that with disbelief and distrust catching her breath, she could speak so calmly.

'And if I have hurt you in my anger, I apologize. But I pride myself in being an honest person and I expect honesty from others, especially, my friends.'

Sugriv eagerly grabbed at the word. 'We are friends, right? I went overboard, I think. And I am sorry, I shouldn't have discussed you with either Amma or Vali,' he said feebly. 'I didn't mean to hurt you in anyway... It's too bad, all this has caused so much grief and unnecessary pain and misunderstanding,' Sugriv sighed. He stretched out his hand in a conciliatory gesture. 'It's a scrape we've got into, but we shall get out of it. The greatest thing is not to let anything come in between our friendship.'

Or our trust, she thought bitterly. *Have I trusted him too easily? Am I being unfair to him?* She passed a weary hand across her face.

'Yes, I made Ruma angry too,' she sighed. 'But I was simply trying to caution her...'

'About me?' he said righteously.

'Yes. About love,' she shrugged. 'But Ruma took it badly and thought I disapproved...'

'Do you?' he asked bluntly.

'Do *you* love her?' she asked with her clear, clever eyes.

Sugriv did not reply for a moment, but looked at her with a slight smile. She wished she knew what he was thinking.

'It's no good deceiving yourself, Sugriv,' she said earnestly. She saw him pale under his dark skin. 'If Ruma has made up her mind to love you, nothing that you or anybody else can say will have the slightest influence.'

Sugriv gave a quick smile of relief, his manner relaxed again; for a dreadful moment, he had thought Tara had seen through his feelings, his lie.

'Oh, well, that's not so terrible, is it? Though her father doesn't think so. He definitely disapproves of me and makes no bones about it.'

'Knowing Ruma, that will make her more adamant,' observed Tara.

He looked up at her, and his dark, lean face had a strangely trapped look he could not hide.

'Ruma has abandoned everything for my sake—home, family, security and self-respect. I've even sent her away two or three times, but she has always come back. And now I've realized that I am as serious about her as well. I think I've got to put up with her for the rest of my life,' he added with an affected grin.

Tara nodded thoughtfully.

'It's a rather funny sensation, you know, to be loved so absolutely,' he answered, wrinkling a perplexed forehead.

'But it's loving that's the important thing, not being loved,' said Tara, quietly. 'One may not even be grateful to the person who loves them.'

Tara looked at Sugriv curiously. It was strange that this shy, reticent, meek man should have aroused in such a headstrong girl so devastating a passion. She could not tell why, but the way he spoke of her, notwithstanding his casual manner and his flippant phrases, gave her the strong impression of Ruma's intense and unique devotion—but not his. It troubled her a lot.

'I know Ruma is wonderful. But I wonder what Ruma sees in *you*!' she said in a jesting voice, but it had the effect of exciting in him a certain indignation.

'As if a woman ever loved a man for his virtue,' he mocked.

Tara gave him a sidelong glance, 'Ruma does—whatever virtue she sees in you! But men are incalculable; I thought you were not like everybody else and now I feel that I don't know the first thing about you.'

Sugriv got the same unsettling feeling that Tara could see right through him.

8

VALI AND RAVAN

'Come out, Tara. It's not a sight to be missed!' A heavy patter of rushed footsteps could not drown Ruma's exclamation.

'Why, what happened?' Tara faltered.

'Vali is back—'

Her heart leapt.

'He has got Ravan in chains and is parading him around in the city!' Ruma laughed heartily, clasping her hands in delight. 'Vali has him held by the neck, and the crowd is cheering him on.'

Scrutinizing Tara's rising bewilderment, Ruma explained in a hurried manner. 'Don't you know Vali has made Ravan a prisoner and brought him to Kishkindh as a victory trophy?'

She was met with a dazed look.

'From what little I have gathered, it all began when Narad, the devilish mischief-maker that he is, sought out Ravan and taunted him about Vali as the most powerful man on earth besides him. Initially, it roused Ravan's curiosity, but when Narad started singing his praises, recounting for him tales of Vali's strength and valour and insidiously letting slip the news of his aspirations to become an independent ruler of Kishkindh, it expectedly riled Ravan enough to promptly declare that he would duel Vali and defeat him. Preparing to confront him in Kishkindh, Ravan was duly apprised that Vali had gone on pilgrimage for the *sandhya-vandana* at Dakshin Samudra. Impatient to meet his new rival, Ravan headed there. He discovered Vali in deep meditation and decided to strike his enemy unawares—'

'Coward!' exclaimed Tara.

Ruma nodded impatiently, 'Treading silently from behind, Ravan is said to have made a grab at Vali, trying to seize his arms, when Vali, instinctively sensing his presence, was quick enough to trap Ravan's head in a throttlehold under his armpit. And that's how he has dragged him all the way here!'

A bubble of laugh slipped from Tara's amused lips. 'Vali when provoked is dangerous! He intends to publicly humiliate Ravan. Let's go!' she urged, suddenly anxious that Vali's volatile temper might kill Ravan.

She rushed out, down the lane, up the high street, thronging with excited people and their chatter, all winding their way up to the market place. She was met with a sight that halted her running feet, leaving her speechless, her heart in her mouth.

Under a banyan tree, stood Vali, strapping and snarling, with a huge man struggling in vain under the stranglehold of one brawny arm.

She gaped, as did the excited crowd, which had gathered thick and fast.

'This is the King of Lanka I hold in my grip!' shouted Vali triumphantly.

Ravan! Tara gave a slight start, throwing the wriggling man a curious look. This was Ravan: the mightiest of the mighty, the richest of the rich, the brightest of the bright, and the scholar-emperor of the golden country of Lanka. But right now, he was reduced to a desperately struggling prisoner in a mortifying stranglehold of a Vanara he had sorely underestimated.

But even as Vali proclaimed his conquest, Tara felt a sudden gust of pride, making the smile in her eyes travel to her lips, euphoria gurgling out from deep within.

'So, what do we do with him?' questioned Vali mockingly, tightening his grip around the hapless man. Ravan's face turned a deep mottled red, the veins bulging at the temples. He knelt there staring blearily at the lusty crowd.

Clearly, Vali was now putting on a show for the crowd. He was answered with a robust cheer.

Over the bobbing heads, Vali's mocking eyes met hers. She shook her head slightly, a faint smile on her lips.

'Leave him,' she silently mouthed the words.

Vali slackened his grasp immediately, releasing Ravan. Ravan now free, stumbled backwards, clutching frantically at his bruised neck, panting heavily. His face was set in a furious, vindictive mask.

'Welcome to Kishkindh,' said Vali smoothly. 'I hear you were on the way here, seeking me out?'

Ravan seemed paralysed. He stood up slowly and passed his hand over his sweating face. He straightened his wide shoulders, composing himself, his thick fingers rubbing his bruised neck. Only his eyes were alive and they regarded Vali murderously.

'I am here for you now,' jeered Vali, his eyes gleaming in open derision. 'What can I do for you?'

Ravan cleared his throat; he could not speak but for a rasping grunt. He suddenly expelled a little hiss of breath through his teeth. 'Salutations, Vali,' he said, in a strangled voice. 'You quite took me by surprise.'

'Apologies but I am not used to being hugged from behind,' Vali returned suavely, his smile engaging. 'I was taken unawares. Now we can hug face to face. Agreed, friend?'

Ravan put his hand to the back of his neck with a grimace of pain. He stood looking at Vali, his hands shaking and his amber eyes blinking. Despite the heat, an icy shiver went up his spine; this was the man who had almost killed him. He felt the sweat running down his back. His breath was coming in great labouring gasps. He tried to control himself and his mounting anger. One glance at the tall, dangerous man by his side forced him to face a new, terrible truth—that he was not invincible, after all—not in his might, nor his power. He could see through the divine boon from Brahma that had granted him near immortality: that even thought he could be killed neither by a Deva nor an Asura; neither an animal, nor super being; a human could kill him. He realized with a cold shock, paling under his fair skin. It was only because of this man, Vali, who had spared his life today, that he was still alive. He shifted his eyes and said nothing.

It was after a long, heavy silence that he managed to sputter the words he despised himself for saying out aloud. 'I wanted to meet you,' confessed Ravan, his beady eyes, cagey. 'I wanted to know if you were as great as the tales about you go. And I wasn't disappointed,' he stated grandly, in an effort to appear magnanimous.

Flamboyance, Tara smirked, apparently makes defeat less humiliating.

'But *I* was—disappointed that is,' smiled Vali thinly, his tone relentless. 'I thought you would give me a tougher fight, if not a fair one.'

For a moment Tara thought Ravan was going to have some kind of a stroke, but he controlled himself with an effort. He shook his head. 'Nothing like that,' he said, his mouth closing into a spiteful slit. 'As I said before, you were quite a surprise.'

'Likewise,' Vali gave the same fixed smile, but his coal eyes glittered dangerously. 'O Great King, you are in my land, in my custody. And what do we do about it?' he asked with elaborate politeness. 'Instead of words like "enemy" and "prisoner", shall we use "friend"?'

Ravan looked at Vali quickly to make sure that he was serious, his eyes widening. He then shut his eyes in despair. This was Vali's masterstroke, Tara smiled in silent glee: he was forcing his captive to acquiesce into a cordial alliance. No war; just truce.

Ravan seemed suddenly to lose his cool. He leaned forward, his eyes snapping fire, and his great face turning mauve with fury. 'You talk as big as you look!' he snarled, shaking a quivering finger at Vali. 'Do you hear? That's all what you are—a big beast of this jungle. A *Vanara*,' he spat. 'I am an emperor—'

'—who is my prisoner right now,' leered Vali, the thin smile still set on his face, his dark eyes glinting. 'And at my mercy,' he added frostily. 'You don't have much choice, O Emperor,' he said, his voice now a soft purr. 'So, what's it going to be—friend or foe, hmm?'

Ravan's face turned the colour of old ivory as he gripped his clenched fist to restrain himself. 'Don't be a fool, Vali,' he said. 'You're only heading for trouble. You can't keep me here. My army will attack you before you can blink. I'll see you right. You know what I mean.'

Vali strolled slowly towards Ravan, standing so close to

him that Ravan could feel the cold rage emanating from him. Vali was a head taller than Ravan, forcing him to look up at his tormentor. Tara thought Vali would almost strike him, but Vali controlled himself. His slit of a mouth pursed and his narrowed eyes were like granite.

'You need to know what *I* mean,' he corrected silkily, putting his hand under Ravan's fleshy chin. He raised his face. They looked at each other. Ravan saw the snarling anger in his eyes and flinched away, but Vali's giant fingers crushed his chin. 'Forget your grand army, I can kill you right now like a dog on the street—not the brave warrior that you claim to be. Or I can display you as my prisoner and make you hang upside down like a hunted beast for the world to see,' he stated tonelessly. 'But again, you have a choice: you can take my hand of friendship—one king to another. Because from this very moment, I declare myself as the King of Kishkindh, free from your yoke, Ravan. I am the king now, and you are a prisoner in the land you once lorded over. As a friend, you have kindly returned our land that you had taken. This part of the Dandak Forest is now independent.'

The crowd roared, all in applause, some screaming for Ravan's blood.

Vali didn't move. He sat down, looking up at Ravan with an odd expression in his eyes that Ravan didn't like. Ravan was forced to face the heaving masses in front of him. He knew he was trapped, had no place to manoeuvre and would have to take up Vali's offer of friendship.

He lifted his massive shoulders; his small amber eyes shifted away from Vali's impassive face.

'Just as you say,' Ravan forced a tight smile. 'We are friends, not foes, King Vali.'

The crowd exploded. Then, over the commotion, Vali

raised his mighty arms, outstretched and high, facing the crowd. A silence fell heavily in the market square.

'Ravan is our friend, our new ally. Please welcome him in Kishkindh!'

The cheer gathered a higher tempo.

Vali continued over the din, 'Henceforth, we are allies; Lanka and Kishkindh shall bond in a new era of friendship of trade and fair exchange—and peace,' stated Vali pointedly, his voice loud and final. 'No more run-ins in the Dandak, no more skirmishes, no more pitched battles at night. Just good old peace. Has a nice ring to it, doesn't it?' he added turning to his new friend.

Ravan thought about this, then nodded. 'Only glad to be of help, Vali,' he said stiffly, his lips twisting in an attempt to smile.

'That's magnanimous of you, King Ravan,' said Vali. No one could miss the irony in his voice. 'I shan't forget it, nor will the Vanaras of Kishkindh.'

Ravan nodded, and started to say something, then caught the look in Vali's eyes. He lifted his shoulders in a despairing shrug.

He bowed low, an oddly humble gesture coming from an arrogant king, thought Tara. He looked the picture of modesty. But Ravan was famous for his charm too.

'I take leave for Lanka, if you permit me, King Vali,' he declared in a low, even voice. 'As a gift of our friendship, please allow me to build you a magnificent palace fit for a king like you,' Ravan gave a slow smile. This time, Tara could detect the mockery in his tone.

No! Tara threw a swift glance at Vali and raising her eyebrows, without speaking gave Vali a look that he was too quick-witted not to decipher.

Vali regarded Ravan, with an expression of complete indifference.

'We build our own armies as we do our own homes, no matter how humble,' he returned imperiously, with the grace of a proud man. He gave Ravan a glance in which Tara discerned a certain hauteur.

Ravan looked visibly taken aback. Vali turned away from him, raising his eyebrows at Tara who gave him a faint nod, her smile widening in quick relief.

'If not a personal gift, consider it a memento of our friendship, the new promise between Lanka and Kishkindh,' persisted Ravan. 'Let the world know of our peace pact.'

'We could commemorate by having a tower of victory constructed,' said Vali, with his sardonic smile. 'Or some monument. How about a grand hospital? To tend to the sick and injured in war?'

Ravan flushed darkly. His face bore a look of frigid disapproval.

'My offer for a palace still stands,' he said courteously. 'It would be my personal gift to you, friend to a friend... And now I shall take my leave.'

Vali stepped forward and embraced Ravan. 'A hug as promised,' he smiled roguishly. 'To our friendship.'

The hold was gentler, from which Ravan broke free, stepping aside, a faint smile on his lips. 'And I take my leave,' he bowed. He shut his eyes, and with a strong wave of his left arm, he seemed to beckon for someone. Or something.

Within a second, appeared the magnificent Puskpak Viman as glorious as was claimed. As it whisked him away, it left behind a motley of open-mouthed people. None had witnessed such a grand spectacle. Tara was not sure what had been more splendid: Vali or the viman. She moved to greet him but stopped.

There was a delighted shriek. Vriksharaj gave a little roar of passion, like a wild beast baulked of its prey, and pushed past into the street. They rushed and threw their arms around Vali's neck and kissed him. Tears streaming down their raddled face, they hugged him, and with a loving gesture stroked his face with both hands. Tara and the others who watched would never have thought them capable of such tenderness. At last, with little sobs of joy, they let go of Vali and announced, their voice ringing clear in the exultant air, 'My son has returned. Your King is here!' Their eyes shone with triumph, trailing to where Tara stood in the crowd. They exchanged a glance—all-knowing and profound. Later, Tara realized, that look of understanding was also one of mutual respect, hopefully changing their fraught relationship for the better.

'Vali, our new king,' announced Jambavan, the commander-in-chief and Vriksharaj's closest aide. Vali and Sugriv were like his own sons. Tara knew his words has the most weight as he was the most powerful nobleman in the kingdom, particularly the animal kingdom in the forest. He was a huge, burly man, particularly hairy, almost resembling a sloth bear. He had the agility and astuteness of a bear, conceded Tara, for which he had held his high position for so many years. Besides that, Jambavan had a special knowledge of the all-curing herb, *vishalyakarni*, which he had received from the gods when the Ocean of Milk was churned for the *amrita*, the elixir of immortality. No sooner had Jambavan given his voice of support to Vali, there was a huge applause from the crowd confirming public approval of the new king.

Vali was back as a hero in full glory, as she had wished, and what a return it was! He had done what no one had accomplished until then: he had defeated the invincible Ravan, the most powerful man on earth. He had fulfilled her condition. Tara drew a long, happy sigh. She wanted to spring out and run to meet him, to throw her arms around him. But social constraint and personal guilt restrained her, and she decided she would wait.

'Tara.'

His voice, her skin prickled instantly. She turned around with a relieved laugh. He had spoken her name in that melting, rich tone of his which came to him so naturally and meant so much to her.

'Welcome,' she managed to murmur, her throat thick with emotions.

'Am I to have the privilege of sitting next to you?' he whispered in her ear, the heat of his breath making her gasp.

Startled, she looked up. Vali gave her a look. He was smiling still, but his smile was a little unnatural. She thought there was a shade of anxiety in his eyes.

'For the feast tonight to be held in my honour,' he said, his eyes smiling and teasing her. 'I shan't have much of an appetite. I would rather be with you,' he said huskily.

She leaned towards him. The love she felt for him was almost torture. She gave him a long look and tried to speak, but her lips were stiff.

'I am suitable enough for you now, I hope?' he added casually, but his eyes gave his words a meaning that she could not fail to see. 'To marry you.'

Her throat constricting with emotion, she stared back at him, her chin tilted. Then, suddenly, her expression softened and she smiled at him.

'It depends,' she said sassily. 'You want to be king first or bridegroom?'

9

NUPTIALS

The day Sugriv had dreaded for the past several months had finally arrived. Tara was getting married. To his brother. He had just finished telling Hanuman about the firework display planned at the end of the wedding, when he glimpsed her as she walked towards the *mandap*.

Tara was a little thinner than she had been before Vali had left, but she was blooming now. She was dressed simply in a yellow raw-silk drape, decked up in wild, vibrant flowers and not much jewellery but for Vali's bracelet. Tara looked ravishing. Ruma had cleverly dressed her up to reveal her youthful voluptuousness. She radiated a warm glow that was palpable. She looked delectably tiny against the towering height of his brother.

Glancing at the large crowd of guests, one could see that the wedding was grand and the otherwise thrifty Vriksharaj had spent lavishly. Almost all the known and powerful were there: Panas; Keshari; Gavaksha; the King of the Golungulas; the Vanara chiefs like Dhumra, Gavaya, Durmukha and Darimukha; Jambavan; and other leaders like Sharabha, Kumuda, Vahni and Rambha. Nila and Nala were present too; people assumed them to be brothers because of their similar sounding names and their childhood friendship. But the guest who stole the show was Ravan, who had come with his cousins Khara, the king of Janasthan, the northern kingdom of Lanka in the mainland; and Dushana, the viceroy of Janasthan.

Are these guests or is Vali flaunting his political clout, Tara wondered as she watched all of them assembled at the venue.

'It is a double celebration,' Vriksharaj chortled loudly. 'My son is the king and he is getting married!'

It was possibly overcompensation on their part, thought Tara, as she sat primly by Vali's side. Vriksharaj had quickly got over their initial hostility since their son's return as the proverbial hero. They now watched the newlywed couple with favourable eyes but not without a certain cynical amusement. So, Tara and Vali had fallen in love with one another at first sight two years ago. Theirs was the kind of love that makes the world a miracle. Vriksharaj gave a long sigh. They now felt like a charlatan denouncing their relationship. But the cynic in them, who believed that in a couple, there is always one who loves and one who lets themselves be loved, disappeared when they saw clearly that the groom and the bride both loved and let themselves be loved. Like Chandra and Tara, both shining in the light of each other's love. Vriksharaj frowned; *but will Sugriv take the same course of actions as Brihaspati?*

In their maternal protectiveness, they had charged Tara to be the reason of conflict between their two sons. Their heart had bled with pain and disappointment when they had heard them quarrelling violently over Tara. Their sons were all they had, all they loved in the world, and, hence, he could not resent anyone but Tara. They had not slept well since

Vali had left and had wretchedly waited for him to return. But watching the quiet sorrow in Tara made them come to their senses, realizing their own grief: they both loved one person as completely as the other. Was their bond with Vali so weak as to snap by the admittance of a slip of a girl? They glanced surreptitiously at his second son. Sugriv's otherwise amiable face was far too often grim and unhappy these days. *The fool*, they thought sadly. Ruma loved him hopelessly; could she possibly make him love her some day? They gave themselves a shake: they would not allow anxiety to spoil the happiness of this day. They could retire now. They recalled his own bitter words when they had gone to Tara to apologize. She had welcomed them with her customary graciousness, which made them feel worse.

'Conveying my regret for what I did to you is not enough,' they had admitted awkwardly, much to her consternation. 'I am not just a neurotic parent but a chief and an elder; yet I was unforgivably discourteous to you. I do realize now that it's only you who can bring out the best in Vali. And that's what a partner is meant to do—give and bring out the best,' they said, putting a conciliatory hand on her shoulder. 'I know I am needed no more—neither as a chief, nor a parent,' they quipped lightly. 'The old have to give way for the new, but I was more selfish in my motive to make Vali chief so that I can hand over this burden to him, for me to finally retire and be what I am—a woman. I lived as a man for the sake of the society, and I wish to die as a woman for my sake.'

Tara, as expected, had forgiven him easily. Vriksharaj could only admire her. As for Tara, by no word or by no hinted gesture, had she given any indication of their exchange to Vali. Vali would never know of the ill feeling Vriksharaj had nursed towards his wife.

'To be the mother to your sons, you shed the father. Now to be the woman, shed the man once and for all,' Tara had told him in her soft, serene voice. 'You have lived so long for the world and for your sons. Now, live for yourself.'

The wedding rites were swift, as Vali had instructed the priest, followed by a simple feast.

'If I have any more of this, I am sure I shall dose off right here!' Tara yawned delicately.

'You can't be that tired...yet,' Vali teased with his rare grin.

He paused. 'I have something to show you... Let's leave once the feast is done.'

'Oh, but we can't, we are the hosts!' she protested. 'And then, we have to go home,' she smiled. 'Our home.'

Vali gave a surreptitious smile. 'Exactly.'

Nodding to Sugriv, he waved and called for a chariot. With Vali pulling Tara with him, they ran towards the new chariot drawn by two horses that had pulled up a few yards ahead. Sugriv was left to piece together a mass of perplexing impressions.

They rode along a road that ran by the snaking river. On each side of it were coconut groves broken by a few great mango trees, the fruit yellow and red and purple, among the massy green of the leaves. They had a glimpse of the silver river, smooth and glimmering, and the sun-browned boys bathing in it. They were chasing one another with shrill cries and laughter, and their bodies, mahogany and wet, gleamed in the sunlight.

'Where are we going?' she demanded with a weak laugh.

Vali remained silent, gazing before him. In the distance, rising from the shimmering blue and green, were twin turrets, supporting a huge dome.

Tara's breath stuck in her throat.

'It's a palace!' she breathed.

'Our palace,' he corrected.

She whirled around.

'But how could you build it so quickly...and so secretly?' she cried.

Before she could finish her sentence, she knew as a sudden realization hit her. 'No, no, not Ravan!' she ejaculated an exclamation of sudden dismay. 'I thought you were too proud to take his charity! Oh Vali, how could you...?'

Vali placed his hands on her shoulders, stiff with indignation. 'It is not what you think. It is not Ravan's gift. It is the fee of his loss, the treaty we duly signed.'

'Whatever. It is funded out of *his* fortune.'

'Not *his* wealth, Tara—it's the price of my conquest; the cost of his defeat. He had to pay not just allegiance but reparations too.'

'Reparations for what?' she demanded. 'There was no war for damages to be paid!'

'But we fought! And won,' he reasoned. 'Mercifully, it was not a war between us at the cost of innocent lives. I prefer it that way; if two egotists want to fight, let it be an open duel, not a battle involving armies,' he exhaled slowly, his tone grim. 'But yes, what got irreparably damaged was his reputation, and he tried to cover it up through the game of friendship, for which he had to pay a price,' Vali gave one of his wolfish grins. 'But I did borrow Ravan's architect whose services he so generously offered.'

'Mayasura! He is also his father-in-law,' she said slowly. 'Ravan married his daughter Mandodari, and his sons Mayavi and Dundubhi have learnt architectural skills and magic from him.'

Mayasura was the son of Rishi Kashyap and his wife Diti.

He went on to become an Asura king and architect of the nether world. He married the apsara Hema and had three children, Mayavi, Dundubhi and Mandodari, and the latter was Ravan's high-minded wife who was said to have taken after her mother's beauty.

Vali gave a small shrug. 'Mayasura may be Ravan's father-in-law,' he said sourly, 'but for me, he is an extraordinary architect rivalling only Vishwakarma, the celestial architect of the gods.'

Tara gave an uneasy nod; the past from a foreign land was throwing a new shadow, silhouetting not just her new home, but her newfound happiness. 'Yes, but by inviting people like Ravan and Mayasura in your kingdom, you are inviting trouble,' she warned, her brows furrowed in a frown. 'Mayasura is a mild man; his sons are not!'

Vali gave an impatient snort. 'I need them to build my house. I am not going to start some war with them.'

'You may not, but they might,' she said quietly. 'They are ambitious and avaricious, and that's enough reason to start a conflict.'

'Well, right now what I am impressed by is that Mayasura is a brilliant scholar and he has just finished writing a book called the *Surya Siddhant*. He is a genius performing miracles!'

Tara smiled tentatively. 'That is why this palace was built so fast,' she turned to gaze at it again, trying to shrug off the heavy cloak of unease swathing her. 'And so magnificent.' The palace loomed from a little hill and only a path led to it, so they got down from the chariot, leaving it by the side of the road and started walking.

'The road will soon be widened,' said Vali.

'Not at the cost of cutting the trees of the forest, hopefully?'

'I wouldn't dare!' he gave a quick grin. 'And I know you like to take your walks, so you can have one for today!'

She halted. 'Wait, Vali. I didn't want a palace. I would have been happy in your old house.'

'I know. But I wanted this for us. It is not just our new house, it is our dream, our future. It is about who we are, what we have today.'

'You, as king,' she said thoughtfully.

'All thanks to you.'

'But not this show of wealth,' she reminded him gently. 'A king doesn't need a palace to flaunt his status. His wise leadership will. And you have amply shown that to the world. So, why this display?'

'Of wealth?'

'No, display of insecurity,' she said evenly, 'or a certain arrogance.'

'You think I am over-reaching?' he questioned dryly.

'Yes, and worse,' she sighed. 'It shows a need to shout to the world that you have arrived! A grand house, a grand throne, a grand army... What next, Vali?'

'A grand wife too,' returned Vali breezily.

By humbling Ravan and gaining half his strength, is Vali becoming like Ravan too? This thought had been niggling her since the day he had defeated Ravan, and it surfaced each time Vali behaved in this new, brazen, uncharacteristic way.

'A grand ego as well,' she returned quietly.

Vali's grin slipped. 'You are exaggerating, Tara,' he gave an impatient frown. 'I simply wanted a palace—not just for us, for my mother too... She has toiled hard enough,' he paused. 'I wish to give her the best in her last days.'

Tara softened, placing a hand on his tense arm. 'But she

won't be staying here. She wants to retire to the forest. Did she not tell you?'

Vali nodded grimly. 'I hope to dissuade her.'

'Let her go, Vali. That is her last and only wish left for herself.'

His face clouded. 'Do I have to relinquish one to receive another?'

'For her sake, let her go, however much it saddens you. And she is proud of you, whatever you do!'

'And you aren't?' he quipped, his tone wry.

'I am,' she said. 'You know it. You have more than proved yourself to me and I do feel guilty of pushing you so hard...'

'Hush, no bad feelings for today!' he insisted, brightening up. 'I want to keep the best for the last,' he said, using the end of her *angavastra* as a blind cloth over her eyes. 'Now come with me,' he whispered in her ear. He held her hands as he led her through a winding path, then up a flight of steps, which she assumed must be the entrance stairway. Then again, they glided over a smooth floor and again up a staircase—a curving one this time. Then he led her to a high, open space as she felt the waft of cool breeze tingling her bare skin. She stood beside a tall window.

'Look at that,' he said, with a dramatic gesture removing her blindfold.

Below them, over the bulky boulders that dominated the landscape, coconut trees tumbled down steeply to the cove. In the evening light, the river bay had various streaks of colours. Beside a creek, at a little distance, were a cluster of huts of a village, and towards the ridge was a round canoe, sharply silhouetted, in which were a couple of men fishing. Then, beyond, one saw the vast calmness of the great river, and twenty miles away, airy and unsubstantial like the fabric of fancy, the unimaginable beauty of the land that was Kishkindh. It was all so lovely that Tara stood humbled.

'This is our land, our palace, our home,' he murmured huskily, encircling his hands around her waist from behind. 'This is the view we always cherished on the cliff, near the pond. I brought it right into our new home.'

She leaned against his chest, feeling his heart thumping against her.

'Yet I've never seen anything like this,' she said at last, her voice thick with emotion.

'Beauty,' he murmured. 'We seldom recognize beauty face to face. Look at it well, Tara, for what we see now we will never see again, since the moment is transitory. But it will be an imperishable memory in our heart. We touch eternity.'

His voice was deep and resonant. He seemed to breathe forth the purest idealism. It was his dream they were watching together. The dream of being the king of his own land—free and independent. Tara had to urge herself to remember that the man who spoke was a warrior and a king.

The sound of footsteps interrupted them. Vali turned around quickly.

It was Sugriv and Ruma. As always, they made a handsome couple.

'Oh, you got a palace fit for a princess!' Ruma squealed in delight. 'And on your special day too.'

'I had intended it to be done on our wedding day and only Mayasura could have achieved the impossible task of completing it this quick and early,' said Vali. He waved an arm to his right. 'The palace to the west is yours, Sugriv.'

'Oh, the smaller one,' murmured Ruma, a quick look of disappointment crumpled her face. 'I thought this was his.'

Vali ignored her obvious grievance, watching his brother's

face darken in embarrassment. 'Please convey our regards to your father, Ruma. I noticed he did not turn up for the wedding.'

Tara was astonished to see Ruma's face lose pallor at Vali's stern tone. Her brows knitted delicately. Was there a conflict between them she was not aware of?

'He has been unwell for the past week,' mumbled Ruma weakly. 'But he should be back at court within a day or two...' She forced a short laugh. 'Surely you newlyweds would like to have a few days for yourself. You and Tara alone,' she said pointedly, with a sly smile.

'This palace is our new haven,' said Vali. 'We shan't leave here.'

Shrugging away the last of any creeping doubts and unpleasantness, Tara surrendered herself completely to his words and the moment. Their love was a great river into which she boldly plunged, uncaring whether she would swim or sink.

She linked her hands through his. 'I am such a fool, we don't need to go anywhere. This is our world,' she told him.

10

MATRIMONY

Tara's happiness, sometimes almost more than she could bear, magnified her beauty. She smiled against Vali's bare chest as she felt the steady thud of his heartbeat. Marriage seemed to have made both of them lazy. Even when they did nothing all day long, days seemed all too short. Tara leaned a little more towards him, her molten honey eyes gazing passionately into his, her mouth slightly open with desire. He put his arms around her. She abandoned herself with a sigh of ecstasy into their shelter, stretching lazily against the length of Vali's lithe body, throwing a leg over his.

'You don't intend to hold court today?' Tara murmured lazily.

She felt him move under her.

'What do you say, should I?' Vali asked turning around, his arms still wrapped around her.

Vali gazed at her. His eyes darkened as they watched her fit perfectly in the contours of his body. Her eyes were half closed, teasing him; her hair, burnished red and flaming, spread over the silk sheet. The sight of her like this gave his heartstrings a strum. Good heavens, she was too beautiful, too good for him to be real, he thought, as he pulled her roughly towards him, his lips tasting her soft ones, his skin burning against hers.

He sought her face with his searching lips, her honey skin damp and soft. She kissed him back fiercely, making blood rage through his veins, his body crushing hers as they moved in a slow rhythm. She did not know what he was saying—broken, passionate words of love—and his arms held her so firmly that she felt like a lost girl who was now, at last, safe at home. She moaned faintly. Her eyes were closed and her face damp with his lips detailing every contour. And then, he found her lips again, and the pressure of his lithe body upon hers shot through her body like a devouring flame, engulfing her with the heat of an ecstasy. She was burning in an uncontainable fire, glowing as though she was transfigured. In her dreams, she had known this rapture. What was he doing with her now, she did not know. She was not a woman—her personality was dissolved, she was nothing but desire, desperate and adoring. Her head sank on the pillow and his lips clung to hers.

'I am no king, I am your slave,' he muttered thickly. 'Your obedient servant.'

A laugh gurgled in her throat.

'But seriously,' he raised his head from the soft curve of her neck, his eyes, molten and red hot. 'I love you.'

'I know,' she smiled softly.

He shook his head. 'No, you don't know why. Not because you are lovely and clever and kind—'

He paused, bestowing her with his slow smile that she found irresistible.

'I love you because you're unafraid. You take risks and gamble with your whole heart. He chuckled softly, his finger stroking her face. But more importantly, you challenge me to do the same. I don't think I could have defeated Ravan if it wasn't for you.'

'I can't take credit for that.'

He traced her lips lightly with his tongue. 'You make me better, you make me whole,' he breathed huskily. 'You make me thorough. You make me take risks to not always take the safest road...'

Her lips quivered, creasing into a smile. 'Is this your way of saying you're—'

He cut her off with a long, hard kiss. 'Silence, woman.'

She gave a little laugh, a laugh of happy love and of triumph.

His eyes were heavy with desire. He broke off. 'I better leave. Sugriv is waiting for me.'

Sugriv, her heart lurched, jolting out of the full exhilaration of unbridled pleasure. Now that they were married, the situation between Sugriv and her still somehow remained absurdly awkward. His demeanour, so grave and self-controlled, left her with a twinge of unease. She was too happy to feel unkindly towards him. If it wasn't for him, after all, she would have never known Vali. And he was her friend, once upon a time...

Tara quickly got up, covered herself with hurried grace and went over to her dressing table barefoot. She began to fix her shingled hair with a comb. She stared listlessly at her reflection in the mirror and shivered with a current of apprehension. It was as though the soft-blowing wind whistled a soft warning. Whenever she saw Vali with his younger brother, she felt jabbed by a needle of dread. Sugriv had managed to assure her, but she still had her doubts. Of course, she was not frightened of him. Rather, it was what he implicated each time she met him that sent a shiver of disquiet down her spine. And as she now had suddenly felt frightened, she grew concerned about Sugriv. Did Vali reckon things were not as they were before he had left? *And what about Sugriv*, she thought uneasily. Would he confess to his brother? Would they quarrel again or would they pretend all was well again? Sugriv was too weak to confront Vali. And if anyone would make a scene, it had to be Vali—the more fierce of the two—due to his predictable temper. But that was their lookout; it was a matter between the brothers. This was about her, a small voice cautioned her. But a louder one taunted her. It told her that she must not be surprised if she got more than what she had bargained for.

The brothers were cordial to each other, but it was a fragile ground that they were cautiously treading. It was no good pretending that all was well. She hoped Sugriv wouldn't look so unhappy. He seemed to be tainting their new-found happiness. Tara was hoping Ruma would make him forget all this, and that he would be sensible enough to reciprocate Ruma's love.

With a burst of panic, she blurted out, 'I think we should get Sugriv married too!' She saw the look of surprise in Vali's eyes. His direct gaze gave her such a fright that she smothered a cry. *Did he suspect something?*

'Ruma is in a hurry,' she hurriedly blustered. 'You know how madly she is in love with him.'

'But does *he* love her?' he interrupted quietly.

She stared at him in astonishment. She hesitated. 'He is your brother. Did he not confide in you?'

Vali shook his head. His eyes were still fixed on her. She tried to read his expressions, but she was nervous and could only discern a strange watchfulness in his gaze.

'Is there anything you wish to tell me?' Vali asked instead. 'Now that Amma is not here, I frankly have no idea what's going on with Sugriv. He's closer to Hanuman than ever before.'

There was again a swooping feeling in her stomach. 'I wish Vriksharaj had waited long enough and got Sugriv married as well before retiring to the forest. Their departure was so abrupt—'

'But expected,' sighed Vali. 'She had it all planned. And I had no intention of stopping her from what she had longed for all these years. I had to allow her to leave.'

Tara remained mum, but when she spoke, it was with a pleasant voice and a natural mannerism. 'Possibly, that's why Sugriv feels left out, with you married and Vriksharaj gone. He has no one but Hanuman...and Ruma. Exactly why he needs to get married!' stated Tara. 'Besides, things are not too great between Ruma and her father,' she tried to keep her voice steady, almost casual. 'He disapproves of Sugriv.'

Vali pursed his lips. 'Sugriv is a suitable boy!'

'Not as much as you,' she said wryly. 'You are the king; he's not. Panas, who comes from a former royal family, would certainly have preferred to give away his little princess to a king and not to a king's brother!'

Vali frowned, looking down at his square, clean fingernails.

'He tried. Panas. He had approached me with the marriage proposal,' he told her in his quiet, modulated voice.

She stared. 'You didn't tell me this!' she exclaimed in swift astonishment. She paused, her brows knitted in a frown. 'Is that why he didn't attend our wedding?'

'Probably,' he shrugged. 'But I refused, of course.' He frowned, his tone now impatient. 'But if Ruma wants to marry Sugriv, she can and she will—she is quite headstrong,' he added with a small smile. 'She'll get her way eventually. So, let's not meddle in this already fraught situation.'

Tara put away her argument, but, for an instant, she regretted that her plans for Sugriv's future were not materializing as smoothly. She almost wished that Sugriv would insist on his own wedding, even when she knew he would not. *Probably Ruma will.*

'You are his older brother, you can take the initiative for him,' she pressed. 'Besides Panas would take it more kindly if you asked for Ruma's hand in marriage for your brother.'

'On the contrary, Panas could it take it the wrong way and feel insulted,' Vali reminded her.

'True. But there is surely no other way, is there? You will have to persuade and convince him. And coming from a king, Panas might just take it as a royal request.'

'Or you could go on behalf of Ruma as well as Sugriv,' said Vali. 'You are the queen now, besides being Ruma's friend and Sugriv's sister-in-law.'

She felt herself go scarlet. Her first thought was that he was testing her. He spoke almost flippantly. When she glanced at him, she was surprised to see in his eyes a gleam of mockery. She could not understand and looked away in embarrassment.

'Vali, as the king and Sugriv's older brother, you can command Panas!' she insisted.

'Let's see,' Vali shrugged. 'I don't want to antagonize Panas further.'

'I think you seriously need to take this up before the situation worsens. Knowing Ruma's impetuous nature, suppose she elopes?' she warned, feeling the frantic need to press the matter more urgently.

Though his face remained impassive, the shadow of a

smile once more crossed his eyes. He did not answer.

'So, will you?' she asked after a pause.

'We could go together,' he said. 'You and I. As the brother and sister-in-law of the groom. As the king and queen of the land.'

She looked at him quickly. She thought she had heard amiss. But now the smile in his eyes had travelled to his lips. His dark eyes were fixed on her.

'But surely I need not come!'

'I thought you'd like to.'

Panic seized her. 'I don't know what you mean. It would be madness for me to go. Panas might get triggered by my very presence—like I was preening and rubbing it in for him that it is me and not his daughter who is the queen...' she stammered. 'It's just asking for trouble. There's no reason for me to go.'

Vali did not answer. She looked at him in her desperation. His face had a sort of dark pallor that suddenly terrified her. She saw in it a look of perplexity. *Is it possible that he has known all along and is playing all of us?*

'I thought you would want to accompany me when I am about to set out on such a personal cause. You are family now.' He was openly mocking her now.

She was confused. She did not quite know whether he meant what he said or she was misreading him. 'I don't understand what you're talking about.'

'You could be of the greatest use; you are an effortless diplomat, a better persuader.'

She grew even paler. 'I'm not going, Vali. It's too much to ask of me.'

'Then I shall not go either.'

She did not quite know what to say. She was undecided whether to indignantly assert her argument or to break out into angry reproaches.

'I'm afraid you're being unreasonably stubborn!'

'I shall not fight my brother's battle, Tara. And besides which, are you sure Sugriv even *wants* to marry Ruma?'

Vali's eyes that shone with bitter mockery made Tara a trifle uneasy. She was not quite sure anymore how to handle the situation. *Should I give up or press further to make him mediate for his brother?*

'You might not like the outcome if Sugriv does it,' she cautioned again.

'You can't fight for him either, Tara, as you always do. He needs to take his own decisions. If he loves Ruma, *he* has to take the initiative. Not you, nor me.'

It was true, but it gave her a turn to realize that he knew it. Oddly enough, even in that moment of fear and worry, it sounded reasonable.

'Let it be about us for now and no one else. Not even my brother.'

There was something in the way he spoke that disconcerted her. But her self-respect and self-preservation obliged her to accept his offer. They did not pursue the matter further.

*

But the matter exploded a few weeks later. It was a perturbed Jambavan who came with the news.

'Sugriv has eloped with Ruma, Vali!' Jambavan declared the news without preamble.

Vali stood stock still, his face expressionless.

'Were you not aware that she and Sugriv have been in love for quite a while?' Jatayu frowned. 'They wanted to marry. But Ruma's father refused. Desperate, Sugriv, with Hanuman's help, abducted Ruma. And now they have run off together. But we don't know where!'

'The fool!' expostulated Vali.

'Clearly to get married,' Tara broke in, flushed with a rush of emotions. 'Find out where they have gone, Jambavan!' she said urgently. 'Find them and get them here! We can have the wedding here in Kishkindh, not in some furtive hiding place.'

Jambavan hesitated, throwing a quick look at Vali. His thick brows scrunched over his eyes, glittering with unsuppressed fury.

'Hanuman helped him?' he barked.

'He would. He is his close friend now,' clarified Tara, catching the hurt look that quickly entered Vali's eyes and that he tried to hide as swiftly. He watched her without a gesture and without a movement of his face. He listened attentively and no change in his expression showed that what she had said affected him greatly.

'Especially, since you left Kishkindh,' added Jambavan a trifle tetchily. He was clearly waiting for Vali's royal order. 'Should I go after them?'

Vali's silence was as loud as thunder.

Tara felt a frisson of impatience. 'It is urgent that we find them, Vali!' She turned to Jambavan and said, 'Do check with Hanuman first.'

'I did. He won't reveal anything,' Jatayu shook his head. 'He's a faithful friend.'

'Friend?' glowered Vali. 'He is his minister. His subordinate.'

'Very loyal nevertheless,' Jambavan reminded him stoutly.

Vali's belligerent manner became more evident as his voice grew on a sudden stern note.

'I command so!' he said imperiously.

Alarmed, Tara stepped towards him. 'Instead of

discussing how loyal Hanuman is and confronting him, seek the runaway couple yourself.' She motioned to the large bird, 'Jambavan, take Jatayu's help. He will be faster. And he is good at searching and investigating.'

Jambavan again threw Vali a questioning glance, frustrating her. Balling her hands into fists and maintaining her calm, she felt that she could be more effective. 'Give your formal orders, Vali,' she said evenly. 'Send for a secret search party. They have to be brought back home with whatever remaining dignity left intact.

'We deserved better, Tara,' lashed Vali, in a strange, distant voice. 'The fool has run away with the daughter of my most powerful noble. Panas is bound to revolt. Am I supposed to deal with that or run after my stupid brother and his love interest?!'

Vali's jaw, always a little too square, protruded with an apish gruesomeness. His beautiful eyes were black with malice. But she kept her displeasure in check.

'We can do both,' she said measuredly. They stared at one another for a moment and then he looked away, calming down. He kept his eyes averted when she spoke, turning to Jambavan. 'Please do the needful. Get them home. Quick.'

With a knowing glance and a heavy shrug of his burly shoulders, Jambavan left the chamber. Snatching the privacy his departure had left behind, Tara rounded on Vali, her tone severe. 'If I am the Queen of Kishkindh, I demand my word carries the needed royal weight.'

'I am well aware you are very well-educated and you are very clever, Tara—'

'Don't patronize me! I'm not just an ordinary young woman. I am your wife, and fittingly, your queen.'

'Undoubtedly. But neither do *I* wish to be refuted in

front of *my* people,' he returned hotly.

'Then you should have given the orders immediately and not waited for me to bring it up,' she snapped, without raising her voice.

'It's not about you, Tara. It is Sugriv whom I am angry with,' he muttered savagely. 'He'll be all right once I've given him a sound reprimand. That should lick him into shape,' he said.

'You should have talked to him earlier—'

'You worry too much, Tara. He'll come back for my blessings. He's loyal and he loves his master.'

Tara, magnificently imposing as ever, snorted like a charger eager for battle.

'He's your brother!' she had fumed. 'Your younger brother!'

'Oh, then he's a good servant who loves his brother.'

Tara regarded him with incredulous dismay. 'You are being a tyrant! And instead of quarrelling with me now, it would be better if you talked with Panas right away before this news reaches him. It is better you break it to him and calm him down before he decides to rebel!'

She leaned forward, staring at him. Her large, luminous eyes seemed to try to bore into his soul. 'What is irking you more—that Sugriv has eloped or that he preferred Hanuman's help while keeping you in the dark?'

The moment she had uttered these words she turned red with shame. Vali did not answer, but in his eyes, she sensed the pain of a wound. The shadow of a bleak smile flickered on his lips.

Vali's face softened, the angry lines dissolving into a hurt smirk. 'I have no false illusions about Sugriv. He is my younger brother, devoted and dutiful. Clearly, I was never his friend, or he would have confided in me about his troubles. If he considers Hanuman his friend, so be it.'

Before she could utter another word, Vali continued, his tone flat. 'Nor do I intend to belittle you. I have no false illusions about you either, Tara. I never had,' he said. 'You are my wife, my love, my queen. I know you can never be silly and erratic and egoistic,' he paused, the short silence stretching between them. She did not misunderstand the words and looked up. There was a gleam of passion in his heavy eyes. 'You aspire for the highest ideals—for yourself and for me—and I know that you can never settle for mediocrity. This is why I love you.'

Tara, visibly moved, was unable to think of anything to say. For a moment longer, he held her in his stagnant gaze.

'So, never doubt my intention or the meaning and purpose of my feelings towards you. Sometimes my respect outweighs my love for you. Never doubt that.'

The sincerity of his words had left her speechless.

'It's laughable when I think how hard I try to seek your approval,' he chuckled dryly. 'To be amused by the things that amuse you... How anxious I am to hide from you my ignorant, vulgar, petty and stupid side! I know how contemptuous you are of inanity, how you respect intelligence... I do everything I can to make you think of me as anything but a fool...different from the rest of the men you know.'

She made a movement of protest but he waved his arm to halt her words.

'I know that you would have never married me if I was a failure, a loser. But I loved you so much that I didn't care. Or rather, I did care enough to give you what you wanted, what you desired, what you thought was best for me. Most people, as far as I can see, when they're in love with someone and the love isn't returned sufficiently, feel that they have a grievance. They grow angry and bitter. I am not like that. I never expected you to love me—I didn't see any reason that you should as I never thought myself very lovable. I was thankful to be allowed to love you and I was thrilled that you deigned to return it.'

'Stop it, Vali, don't make feel so small against your magnanimity!' she cried, turning scarlet.

Vali gave a self-deprecating laugh. 'I am not all praises, Tara! You have the most blistering tongue. No one could say such bitter things. On the other hand, no one could do more charming things.' His words sounded chillingly odd. 'It may be that, like some historical hero, I am too proud to fight either you or Sugriv.'

Vali said it with a pinched face, which did not validate his words. Fear froze her heart. 'What do you mean?' she whispered, pausing for one terrifying moment, as if challenging herself to utter the next words. They would change the course of this conversation and their life. 'That you won't fight me over what, Vali?'

Vali's coal black eyes gleamed.

'Sugriv.'

His ironic tone had a bite that made her wince, and she knew then that he had known all along. She froze, struggling for self-control, her hands clenching and unclenching spasmodically. 'That fight you had with Sugriv before you left Kishkindh was—'

'Over you, yes,' he watched her lips tremble, and he felt like a brute making her say it.

'I love *you*, Vali,' she said quietly, 'not him.' She threw up her hands in a gesture of lassitude. She was exhausted.

'I know. I don't doubt it. As I said before, I can never

doubt you.'

She flushed, pained at the passion in his voice. Suddenly, she pulled herself together. She looked at him with haggard eyes. She clasped her hands over her heart as though its beating was intolerable.

'I don't want to come between you and your brother. Yet I inevitably have.'

'You are more than my wife; you are dearer to me than anyone in the world. No one can come between us, not even Sugriv.' The words were ordinary enough, but to her troubled mind there was in them something hortatory and had the most adverse effect. The silence of their surroundings seemed to gather body, so that it became an almost tangible presence.

She had to break it. 'But he *is* coming between us.'

She sat down. She seemed to make an effort over herself. 'It's affecting all of us now,' she cried. 'Vali, I fear for all of us!'

'Frankly, I don't care about his feelings for you.'

The calm emanating from him was palpable. He oddly seemed to bear no resentment. She felt slightly outraged at his lack of spirit. Perhaps he guessed what was in her mind, for he said, 'Who wouldn't fall in love with you, Tara? You were his first friend, his closest one. That was only natural, wasn't it? I love my brother, I know him too well,' he gave a half-sigh. 'Initially, I was jealous...and furious. That's the reason why we had a fight just before I left Kishkindh. But love knows no reason; it is irrational. I can't blame *you* for him loving you. I would have if you were the one who was in love with him!'

His twisted humour had a grain of truth. She paused, looking at him with those reflective eyes of hers. 'You certainly are more thoughtful than any man I've ever known.'

She looked at him quickly. He lowered his eyes. His

answer, seemed to her strangely humbling. She was conscious that he regarded her with a love so profound that the fact of his brother's feelings for her did not have the slightest effect on him. She felt tears well up in her eyes. She blinked. 'You have a knack of making me love you impossibly more!' she said huskily, leaning towards him, her arms encircling his waist, her bracelet clinking as she did so. She had reached that stage of exhaustion where misery and fear had drained out of her, relief and tenderness had seeped back into her tired limbs.

'Never as much as I do, Tara,' he muttered thickly.

His arms tightened around her limp frame, holding her. 'Now *I* am jealous!' she laughed.

He gave a wolfish grin but his eyes grew thoughtful. 'It seems to me that when jealousy creeps into love it can only be because one is not sure of their love. Jealousy comes out of distrust, your own uncertainty. And I am so certain of us!'

'I dare say that's quite logical,' she smiled, 'but most men are made differently.'

He kissed her on her smiling lips. 'You see, I am not most men. And you simply don't know how much I love you!'

11

THE TWO COUPLES

Two seasons later, Tara had made an unforeseen discovery. She had gone to the clinic as usual and had set about her first work of seeing that the children were washed and dressed. After the freshness of the morning, Tara found the air in the dormitory to be particularly fetid, making her a little uncomfortable, and causing to fling the windows open urgently. All of a sudden, she felt desperately sick. And with her head swimming in sickness, she stood at the window trying to compose herself. It had never been as bad as this. Nausea overwhelmed her and she vomited. Her loud cry frightened the nurse. The older girl who was helping around ran up to her. Seeing Tara unnaturally pale, she stopped short with an exclamation.

'You are unwell!'

'It is quite evident,' Tara brushed off casually. 'I am with child, my dear.'

Tara would have preferred if Vali had been the first person to get the news.

'Ah! What happiness for your husband!' exclaimed the old midwife who looked after infants at the clinic. 'Vali will be overwhelmed with joy. You have only to see him with kids! And the look on his face when he plays with them—to see how enchanted he will be to have one of his own!'

For a little while, Tara was silent, caressing her bracelet with a fond smile. She knew how Vali would react. The two nurses looked at her with tender interest and the mid-wife patted her limp hand.

'It was silly of me not to have suspected it before,' said Tara. 'In any event, I'm glad it's not some illness. I feel much better. I will get back to my work.'

'I insist that you rest,' said the midwife sternly. 'What would our good doctor Sushen say if I let you be imprudent? Come tomorrow, if you like, or the day after, but today you must go home. Go tell Vali! Would you like me to let one of our girls go with you?'

*

Vali wasn't there when she reached the palace. Tara went to her chamber and lay on her bed, thinking. What she had learnt that morning filled her with joy, confusion and consternation. Ever since she had come home, she had been trying to think. But her mind was blank, and she could not collect her thoughts. Suddenly, she heard a step. The feet were heavy and firm. With a quick breath of apprehension she realized that it could only be her husband.

There was a moment's silence and then a knock on her door. 'The nurses said that you weren't very well. I thought I had better come and see what the matter was.'

'Didn't they tell you?'

'No. Sushen said that you must tell me yourself.'

Oh, her father knew too. She felt a sudden gush of happiness.

'We are going to have a baby,' she said.

He did now what he seldom did—he looked her in the face, his eyes bewildered. She hesitated, suddenly unsure. Then she forced herself to meet his eyes.

He said nothing. He made no gesture. No movement on his face or change of expression in his dark eyes indicated that he had heard. She felt suddenly inclined to scream. The silence felt intolerable to her.

'Say something!' she demanded, but there was a plea in the command.

'As always you have left me speechless,' he muttered, the frown melting from his brows, his smile widening. Joy grabbed his eyes and they shone with gleaming brightness. He could not stop tears of happiness from welling up in his dark eyes, only to fall down his lean cheeks.

'Don't mind my crying,' he said, grinning through his tears. 'It's nothing really; it's only that I can't help the water running out of my eyes.'

She could not prevent a smile, not of amusement but a tenderness that crossed her face. She hugged him fiercely, bringing his face down to hers.

'Vali, this was expected from you!' she giggled, feeling her face damp with tears—were they his or hers? 'You cry when you are overwhelmed.'

He paused for a moment, hesitating, as though for reflection. 'I've been thinking about what you just said. It seems to me that it would be better if you went away to your father? You will be quite safe.'

Her eyes widened in disbelief. 'I am safe here, silly! And what will I do at my father's place? I am not sick, I am having our baby.'

'You will need a good deal of care and attention. I don't

think it's fair to ask you to stay here.'

'Then you better see to that you give that attention to me,' she said glibly. She gave a laugh, intending to permit nothing of the sort. It felt so comfortable to her to lie on the bed, with Vali by her side. She held his hands. 'I nursed you once. Now it's your turn,' she dimpled.

'As I said once, I am your servant. I shall always obey you,' he drawled.

She nestled up to him, hearing the steady beat of his heart. 'I'm glad she'll be born here among the sound of the river and under a wide blue sky,' she murmured against his broad chest.

'Have you already made up your mind about the sex of the baby?' he murmured, with his thin, dry smile.

'I guess you want a boy as the heir to the throne,' she shrugged. 'But I want a girl.'

'Like you,' Vali said softly.

'Yes, but I'm not going to bring a girl into the world to love her, bring her up, only so that some man may want to marry her and provide her with board and lodging for the rest of her life through marriage.'

She felt Vali stiffen. It shocked him to hear these words from her mouth. His bushy brows shot up in stunned incredulity. 'Is that what we are, Tara? Just sleeping together under the guise of marriage? You are my wife, my partner in all that I have and do, not a boarder or lodger, for heaven's sake!'

'Let me be frank just this once, Vali. It might not be so with us, but it can be for her, as it is for many girls. I'm determined to save my daughter from all that. I want her to be fearless and frank, considerate and kind. I want her to be a person, independent of others—a free individual.'

Vali gave a slow, knowing nod. 'Do you realize you are describing yourself, Tara?' he laughed softly. 'You want another mini Tara. And I don't mind a girl at all, if she's going to be anything like you!'

He began to kiss her. He sought her face; he sought her lips. She moaned faintly. Her eyes were closed and her face was wet with their mingled tears. When he lifted her off her feet, she felt very light in his arms. He carried her, and she clung to him. Her head sank on the pillow and his lips clung to hers.

It was after a long time that he broke away. For one instant, she clung to him more closely, but she felt his desire to leave. So, she released him.

'I need to tell Sugriv the good news!'

They had a strange bond, these two brothers. Although Vali laughed at him and squabbled with him, he was accustomed to him. He could not do without his brother. Tara had seen the anxious look as he waited for the news of Sugriv's return after he had eloped. She had felt his worry, his disquiet, his concern in each step as he paced the chamber, rushing to the window at the slightest noise on the street.

Vali had a certain tolerance for the peculiarities of others, and he accepted Sugriv more as a son than his younger brother. He was fiercely protective of him, as he was fiercely dismissive when angered. Perhaps Sugriv amused him, unconsciously, because he could chaff him as the older brother. His humour consisted of sarcastic banter levelled at Sugriv's exactness, his soberness—all effective targets. And he could make everyone laugh at the expense of Sugriv. Tara found it cruel.

It was Tara who had suggested to Vali that he hold a grand wedding for Sugriv and Ruma. Perhaps, it was her way to show to him—and to the world—that all was well between the brothers.

Tara grabbed his hand, slanting him a direct look. 'Don't gloat about this to Sugriv,' she cautioned.

Vali frowned. 'I am simply telling him the good news of being a father. Should not my brother be the first person to know? Especially, since Amma is not here anymore?' he paused, releasing his hand from her grip. 'You certainly have the worst opinion of me.' It was Vali's turn to thin his lips. 'Do you ever wonder what he feels for me, Tara?' he asked quietly.

Tara again felt the stab of conscience knifing her. *Why am I again meddling between the brothers?* She bit her lip, his injured look shaming her.

'I don't doubt you,' she apologized immediately. 'But it's the situation we are in,' she muttered, laying a placatory hand on his tense arm. 'They, too, have been trying to have a child for a long time,' she said quietly. 'We need to be sensitive about that.' She sighed with an imperceptible nod of her head. 'But you're right; he should know. I should let Ruma know as well. She'll feel hurt if she gets to know from Sugriv or someone else.'

'Agreed. Ruma is your friend first, sister-in-law later,' he remarked wryly. 'But remember, she is the much-peeved daughter of a peeved father.'

Ruma, sighed Tara with affection. She had made a beautiful bride, swathed in a silk red robe, her feet bare and bejewelled. She was crowned with a wreath of white scented flowers, pearls and gemstones. But after the wedding, Ruma had found it hard to reconcile with the fact that her social position was determined by her husband's. Of course, everyone was polite and treated her with royal reverence, but she had understood quickly that, from a social standpoint, the brother of a king was of no particular consequence; his wife, even more so.

But there was courage in Ruma that was admirable. She let no one in her immediate circle—which to her was her world—see how mortified she was due to the collapse of her hopes. She made no change in her style of living. By careful management, she was able to throw as showy feasts as she had done before, and she met her friends with the same bright gaiety that she had so long cultivated. She had a hard and facile fund of chit-chat, which, in the society she moved in, passed for conversation. She was a useful guest among persons to whom small talk did not come easily, for she was never at a loss of a new topic and could be trusted immediately to break an awkward silence with a suitable observation. Ruma was too proud to complain to Tara, not allowing her the realization of her humiliation and her subordinate position. Tara sensed it, half-dismayed, half-anxious.

Now pondering over Vali's comment about Sugriv's reaction, Tara wondered how little she knew Sugriv. Vali had laughed it off insisting this was how it had always been between them as brothers. But both Vali and Tara knew that there was nothing Sugriv could stand less than a chaff.

*

Sugriv woke up in the middle of the night—the breathless night of the rainy season—and brooded sullenly over the gibe that Vali had uttered carelessly days before. It rankled. His heart swelled with rage, and he pictured ways in which he might get even with his bully of a brother. He had tried answering him, but Vali had a gift of repartee, smooth and obvious, which gave him an advantage. The superiority of his intellect made Vali impervious to delicate feelings. Worse, Vali's self-satisfaction made it impossible to wound him. His loud voice and his bellow of laughter were weapons against which Sugriv had nothing to counter. He had learned that the wisest thing to do was to control himself. But his resentment festered, and he watched Vali vigilantly. He knew Vali held him in low esteem; it increased his antipathy for his brother. And it gave him singular pleasure to know that Vali was entirely unaware of the animosity he felt for him. Vali was a fool who liked popularity and blandly fancied that everyone admired him.

Sugriv's marriage to Ruma had not mitigated the hostility he felt for his brother. In fact, he felt more mindful of it under Ruma's observant eye and critical tongue. Vali's intimidation spilled in the court and administrative matters. Despite having accorded Sugriv the position of the prime minister, Vali took upon himself to look into the tiniest matters of the state.

The current strain between the brothers was related to a project of road building. The facts were peculiar. Vali had a passion for building roads. When he had come to Kishkindh, there were but a few tracks here and there. But in the course of time, he had cut roads through the country, joining villages together. And it was to this that a great part of the land's prosperity was due. While in the old days, it had been impossible to get the produce of the land—copra, chiefly—down to the coast, where it could be put on the riverboat and taken to the nearest towns, now, transport was easy and simple. Vali's ambition was to make a highway right around the kingdom; in fact, a major portion of it had already been built.

'In two years, I shall have done it!' he exclaimed in casual arrogance.

For no particular reason, except for perhaps the pride in the economic efficiency of his administration and the desire to display this efficiency against the wasteful methods of the other authorities, he got people to work for almost nominal wages. Because of this, he had been having difficulty with the village chiefs lately, and the talks had fallen through.

'I don't want you to side with them, Sugriv,' Vali had uttered. 'You are supposed to be on my side, not theirs!' he had barked.

Sugriv, silently, without a movement of his long, sallow face, had said what he had already said before, 'I was trying to make you see reason.'

Tara had noticed Sugriv put up with his brother's rebukes with a sullen smile. To her, Vali's behaviour seemed unfair. After all, the king had trusted his own instincts over the evidence as well as the wisdom of his prime minister.

Vali clenched his fists and stood akimbo, straining the muscles of his jaw. Tara, horrified, thought that Vali would spring on his brother.

But just as suddenly, his temper cooled. Vali chuckled, shrugging. 'I am not going to waste my time with a pack of fools,' he said. 'Talk it over again. You know what I have offered. If you do not start in a week... Well, we will see what happens then.' His words carried a hidden threat he intended to carry out.

If Vali was loved by his people, he was feared too; and he took it as a compliment. But Sugriv assumed it to be the drivelling sensibility of an arrogant king. Like his brother's feelings towards his subjects, Sugriv had immense sympathy for the people. But unlike Vali, Sugriv could never have a rapport with them or reframe his mentality on the same level as them. His attitude towards them was very distinct from the deep kinship Vali had with his subjects. The humour of the people was coarse, as was their language. But Vali could bring himself to be one with them, never at a loss for a crude remark, which the sensitive Sugriv found offensive. On the other hand, Sugriv looked after them because that was his duty as their minister—like a man who looks after his domesticated animals. Possibly, this detachment made him a good administrator.

But Tara had also observed how Vali could be insecure about his authority—possessive of and controlling his court and ministers. He watched them suspiciously and, if they did anything he disapproved of, he was able to make their life so unendurable that they would be glad to quit and leave of their own accord.

Nothing, despaired Tara, could bring these brothers close again, her frown deepening. With battling bouts of queasiness, the days were uncomfortable enough without the brothers fighting. She groaned, glancing sideways into the mirror. Her pregnancy had blunted her features and she looked gross and blousy. Or was it her downheartedness talking?

'If you scowl so hard, you are bound to get a scowling baby!' chided Ruma, as she entered the chamber. Ruma stood with one elbow on the windowsill with a grace Tara almost envied. Ruma had a poise, which was one of her most charming gifts and which she was able to assume without intentionality.

She couldn't have felt scruffier, Tara rued, her brow furrowed. 'Just a giddy spell,' she grumbled.

'Have some lime juice with honey and ginger,' instructed Ruma, imperiously motioning to the maid to get the needful.

Tara did not mind the arrogance that came naturally

to Ruma. Somewhat like Vali, she observed with resigned amusement.

'Just another two months and this will be over!' Ruma threw her a reassuring smile.

'You always know better!' she returned with a grimace, settling into the pillow, regretting the words the moment she said them.

Ruma's face hardened, her voice forceful. 'What I do know better, Tara, is that I shan't have a child sooner or later. Never!' she pronounced with violent vehemence.

'Ruma, I did not mean—'

'You need not say it, Tara. God's been kind and I shall be spared of having a child with a man who loves me less than I love him!'

Tara went white; the accusation on Sugriv was straight and square. Again, the harshness of her words shocked her into a stunned silence.

Ruma faced her now, her eyes flashing with passion. She couldn't get the words out quickly enough. 'Not even for the sake of an heir!' she rasped. 'Not that our child would ever be a crown prince, but no, I don't wish to have his baby. Not out of duty, not out of pity!'

Tara listened to her open-mouthed. Consternation was written on her face.

She interrupted her with a frantic interjection. 'Ruma, give yourself time.'

'I am tired of waiting!' she cried in angry frustration. 'I thought I will give him time, but it is as it was... Sometimes, I wonder if he ever loved me at all! It was just me loving him...'

When she finished, Ruma hung her head, and Tara saw two tears trickle down her cheeks.

'I really have lost him, Tara,' she choked.

Ruma turned away from her and wept, leaning her face against the back of the chair. Her lovely face was twisted with the grief she did not care to hide. There was nothing Tara could do. She had a vague notion of the unavailing regret that afflicted her but nothing could have prepared her for this display of grief and anger. Helpless, Tara thought it would do Ruma good to cry. Finally, she placed a tentative hand on the other woman's shuddering shoulder.

The tears and smile died on Ruma's lips. 'What a mess we are!' she said with a bitter laugh. 'I guess our only saviour will be this child—our only hope!'

*

As Ruma had expected, the miracle happened. One hot, drenched afternoon, the arrival of the baby—as stormy as the weather outside—changed everything. It was a boy—just as Vali had wished and the world had hoped. She saw the unadulterated delight flooding Vali's face.

Tara was exhausted. She silently pressed Vali's hand in weak acknowledgment.

'I had hoped it would be a daughter as lovely as you, but yes, I am as glad that I have a son—who, unfortunately, seems to be the living image of me!' he rambled in unconcealed elation.

With his very first cry, the baby brought the two brothers running back together, both grinning foolishly, hugging, arms around each other and a happy swing in their steps, performing a victory dance.

'Congratulations brother, you are now a father!'

'Congratulations brother, you are now an uncle!'

A smiling Ruma carefully placed the baby in Vali's arms. 'The father can name his son,' she beamed.

Vali shook his head, glancing at Tara, his eyes tender. 'No, the mother has that honour. She brought him into the world.'

Tara lay in complete fatigue—on her back, with arms stretched by her sides. Her face was grey with exhaustion, her eyes dull and lifeless, half closed, and her jaw hung loose. She tried to form a smile as she saw Vali, but in her feebleness the lips scarcely moved. Pale and weak, she struggled to sit up, but that hint of a smile was strong.

'The symbolic ornament of our love, Vali—' she paused, gazing beseechingly at both the men, 'the bracelet, which shall join all of us.' She smiled, her eyes shining. 'Angad.'

12

THE CURSE

Tara went out on to the terrace of the main palace and watched Vali walk down the palace steps. He waved his hand at her. It gave her a little thrill as she looked at him; he was much older now, the father of a twelve-year-old son, but he had the lithe figure and the springing step of a boy. Yet her sceptical eye could see through his ebullience; he looked a lot more mature. He had broadened and put on flesh, his features had lost their softness and the texture of his cheeks was growing coarse.

'Is Vali indulging in some face-to-face wrestling match again?' cut in her father, Sushen, who sat beside her as they basked in the morning sun.

Tara shrugged. 'He prefers mediating. But sometimes he likes to respond with a fight instead.'

He looked at his daughter with raised eyebrows.

'He thrives on such fights as if to boast of his superior skills!' he wrinkled his forehead. 'Vali should take out time for Angad; these are his growing years,' he remarked in a voice of disapproval. 'He needs a father who's there.'

'Angad already does have a present father—Sugriv!' she

said vehemently. She took a deep breath, calming herself down, and added, 'He has us.'

'You were pretty generous in giving way Angad to Ruma,' said Sushen, observing Ruma watching Angad expertly climb the tall sal tree in the garden below. 'Was it because she cannot have children?'

Tara smiled almost imperceptibly, finding his remark highly significant.

'Ruma is Angad's *chikamma*, his other mother,' she fondly explained. 'Both of them are happy. That's what matters,' she said lifting her shoulders lightly. 'Besides, I have my children at the orphanage and the school. And my patients too.'

His thin lips extended in a frosty smile.

'Exactly! Ruma has been heard saying it's because you are so busy with other kids that you have no time for your son. And it's on her to look after him. Not all are extraordinarily selfless like you, Tara.'

She stiffened, then looked sideways at him, her thin face expressionless. 'She has a point, doesn't she? I do have other children to look after. In any case, I wouldn't let a small insecurity come between Ruma and me or between her and Angad. I know she loves Angad selflessly.'

The growing years had strengthened the bond between the boy and Ruma and Sugriv, with their love centred on Angad. And she could not disagree with Ruma when she claimed that Angad was growing up in her lap, pampered by his chikamma and *chikappa*. Even though many servants waited on him, it was Ruma who gave him his morning tumbler of warm milk. Afternoons saw him with playing with Sugriv. Later in the night, Sugriv and Ruma would take turns to read to the little prince before he went to bed. It was a promised ritual between the boy and his uncle and aunt.

Mornings were reserved for his father: Vali would train him in mace fighting, and climbing ropes and the highest trees in the forest.

'Is that how you look at it, Appa? I believe Angad is fortunate to have two sets of adoring parents.'

'Something you missed yourself?' said Sushen perceptively.

'You overcompensated!' she smiled. 'I never lacked love, nor does Angad. He gets a double dose!'

'Motherhood is often possessive, even jealous,' cautioned her father.

'Then it's not love; it's selfishness—ownership,' Tara retorted.

Sushen shook his head in mild bewilderment.

Suddenly, a bellowing roar rent the still air, so loud that she was sure the entire city had heard it.

'Come out and fight me, Vali!' The howl echoed through the palace walls, quaking the pillars.

Heart thudding wildly, she peered down. Far ahead, just outside the front entrance of the palace, an Asura, huge and formidable, was hollering for Vali.

She straightened her back, alert, her eyes darting down towards Angad in the garden, who was scampering up another tall tree skilfully. Ruma was pleading with him to come down.

With urgent steps, Tara rushed down to the garden. She gathered herself on reaching and approached Ruma.

'Who is that?' Ruma asked Tara, her face frozen in bewildered fear.

Before she could reply, she caught sight of Vali, approaching them from the other end of the garden, bringing instant relief, calming her nerves.

'Dundubhi,' replied Vali, his voice flat, his face grim.

Mayasura's son, Tara swiftly comprehended, and Mandodari's brother. But why had he come all the way from Lanka?

'Invite him in,' Tara said equably. 'He is Ravan's brother-in-law, after all.'

Vali gave her an incredulous look. 'Does he seem that he wants to be invited in, Tara? He's clearly in a mood to fight me.'

Noticing Ruma's startled expression and her son's curious one, Tara said calmly, 'Take Angad inside, Ruma. My father wants to meet him.'

The moment they were out of sight, Tara turned towards her husband, her face worried. 'What does he want to fight you for?'

Vali shrugged his massive shoulders. 'I don't know. But he needs to be taught a lesson for challenging me in front of my people!'

Tara gave a shake of her head. 'How can you say yes to a fight without knowing what you are fighting over?'

'Dundubhi has always been an impetuous fellow, quick to pick a fight.'

'And how do you know that?'

'Might makes fools lose reason,' Vali stared at her, his face tight with frustrated rage. 'Dundubhi considers himself a mighty Asura like Ravan. His sheer size has made him believe he is invincible. And he has got used to intimidating people with this formidable reputation if not his formidable appearance! In short, he is an arrogant fool, itching to fight!'

'If he's a fool as you say, he's best ignored,' said Tara in her clear, calm voice. 'Fight against a worthy foe.'

'Should I leave him barking at my door, then?'

'You are not the first one he is challenging, Vali. Dundubhi seems nothing but a big bully. A few months ago, I had heard he dared Varun, God of the Seas. The wise Varun knew better than to fight him and smartly directed him to Himavan, God of Mountains. Himavan, cleverly in turn, seems to have evaded an open confrontation. He must have suggested you as a foe worthy of Dundubhi's strength. That's why he has come thundering down to Kishkindh. Go to him and talk him down.'

'Such fools don't understand words. They know only one language—battle. And I am ready to give him a thrashing.'

Her expression of annoyance changed to that of exasperation. Her fingers gripped his wrists. 'If what you say is true, he won't know when to stop, and the thrashing will end up in killing.'

She saw Vali's lips settle in a stubborn line.

'If you kill him, you won't be resolving the current crisis; you will make matters worse,' she persuaded. 'Dundhubhi is Ravan's family. There will be retaliation for sure. Don't do it, Vali. It is senseless!'

'Someone has to drive sense into that fellow!' barked Vali. He rubbed the back of his neck. His eyes gleamed just as they did whenever he was eager for a challenge.

Worried, Tara paced back and forth. She halted, looked up at Vali, shaking her head. 'Words can be powerful weapons; they can disarm too. As you say, he's an arrogant fool. Indulge him with praise and persuasion. He is sure to back down.'

Vali's face was now set, pale, mask-like. His eyes were dark and seemed to have receded deep into their sockets. He regarded Tara for several moments before he replied, 'He has openly challenged me in front of all my people, in front of my palace. He is outside right now, awaiting my response. I can't refuse the challenge.'

There was a long pause. Tara felt a chill run down her spine. 'What are you trying to tell me?' she said at last, now no longer able to conceal her anxiety. 'That for some ego pampering and senseless bravado you are going to fight that fool? Then you are a bigger fool! With your vile temper and stubbornness, you refuse to see reason!'

Vali gave a mirthless smile that lent his face a strange, frightening expression. 'I am being reasonable—I have to tackle him or he'll destroy this palace and our city. It's a duel, Tara. A contest between two equals.'

Tara, startled by the expression on Vali's face and by what he had said, blurted out, 'He's not your equal, surely! It is a contest between two egotists to prove a point! You know you will win. I am sure of that; you are sure of that. Yet you want to kill him. But at what cost?' she persisted, her voice rising, hoping he could hear reason.

Tara stopped, her face blanching, as a thought struck her.

'Are you doing this to gain more strength?' she said slowly, her voice shaking in a hoarse whisper, horrified at the new dawning truth. 'You know you draw half of the strength of your rival when you defeat him. You did it with Ravan first, and with several others, all these years. And now with Dundubhi...'

'Winning is not merely a show of strength but the display of your rival's weakness—his defeat.'

Tara played agitatedly with the shells on her bracelet, dread beginning to rapidly mount. 'Tell me, Vali! Say it! Have you taken half of Ravan's power only to become a different person? Are you like him now—thirsting for blood and violence in the name of power, glory and honour?!'

Vali said nothing, compressing his lips into a thin, cruel line. Tara stared at his hard face, with fear and suspicion. But she had hope that if she were patient, some unmistakable sign of her husband's reason would reveal itself.

'You think I'm mad, don't you?' Vali asked, reading her thoughts. 'Sugriv too says I'm mad and unreasonable. God knows what that means. Well, I'm not all that crazed. I just have a weakness—I cannot refuse a challenge—not yet, anyway.'

Gingerly touching the dagger at his side, the blade between his thick fingers, he appeared quite at ease. He spoke quietly and fluently, not hesitating at all, as if he had rehearsed the words over and over again as an actor learns his part. 'You are overdramatizing this, Tara,' he said his face a little flushed, his eyes brighter.

'Taking on his challenge will do us more harm than good,' she said swiftly, running a shaky hand through her hair. It felt damp. Her neck and palms were damp, too. She realized that for the past several minutes, she had been sweating profusely. White-faced and tense, she decided to say nothing more, struggling to submit to the stubborn face of her husband.

Her listless eyes followed Vali as he walked out of the garden. She listened to his determined tread as he strode out through the archway leading to the palace gates, where Dundubhi was waiting for him. She heard the gates open and then clang shut. Then, the garden became strangely still and silent. She shuddered, clenching her fists, waiting for him to return with blood on his hands.

Opening her eyes, she ran towards the palace ramparts, preparing herself to witness a fearsome battle she could not halt.

Exulting on his daring exploits, Dundubhi had destroyed his own chariot, crushing it with his bare hands.

'Dundubhi, your show of strength does not scare me! Do not allow your head to swell so!' roared Vali. 'Beware! There lives one who is mightier than you—me!'

'Oh yes!' Dundubhi emitted a wild snarl. 'I hear you strut on the shores of the Pampa Lake, assuming leadership and asserting your power in Kishkindh. You took it from Ravan. But I am here now to snatch it back from you!'

With these words, Dundubhi gave out a snort so loud and so strong that the wind's whistle in the trees could be heard by Tara. Grunting, Dundubhi changed himself into a formidable buffalo and charged at Vali. Vali stood still, magnificent and confident, the golden necklace of his father glinting in the sunlight.

Tara watched from the rampart, apprehensive and tense. Just then, a small movement caught her eyes. She turned to see Sugriv standing at the palace steps; he shook his head at her. Undoubtedly, Vali had ordered him to not interfere.

Vali and Dundubhi lunged at each other and grappled with each other. Each time they struck one another, Tara winced, shutting her eyes, only to open them again to a gorier sight. The ground trembled. Dundubhi ploughed the earth with his horns and bellowed, parading his lofty pride and his impregnable power. His fury was reaching new heights with every step. He cast terror all around. When he dug his horns into the earth, huge trees ended up uprooted on the ground. His ferocity shook her heart. Vali stepped forward at that very instant and fell upon him, stopping him by the horns with his hands. The two foes struggled for victory, like wild tuskers entangled in mortal combat. Minutes stumbled into hours, but neither was willing to let go.

Tara looked up at the sky. The sun had moved high up, fierce and bright. It had been more than six hours since the fight had begun. She unclenched her fists, her heart still hammering.

Dundubhi was getting weaker; he too had realized it. In a desperate attempt at saving his life, he sank to his knees in a gesture of surrender. Tara heaved a sigh of relief. *It is going to be over soon.* She reckoned Vali would let him go now since it was clear he was the winner.

She had half risen to tell him so, when she saw Vali raise his mighty arms, roaring with fury over the whimpered pleas of the demon bull still on his knees, pleading with Vali to spare his life. She stood stunned as Vali gave a wild cry and bend down to tackle the cowering Asura who was staggering with pain, his face bloodied. Her scream froze in her throat.

Tara heard a terrible screech rent the air. She stared down at the fearsome sight. Vali, with a last mortal blow, snapped Dundubhi's neck with his bare hands. Then, he seized him by the horns, swirled him around and threw him away. Dundubhi crashed into the ground, like a mountain collapsing. His smash resounded like a violent earthquake.

She heard Vali roar once more, so intoxicated with his victory that he tore the corpse apart.

'No! No, Vali, no!' she screamed. 'Leave him some dignity!'

But Vali could did not hear her protests over his war cry.

Her horrified eyes saw him pick up one half of the corpse by the leg and whirl it around several times before hurling it as far as he could, followed by the other half—one to the south and other to the north.

'Stop it, Vali!' she screamed in horror, shocked and shaking. 'You are a beast! No, not even an animal does this to his fellow beings! You are a monster!'

Sickened, shuddering in revulsion, she heard him come up the steps to the rampart, the stench of blood on his bare torso assailing her.

She spun around, away from him, her face white. 'What have you done?! How could you? You were a warrior, honourable and brave. But, not any longer... You are a brute, a savage! What you did just now is nothing but barbarism,' she choked, fear, fury and repugnance strangling her words.

Not being able to bear being near him, she fled to her chamber. Finally, in that much needed isolation, she surrendered herself to a passion of tears. Revulsion and rage almost drove away her grief. The love, which had been a tower of gold, crumbled like a hut of straw in a storm.

She recalled how she had pleaded and persuaded with him, how she had knelt before him, beseeching with him, but he had not granted her request, refusing to see reason. Suddenly, she abhorred him—for his savagery, his viciousness and the sheer barbarity of his actions. She could not conceal his faults that stared her in the face from herself any longer. Vali was a ruthless egomaniac. He cared only for himself—his power, his ego, his ambition. Tara found a bitter fascination in stripping her idol of the finery with which her blind love had bedizened him; she saw him more accurately now, and he was a fiend. But most unbearable of all was the humiliation she now had to go through—to be the wife of such a monster.

*

The morning sunshine had given way to dark clouds, shortly breaking into a storm. The rain poured down, unceasing, and the despair of nature ate into her soul. At last, she was exhausted. Losing track of time, she lay half-insentient, feeling no pain, her brain vacant and weary. When a maid came to ask if Sugriv might see her, she hardly understood what was being said to her.

'Typical of Sugriv to stand on such ceremony,' she muttered ill-temperedly. 'Ask him to come in.'

Her husband's brother came to the door and hesitated, growing red. The expression in his eyes was that of pain and bewilderment.

'Where is Vali? I haven't seen him since he killed Dundubhi.'

'Angad has been asking the same,' Tara mumbled, stroking her son's head who had walked in with Sugriv and was now seated by his mother's side. She raised puzzled eyes at him. 'What day is it?'

'It was yesterday that the incident happened,' he said patiently, taking in her puffy face and red, tear-drenched eyes. 'I just came to check if you knew where Vali was.'

Tara frowned.

'Appa often disappears for many days or weeks on end!' piped in Angad, his tone defensive. He gave his mother a worried look. 'Are you unwell, Amma? Appa will be back soon. He killed that horrible man!' he glowed, his small eyes shining.

He disappears because he is fighting some odd duel, or bashing someone senseless, Tara thought wearily, moved by her son's swift defence of his father. Previously, during such times, it was Sugriv who had stayed with Angad, explaining that his father was a hero, fighting not just for his reputation, but for the honour of all the Vanaras of Kishkindh. Such indoctrination had probably made Angad fiercely proud to be Vali's son, and she was not sure if she should be grateful or wary that he had an uncle like Sugriv.

Sugriv was a little pained at Tara's manifest indifference, yet took it as a just punishment. 'Angad, go to Chikamma. She's waiting for you to have dinner,' he said, his voice mild. Watching the boy swiftly leave the chamber, Sugriv, relaxed and crossed his arms.

'There was another thing I wanted to let you know...' he hesitated uneasily, regarding her pale, damp face.

'What is it?' she said wearily, tightening her lips in a manner he had become accustomed to.

'Well, it's about Vali,' answered Sugriv, with certain gravity.

'Tell me,' commanded Tara. Her eyes turned hard and her breathing sped up.

'It has to do with when Vali flung away the carcass of Dundubhi,' Sugriv cleared his throat. 'One bleeding mass of flesh and bone fell on the great seer Rishi Matang's hermitage, raining a shower of blood over the holy area, polluting the ascetics and the ashram. Rishi Matang had gone to the river for his ritual bath. When, on his return, he noticed the blood splattered all over his ashram with the torn half-corpse of a terror-striking monster, he could not contain himself and pronounced a terrible curse on whoever was the perpetrator,' he said with a slight frown and an uneasy shrug.

Tara felt a coil of fear in the pit of her stomach.

'On Vali?' she whispered hoarsely, chilled to the bone.

'Yes,' said Sugriv shifting his feet. 'Through his powers, the rishi found out that it was Vali who had done the deed. His usual tolerance gave way—'

'What did he say?' she demanded, her voice low and urgent.

'That if Vali approaches that hill or even casts an eye on it, his head would explode into pieces.'

'Does Vali know about this?' Tara interposed, keeping her voice steady.

Sugriv again gave a light shrug. 'Sooner or later, he will know.'

'What will I know?' announced a loud voice.

Sugriv turned speechless for a moment.

Vali had arrived at last, and she did not hurry to meet him. Tara took it upon herself to tell him, her voice low with suppressed fury. 'That you have won an accolade...in the form of a curse,' she said, her voice icy.

Vali threw her a sharp look, discerning the sarcasm in her voice. 'Is that how a wife welcomes her victorious husband?'

Tara, almost dismayed, looked at her husband with horrified astonishment. She scarcely recognized him now. He had not cleaned himself up yet. His enemy's blood had stained his dark skin; his hair was matted with it and his eyes were bloodshot. In all the years of their married life, Tara had noticed him change. But with her great faculty for idealization, she still carried in her mind his image as he had appeared when she first saw him—the serious, quiet youth. Other people had discerned the changes in him as well; spiteful tongues had said that he was morphing into an uncontrollable tyrant. But as his wife, she had seen everything but said nothing. Her hopeful love had given her reasons to believe in him, to see what she wanted to see. But seeing him now, anew, she recognized the changes. In front of her, stood a different man, almost a stranger. *A barbarian.*

'You're a victor?' she asked, with a smile, such a question in such a tone revenged her for much. 'Or none the wiser of the curse you have earned?'

She purposely spoke in a rather formal and elaborate manner, her eyes glittering.

'What curse?' he asked shortly.

'After the despicable killing of Dundubhi, you committed another atrocity of hurling his body away,' she began, her voice soft but forceful, 'a part of which fell hundreds of miles away, on the hermitage of Rishi Matanga. For the desecration, he has pronounced a curse on you, Vali. That your head will explode if you even glance at or ever step onto Mount Matanga, where he lives. You have now upon you a curse, which you cannot avoid.'

Grim lines marked his craggy face but Vali gave a thin, sure smile. 'I can avoid it, Tara. I will never see or step on that hill. Simple.'

'A king cannot go to his own land because it is a death trap for him,' she returned his smile, mirthlessly. 'Not very honourable, is it?'

She saw the flare of fear and fury in his eyes. But almost instantaneously, he returned to his old self—cheery, jovial, red-faced and in good humour.

'Here I am again!' he proclaimed, as a warrior returning from war. 'All fit and fine, and better off than I was—I have now gained Dundubhi's strength, which he was so boastful of!'

'And gained a deathly curse too,' she said quietly.

'A small price for what I got,' he shrugged his heavy shoulders, but she detected a flinch of fear assailing him. 'You see I've got what I wanted. No one will dare challenge me pointlessly,' he purred, his voice low like a growl. 'By heavens, it does me good seeing that I have won... Now, confess—weren't you unreasonable to make such a fuss about battling him? I couldn't have helped it, now could I have?'

He avoided her angry stare and continued with a jarring laugh, 'I am what I am—Vali, the fighter who won't shy away from a bloody good fight if anyone challenges him,' he pronounced, rubbing his hands. 'Now, I am back, fully refreshed and we'll have our dinner!'

Vali kissed her with marital possessiveness. The strong scent of blood and gore wafted into Tara's nostrils. Yet it was the same masculine odour that once had made her nearly faint with desire. She turned away, hardly concealing a shiver of disgust—

Which Sugriv did not fail to notice.

13

COMBAT AND CONFLICT

The tyrannical love that had captured her heart could not be easily overthrown. While she recovered from her rage, the love that had seemed crushed flared up again—like a conflagration, briefly doused, but blazing with a new force. She was dismayed by her extreme helplessness and could no longer repudiate that his love was unlike hers; he possibly loved himself more than he loved her. His obstinacy was as evident as his self-absorption. She was still hopeful to see in Vali her ideal man. She imprudently believed that he was still the man she had fallen in love with years ago, that she could change him to what he was before. Except that, in her aching heart, she had a gnawing suspicion of his true character.

But it seemed that the more passionately she yearned for her husband's rationality, the more apparent their differences became.

As time went on, the calm between the storms was shorter. Every quarrel left its mark and made Tara more susceptible to horror. Realizing that Vali could not answer her expectations, she became more disappointed and less exacting.

Their disagreements were a proof to her that it did not take two persons to make a quarrel. Vali was an exemplar of good temper when it came to her, and his equanimity was imperturbable whenever they argued. However fractious Tara was, he never lost his composure. Vali had, she was forced to admit, that magnificent ability of assuming that he always did right—the most immeasurable talent of the true self-aggrandizer. It was this sense of infallibility of his that pleased him so much and had edified his reputation that caused her the utmost frustration. After every quarrel from which Vali would egotistically stomp off, Tara's rage would be taken over by regret and frustration. She would ask frantically how she could make her husband see sense. Finally, in dread and uncertainty, she would desperately wait for his return.

On his part, Vali would take the first opportunity of taking her in his arms and making the most abject apology. Then, having mollified her, Vali would again make himself to be the golden idol, clothed in righteous garments of true honour and valour, his word the law and his deeds perfect. Tara, like the others, became a mere spectator, offering sane counsel and nothing more. Their love—or rather her advice, she bitterly acknowledged—was like a wave over a barren rock, just as the sea that breaks in waves and scatters into foam, while the rock stands unchanged.

Peace was uneasy; the calm, troubled. As she had dreaded, a week later, another yowl similar to that of Dundubhi ripped the uneasy calm in the palace. Tara shuddered. Revenge had arrived at their doorstep.

'Come out, O vile Vali!' thundered the strident voice. 'You killed my brother through deceit and sheer brutality. I shall now show you what barbarity means. Come out, Vali!

Let us fight and I shall kill you the shoddy way you murdered my brother.'

'It is Mayavi,' Tara said dully.

Vali shrugged his heavy shoulders. 'I am ready for him!'

'But I am not!' she cried, rounding on him with unmitigated fury. 'How often will this happen, Vali? Some person challenges you for a fight and you promptly forsake everything to prove your might—or rather, to indulge your ego! But why this hunger for violence, why this thirst for blood? Oh, who am I asking but a monster!' she wiped away angry tears from her eyes. 'A king who doesn't wish peace, neither for himself, nor for his family, his people or his kingdom!'

Vali was silent for an instant and looked at her with eyes in which there was a sudden perplexity. 'But I do it exactly *for* that—to avoid violence and war,' he said stubbornly. 'I would rather face the enemy myself face-to-face, in a hand-to-hand combat, than engulf my family and people and country in war. Is that not less bloody?'

With a shuddering breath, she walked up to him, taking his large hands in hers. 'Please talk to him first, pacify him; he's a wounded man grieving the death of his brother. Apologize, persuade, placate, plead. Oh, do anything to appease him!'

'He's a brother lusting for the blood of his brother's murderer,' cut in Vali strongly. 'He won't see reason. He wants revenge, not platitudes.'

'Then was it necessary to kill Dundubhi in the first place?' she cried, her breath trembling in renewed anger. 'Couldn't you have subdued him and made him surrender? I saw it— he was begging for his life, yet you mercilessly, butchered him!' she gave a visible shudder. 'Now his brother demands a battle. Another challenge, another duel, another killing,' she said wearily, her shoulder sagging, the anger spent. She turned hopeful eyes on him. 'You are more powerful than him, Vali. If there is a fight, subdue him and make him see reason. Don't kill him as you did Dundubhi.'

Vali shook his head. 'Tara, if you let a wounded animal go, he is bound to come back and attack you again,' he grimaced. 'If I had let Dundubhi go, he would have come back, and harmed you and Angad in his mad fury! It is all of you I need to protect, not monsters like Dundubhi and Mayavi. If I have to kill them all, so be it.'

'Then, let someone else handle it—Sugriv? Hanuman? Or the Kishkindh army? Let your general and the military handle this problem.'

Vali gave a violent shake of his head. 'Should I send someone else to save my skin? It's a personal combat, and I shall fight him myself,' he said with finality. 'He is mocking me by inviting me to an open fight and, worse, accusing me of deceit. I will not show any mercy to an enemy who insults my honour and reputation!'

'Oh, how can I make you understand?' she cried, roiling in frustration. 'I do everything I can to make you see sense and I can't—you're a rock and a stone wall!'

Vali appeared to be totally unconscious of his wife's distress. He was like a king reigning in his world; he did not see Tara's lips curl over some foolish remark of his, nor the angry contempt with which she treated him these days.

'I don't know about that. I can truly say that after God and my honour, I treasure nothing in the world so much as you and your opinion,' he replied, taking her remark with vehement seriousness.

'Then why don't you heed my words? You thrive on

violence and blood and gore. You've forgotten you are supposed to be an honourable hunter, a noble Vanara,' lashed out Tara scornfully.

'And that is what I am, what I am doing,' answered Vali, with a certain gravity. 'You can be sure that I would do my duty.' He paused, and continued with quiet anger in his eyes. 'But oh, I'm sick of your duty. You din it into my ears morning, noon and night. I wish to God you weren't so virtuous—that you were more human!'

'How would a monster know what a human is?' she retorted furiously.

Without another word, he went to the dresser, took out the sapphire studded gold necklace Indra had bestowed to him and put it on. It now flashed on his broad chest.

'My lucky charm,' he said grimly, glancing at himself in the mirror.

He forced a smile, his voice retaining the gentle, persuasive tone, the effect of which he was fully aware of.

'But you're my first lucky charm,' he stated, giving her his roguish charm she could never resist.

She looked at him through her angry tears and replied, 'And your ego is your curse.' Drained, she stood up and, turning to him, limply stretched out her arms. He walked to her. She put her arms around his neck, and pressed her face against his. 'All we do is argue these days! Oh, Vali, it seems so long since we spent any time together,' she said, pulling back and looking up at him. She had to find a way to distract him. 'Let us not talk now. Let us not waste a minute. Kiss me.'

His desire raged. Vali had never heard from his wife a command so calmly administered; it impressed him. He kissed her, holding her to him while his heart hammered in his chest. He tightened his arms around her, firming his kiss. She leaned into him, her dark and shining eyes gazing passionately into his, her lips parted with desire. She adored him; she was angry with him. For one instant, she clung to him more closely, and then she felt his desire to let go, and she released him.

He released her too, and she felt oddly bereft. Her trick had not worked.

His smile was amused and complacent. 'I shall be back in a flash!' he grinned. He gave her that charming smile of his, which she had always found so irresistible. 'You know I hate to let you go,' he murmured thickly. 'But I have another fool to defeat.'

She watched his retreating back, absently turning her bracelet around her wrist. She loved him, she thought dully, but hated what he had become. As she again stood at the terrace, witnessing the fight, it was like a sickening déjà vu.

Mayavi roaring at Vali made him look more monstrous, seeming even larger and more menacing than his brother, appearing to be twice as strong. As was his stance, Vali stared directly into his enemy's eyes—his dull, calm ones into the flaming red eyes of Mayavi.

This was meant to be a terrible fight, and Vali intended to engage in a fair one-to-one combat. But, on Tara's instructions, Sugriv had been told to accompany him for supplementary support if the Asura had any accomplices who might attack deviously.

'I give you a fair warning, dear friend,' said Vali with a mocking sneer. 'You are in Kishkindh, and I would treat you as my guest, were it not for your war call. Let us make peace.'

'Do you expect me to bow to you, you murderer?' snarled Mayavi, his florid face turning purple with fury. 'You killed my brother in a most hapless way!'

'No. Flee in fear, Mayavi, for if you don't, I shall kill you too,' returned Vali, his voice low and even. Mayavi returned the stare and spit at Vali's feet.

Watching, this Tara's heart sank. There would be no coming back from this as she saw her husband's empty eyes well up with rage and challenge. And the battle began.

As soon as the bout started, Tara could visibly see Vali's boon taking effect. Vali was extracting and absorbing half of his opponent's strength. The fight continued for hours without a break, both fighters almost evenly matched. However, Vali's gained strength proved to be advantageous; Mayavi began to visibly fatigue, his sapped body taking more and more devastating blows from Vali's bare fists. Bloodied and considerably weakened, Mayavi lifted his arms limply. *He is surrendering,* thought Tara, clutching her fists together, relief flooding her heart.

Vali thought so too and relaxed, this time ready to let his enemy go. But Mayavi took this opportunity to kick sand into Vali's eyes.

Vali roared as he was momentarily blinded. Tara thought Mayavi would pick up his fallen mace and attack Vali, but his weakened state made him panic with the quick realization that he would lose the fight and be shown no mercy. Mayavi found an opportunity to flee for his life and started running towards the forest. Vali swiftly seized the situation. He turned his furious, bloodshot eyes towards his brother. Sugriv, as usual, was standing like a silent sentinel, watching and guarding his elder brother.

'Catch him, Sugriv, don't let him go!' he growled, rubbing his eyes angrily, water streaming from them.

Tara gave a strangled cry. 'Sugriv, don't! Let him go,

Vali, please!' she cried, her voice hoarse with fear. 'He is defeated, don't chase him. Come back!'

Sugriv looked momentarily baffled before making a dash for the fleeing figure. Vali had recovered his composure and with a wild roar, followed his brother, hot on his heels. Mayavi shrank back in fear when he saw the brothers charging towards him. Realizing that he was no match for their combined might, he quickened his pace, fleeing for his life.

Tara sank slowly to the floor, her hands clutching her chest as her heart hammered away. They were gone as fast as the whirling wind and they would soon come back victorious with their gory trophy. Now, all she could do was wait for Vali to come back.

14

WAITING

The verandah of the palace that ran alongside her chamber was shadowed. Tara's heart constricted with dread. Her unfocused gaze scarcely noticed the blue river and the crowded harbour that would always catch her attention when she would look outside her window. Today, Tara could think only of Vali.

Vali had not come back since that day a month ago, nor had Sugriv. But even as she tried to reassure herself and a panicking Ruma, her heart thudded fearfully against her ribs. She gladly handed Angad to Ruma to keep her fully occupied and, more significantly, to keep her fears at bay. Two worried women would not save the day or the situation, Tara thought grimly.

The thought of Vali being missing drove her insane, her mind unravelling in constant fear. She would think of him injured, lying helpless, but then where was Sugriv? He would surely be on the lookout for his brother, wouldn't he? *Would he,* a small voice taunted her. She shook her head violently, asking herself how she could have possibly divined such a horrible doubt.

Her eyes grew vacant, the image of Vali lingering long in her dilated pupils. She comforted herself with the idea that he would certainly be safe and that he would come back—vociferous in his victory, as was his ritual.

And then, one cloudy morning, Sugriv arrived at the palace gates. Before Ruma could collect her composure, she flew down the staircase and flinged her arms around him, tears of relief streaming down her face. But his weary eyes looked up at Tara over his wife's shoulders.

The look made the colour drain from Tara's face, her heart lurching to an abrupt halt. She fled to her chamber, as if to escape from some terrible truth Sugriv was about to tell her.

She heard him come into the room. Her heart was beating wildly and her hands were shaking. She sat rigidly on the settee, holding herself straight as though she was prepared for the worst. Suddenly, she felt a cold chill pass through her limbs and she shivered. Sugriv's face was deathly pale. His dark eyes, immobile and inscrutable, seemed unusually large. He knew everything. And he wanted to tell her something.

There was sinister silence between them. *When is he going to speak?* It was dreadful that she could not control the trembling of her lips.

'Where is Vali? Is—is he in trouble?' she asked, standing unsteadily on her feet. 'Say it, Sugriv!'

He shook his head. He wanted to be brutal and tell her everything, but looking at her ghostly face, seeing the terror in her large, luminous eyes, the quivering of her lips, the sudden clenching of her fists, it was impossible for him to give her more than a hint at what had happened.

'No, he's not in trouble. It's worse than that.'

Terror clutched at her throat, she approached him. She

grabbed him by his arm. 'I'll never forgive you for this,' she said, trembling. 'If anything's happened to him, I'll—'

'Tara! Oh, Tara!' he whispered hoarsely, holding her wrists. 'He's dead, Tara. Mayavi killed him,' he announced flatly.

She sat down suddenly, as if the strength had gone out of her legs, and her face went white under her mask of poise.

His voice sounded strange to her. His tone was raised towards the last sentence in order to give his remark a tragic air, but it was forced. She wondered if he saw that she was shaking. It was only by an effort that she did not scream.

'No, no, no one can kill Vali,' her voice came out in a husky whisper. 'He is invincible.'

Sugriv dropped his eyes.

She looked fearfully at him now and saw that his eyes were fixed on his feet. His gaze would not meet hers. She realized that he could not bear to look at her. His voice, as a rule, was polite, but now he spoke in a flat note.

He could see at once that she believed the news. Her soft little face seemed to fall to pieces. She fell back against the settee, her hand across her eyes. The column of her throat jerked convulsively as she grappled with the news. Grief seared her, cleaving her bleeding heart.

'Oh don't!' she moaned. 'He can't be dead. He can't!'

He rushed to her side.

'You are not alone, Tara, I am there...' he said. 'There's Angad—'

'But I am alone now,' she said, looking up at him dazedly. 'Oh, Vali! Vali! Why didn't you listen? How could you leave me alone?!' It was the anguished cry of a wounded woman and it disturbed Sugriv. He put his hand gently on her shoulder, but she barely noticed it, her body wracked in dry sobs.

'Vali is indestructible. You know that, Sugriv!' she said wretchedly, looking up at him, her face pinched. 'Why did you return without him?!'

'I waited. I waited for days for him!' said Sugriv, his eyes imploring.

'I asked you to be with him, didn't I?' She didn't sound angry, but just as if she were thinking aloud in a daze. 'If you had guarded him as you had promised, this wouldn't have happened. I told you he couldn't look after himself. But you wouldn't believe me. He wouldn't believe me either.'

'You saw what happened, Tara,' Sugriv paused, his voice shaking. 'Realizing he would lose the fight and be shown no mercy, Mayavi took an opportunity to run for his life after kicking sand into Vali's eyes. Vali and I chased the fleeing Mayavi into the forest. But Mayavi knew where he was going. Hoping to lose us in the chase, he ran into a cave, which was clearly his hideout. It was an entrance to the underworld. We were forced to stop, wondering what to do next. It was then that Vali decided that he would follow Mayavi into the cave alone. I was to wait outside the entrance and keep watch. I entreated him to turn back but Vali had no intention of letting him escape. I suggested we go in together as we always did in times of battle but Vali was adamant! He was sure Mayavi would cheat in battle again, and with the strict instructions that I wait outside, Vali disappeared into the cave.'

'Despite your warning,' she said hollowly.

Sugriv was taken aback. His leathery complexion turned a dark red. Her tone was so flat that to his confused mind, it seemed she was accusing him. Or was this something he only felt because of guilt? Was he secretly relieved that Vali had died in that cave? And perhaps his anguish was greater because of his guilt, especially when she had trusted him.

'Yes, I implored him to not pursue Mayavi but Vali was hell-bent on capturing him. I haven't seen him more murderous!' said Sugriv with a heavy exhale of his breath. 'After Vali vanished into the yawning darkness, I waited for a long time, peering into the cave as far as the eye could see. Every morning, I would walk to the cave to check if Vali had emerged. I even placed soldiers at the mouth of the cave to escort Vali home when he would emerge. We saw nothing and heard nothing untill, finally, one morning, the cry of the wretched Asura resonated through the cave. Was it a cry of agony or of victory I couldn't fathom, but I waited, straining and praying to hear some sound of my brother, but the cave remained deathly silent. When the deafening silence went on and on, my heart sank, and then, to my horror, I saw a trickle of blood flowing out… All I could infer was that Vali had been killed. I felt torn between my desire to rush to help and avenge my brother's death and my duty to protect the kingdom from the savage Asura. If Mayavi came out of the cave, he might well be unstoppable. I was forced to rethink. Besides, would I be able to overpower a foe who had already overpowered my more powerful brother? Deciding that discretion was the better part of valour, I was forced to devise an alternative strategy. With the help of the soldiers on guard, we managed to move a giant boulder to seal the cave. Feeling reassured that this would keep the Asura at bay, I have returned to the kingdom.'

But perhaps Tara had keener intuition than he knew, for as he went on with his explanation, her eyes grew colder and her lips closed upon one another more tightly. Now and then, she looked at him closely. And, if he had been less intent on his narrative, he might have noticed her expressions.

'Did he tell you that in so many words or is that the impression you had gained from his manner?' Tara's glistening eyes shone with desperate anguish. They made Sugriv a trifle uneasy. He was not quite sure that she believed him.

'Vali said it over and over again,' he said stiffly. 'And I had to follow his orders against my wishes. I waited with the soldiers, screamed out for him, but there was no response. I wanted to rush into the cave but was subdued by my men. They were too frightened. They said if we opened up the cave, Mayavi would re-emerge and again attack us, laying claim to Kishkindh.'

His reasonable tone could not placate Tara, who, accustomed to Sugriv's obedience all her life, could not bear to hear him voice her worst fear. Blind, incoherent wrath arose in her heart. It seemed to choke her, and she felt the blood vessels in her temples swell and throb. Anguish made her more vindictive than she would have imagined herself to be.

'Did you not for a moment consider that Vali might have killed Mayavi and that it might be Vali who is now stuck in the cave?' she lashed out.

Sugriv looked shocked. 'I waited, Tara. We waited for one whole month.'

She sat upright, her tears halted.

'But not enough, Sugriv!' How can you assume he's dead? Where is the dead body? Get me that and I shall believe it!' she passed a trembling hand over her eyes, flicking away the tears impatiently. 'I don't want your sympathy, I want you to search for him!' She got unsteadily to her feet. 'If you had been a proper brother to him, he would be here with us right now!'

He went white, stunned by the suddenness of this attack.

He remained motionless, staring at her.

'I did my best, Tara, you know it!'

'All I know is that you did *not* do your best to save him! Why didn't you check inside the cave before you blocked it?' she demanded fiercely. 'Because you did not want to take a chance, did you? If there was even the remotest possibility that Mayavi was dead and Vali alive, you removed that likelihood.'

'What are you saying, Tara?' he said hoarsely.

'That you did not do enough for him. That you would rather have him dead!' she cried. She clasped her hand to her mouth in horror, the moment she said it. Oh, what was she saying? Was it the angered resentment that Sugriv was alive and Vali dead that made her utter such an awful accusation?

It was true, but it frightened Sugriv now that Tara had unconsciously sensed it. While she was horrified that she had voiced her doubts aloud in her grief, he wasn't. Oddly enough, even in that moment of fear and anger, her accusations excited his indignation. He faintly sneered.

'And why would I want my brother dead?'

She was a little startled. There was a light in his eyes that made her uneasy.

'You know why! Don't make me say it.'

His jaw tightened. 'Say it, Tara,' he said quietly.

'Because you want the throne. Because you want me!' she spat, her lips trembling.

He watched her without a gesture and without a movement of his face. He listened attentively and no change in his expression showed that what she had said affected him.

'I have no illusions about us, Tara,' he started slowly. 'But you are being unfair... I didn't kill Vali—or ever intend to—as you so vilely accuse,' he said, his eyes quietly smouldering.

'I know why,' he said. 'It is because you know I love you, isn't it? Is that reason enough for your wicked suspicions?' Sugriv stood looking at Tara, his livid eyes searching her pinched face.

'Tara, I know you love Vali. I know you are his wife. But you may as well know my true feelings. I am sure it won't hurt you. Well, it gives me no pleasure just to tell you over and over again, but I love you... I think right from the time I met you. Long before him!' he added bitterly. 'I did everything I could to conceal it and make you think that it was not so, even if you and Vali treated me as a big fool. I knew that you had married for love and that I had only married Ruma for convenience. I loved you so much, I didn't care in what capacity I could love you. Most people, as far as I can see, when they're in love with someone and the love isn't returned, feel that they have a grievance. They grow angry and bitter. I wasn't like that. I never expected you to love me; I didn't see any reason that you should. I was content being near you, as a friend, even as your brother-in-law. I was thankful to be allowed to love you, and I was satisfied when you were pleased with me or when you treated me with good humoured affection. I tried not to overwhelm you with my affection. I couldn't afford to do that! I couldn't have been able to bear knowing that I was causing you trouble. I was ready to receive any favour from you, however small,' he exhaled, his voice shaking. 'But the fact that I love you does not give you the right to heap this terrible allegation on me, Tara!'

Standing there, his face tortured, his eyes glittering with fury and hurt, his big hairy hands tightened in to fists, Tara felt an overwhelming wave of shame wash over her. There was an intense, savage sorrow coming from him; Tara could feel it. It shocked her.

'It's not my fault that I don't love you,' she said simply. 'But yes, it is my fault for having my suspicions...for this accusation. I—I am sorry.'

Again, Sugriv raised his burning eyes and looked. 'Fair enough... No matter how unfair you were earlier,' he said.

Tara stepped back quickly. His strangely calm voice startled her now. His coal-coloured eyes were expressionless, bereft of the earlier rage and resentment, but there was something shadowy in their black vacancy. He turned suddenly disconcerted as she twisted her bracelet on her wrist.

'I promise you—I never wished Vali dead,' he continued, observing her nervous gesture with a fixed stare. 'Ever.'

His face was impenetrable, and it again reminded her of Vali, frightening her.

'I take your word when you say you tried to save him,' she broke in, bitterly. 'Go search for him, he's not dead—not for me!'

His eyes dwelt on her face speculatively.

'No, Tara, Vali *is* dead. Believe it. And believe that I am here. I shall be here, always by your side.'

✴

15

LOVE AND LOYALTY

Jambavan and Tara stood in the latter's chamber, coming to terms with the past and future. 'It's been decided—Sugriv has to be made king,' said Jambavan flatly. The finality in his voice made Tara wince.

But Vali is not dead, she told herself, clutching at her bracelet. She could feel it in her gut, her soul.

A visibly sorrowful Sugriv had informed the waiting courtiers about the demise of their valiant monarch and had ordained a period of state-wide mourning. After the mourning period had ended, the ministers had asked Sugriv to take up the role of the king, pointing at the absence of any other qualified heir—Angad was still a boy. Still afflicted by memories of Vali, Sugriv resolved to carry on his brother's legacy and accepted the royal mantle.

Tara had been blankly observing all that was happening around her, half dazed, half disbelieving.

'The tribes had only recently been brought together by Vali. Hearing the news of his death, they are most likely to disintegrate and start fighting among themselves again. I know you have personally spoken with each one of them,

Tara...' Jambavan trailed off.

The worried note in his voice made her sit up. He was politically the most powerful ally to have, and seeing him in this state made her momentarily forget her anger and grief. 'As Sugriv should have,' said Tara pointedly. 'Please guide him, Jambavan, he seems lost.'

Jambavan nodded his hoary head. 'Yes, he should have but he is banking on you. He is well aware that you have more convincing power than him, and that they will listen to *you* as the bereaved queen of Vali.'

Tara lifted her narrow shoulders and spread out her hands. 'Right now, they need an able leader, be it the bereaved brother or the bereaved wife.'

'Exactly,' nodded Jambavan again, in a voice as burly as his size. 'That is what places you in a position of such prime importance now, Tara,' he remarked, giving her a sympathetic look.

From the time Tara had first seen Jambavan walking along the main street, she had been utterly fascinated by this man for his towering, hulking form, his benign expressions, the gravity in his demeanour, his copper-brown, unruly hair; he had made an ineffaceable impression on her. Later, when she had grown up, she had seen him in court. There, his quiet, dignified manners, his candid estimations and his intimidating appearance made her respect him even more. Jambavan had been Vriksharaj's friend for the longest time. Even when they had retired to the forest, he had taken over the mantle of a foster father for Vali, guiding him, supporting him at every turn. Vali, too, had been in awe of him; he was very proud to have such a man as his mentor. Aged and wise, Jambavan was courteous and dignified, but he never failed to be brutally frank, not afraid to mince his words. Right now, looking at this tall, stately man, she had the same impression, giving her the much-needed confidence in his straight and outspoken words.

'Vali and Sugriv are like my sons, I love them both, but Tara, you hold your own,' he continued quietly. 'You are the daughter of a respected physician, as respected as him. As a healer—and as a queen—you are loved and admired by the people. When you say something, you are endorsing it. Now you need to endorse yourself as queen and sit on the throne...'

Tara exhaled painfully, her heart contracting. *Time and throne wait for no one*, she thought bitterly.

'As Sugriv's wife,' he added pointedly.

No! She gasped. 'No,' she repeated, her voice betrayed her dismay.

'You seem to know everything, yet you don't realize the significance of my request?' Jambavan said, looking at her severely. 'I suppose you know what is at stake?'

She said, 'Yes, I have to consider Angad's future too,' she said carefully. 'Ours being a matrilineal clan, the kinship is passed down through the maternal line. As Vali got through his mother Vriksharaj, as Angad will get through me—'

'As Sugriv has a right to, as Vriksharaj's remaining son,' Jambavan interrupted, reminding her. 'If Sugriv gets an heir, Angad will lose his right to the throne,' he paused dramatically. 'Unless you marry Sugriv.'

'What an ironic custom! It's meant to protect the female lineage, yet binds you more than frees you as a woman. First Vriksharaj, now me...' Tara shook her head violently.

'Vali is dead!' Jambavan said forcefully. 'You know it.'

'I don't!' she retorted fiercely. 'Until I see it, I shall not believe it. He is missing, Jambavan. He will come back...' she pleaded, watching Jambavan's perplexed face. 'Until then, let

Sugriv rule the kingdom. But I beseech you, don't demand me to be his queen... Oh heavens! No, it is nothing short of appropriation!' she said, her voice now strident and angry. Jambavan gently patted her shoulder. 'It is inevitable,' he sighed.

She stared wordlessly at him, still shocked.

'The coronation needs to be done fast before all hell breaks loose,' Jambavan said, getting to his feet. His face still wore a worried look. 'Now with Vali no more to hold Ravan back, I don't want Ravan's cousins Khara and Dushana invading our land,' he cast her another worried glance. 'You have to be seen by Sugriv's side, Tara. For your sake, as well as his. That is the surest, swiftest way the people will accept him without any doubts or misgivings. You have to show your support to the new king.'

'That I shall,' she said in a dejected whisper. She raised her small chin in sudden determination. 'But I cannot be his wife—not without Ruma's permission. I need her sanction for this arrangement.'

His eyes gleamed with a new understanding of this woman; she was playing a sure game. Sitting there, her hand in her lap, her face wan and serene, Tara impressed Jambavan. There was an intense, silent power emanating from her; he could feel it. It intrigued him a little.

'Talk to Ruma and Sugriv before the coronation,' he counselled. She gave a grave nod and sent a messenger for both of them to meet her that afternoon.

✳

Sugriv arrived first. She saw him enter the chamber hesitantly. She realized how closely he resembled Vali, but lacking the raw magnetism and roguish charm of her husband.

'Where is Ruma?' Tara said stiltedly

'She is checking on Angad before coming here. How are you holding up?' he said, tentatively touching her shoulder as if to console her. She shrugged it off violently.

'I want to speak to both of you,' she said through stiff lips.

'I'll get him,' he muttered savagely. 'I'll fix Mayavi for this.'

'You still haven't found him to fix him,' she scoffed. 'Nor have you recovered Vali's body to declare him dead.'

Sugriv did not say anything. He was unsure what to say to her as she sat looking out of the window, impassive and bitter in her loss.

'Vali is dead. And the land needs a ruler...but I don't want to be king, Tara,' he said helplessly. 'However, it's demanded of me,' he heaved a long sigh, sliding her a sidelong glance. 'Just as it is demanded of you—to marry me.'

She turned to look at him, revealing to him the anguished frustration in her eyes. 'I don't want to,' she said.

'It doesn't matter what we want or believe,' he said blandly. 'It is what the people want, what is expected from us. That is why I want you to be my queen.'

She winced. 'That is what I wanted to discuss first with you. And Ruma.'

'You know that's what the courtiers are also requesting, don't you?' he continued urgently.

She turned away, feeling physically sick. 'Do I have a choice?' she lashed, her fists clenched so that her knuckles shone in the sunlight.

'Neither do I! Not this way!' Sugriv said, between his teeth.

'But this decision should be between you and me, not the others. I *don't* wish to be your wife, Sugriv!' she cried, desperation dulling her eyes. 'I love Vali. He means everything in the world to me. Please... I don't want to hurt you or humiliate you, but I just can't follow why you can't get it! You are my husband's brother, nothing more.'

'Not even your friend?' asked Sugriv, feeling a flare of fury at her words. He turned to look straight at her. 'I know how you feel about this,' he said. 'But being angry and bitter won't help. Vali was my brother. But, more importantly, he was a friend...'

Tara simply looked at him oddly, infuriating him further.

'...and I'll miss him,' he said stiffly. 'He meant a lot more to you than he meant to me and you'll miss him too. But we can't do anything about it. All we can try to do is to remember him as we knew him and just think that he's gone away. Then neither of us will be sorry for saying things that might not be true and hurting other people.'

She gave a slow nod. 'Yes, we are the face of the throne now, Sugriv. We have to be together.'

She saw hope spring in his eyes.

'But not necessarily as *your* queen. Not as *your* wife,' she reminded him. 'For that I need Ruma's consent.'

'Ruma knows the situation we are in,' he said quickly. 'She comprehends the politics of the throne possibly more than—'

'Me?' she said ironically. 'I am the widow who has to marry her brother-in-law to retain power, prestige and the throne. So possibly yes, what you say is true. Ruma knows better. And you understand Ruma very well.'

He flushed, fear leaping into his eyes. And before he could protest, Ruma appeared, as stately as always. Tara came forward to embrace her. But the moment the messenger retreated from the chamber, Tara dropped the formality of her manner, thawing to a more affable demeanour.

'I wouldn't have called for you unless it was necessary.'

'I can understand your pain,' said Ruma, clasping her hand in a gesture of comfort. 'I have been looking after Angad so that he does not disturb you... He's so greatly upset too...'

Tara pressed Ruma's hand reassuringly. 'And I shall ever be grateful for this. I could grieve because you were there for me, Ruma. I know how much you care for him.'

Sugriv smiled and took his wife's arm.

'Well, now that you are here, come and sit down.' Tara crossed her arms across her chest. 'I shall get to the point for why I called you here, Ruma. I wanted your opinion. It has been proposed that Sugriv is to be the new king and, to show solidarity and strength, he has to wed the widow of his brother and previous king...' she paused to give time for Ruma to register the words.

Ruma's eyes widened in shock.

'As is the custom,' Sugriv quickly added.

Ruma looked at him quickly and she saw that his face was red. She felt the pressure of his arm on her shoulder increase. She tensed, her body stiffened. There was a moment's silence. Next moment, Ruma moved away from her husband and sat down next to Tara, keeping a safe distance. She was somewhat disconcerted at the manner in which he was reacting to this news. She had expected him to take an angry, indignant stand and assure her this was nonsense. Her eyes hardened, as did her voice.

'What do *you* say, Sugriv?' Ruma asked in a brittle voice.

'This is a bloody mess we've got into,' he said at length. 'But it's no good losing our heads. Arguing isn't going to do us any good, you know.'

'We are not arguing, Sugriv, we need to discuss this among us—the three people to whom it should matter,' said Tara, with a hint of cynicism in her grave eyes.

For a moment Ruma looked away. She did not mean to let Tara see that anything she had said, had affected her. She heard Tara with apprehension, for she had a pretty good idea of Tara's shrewdness and straight-forwardness.

'It's the situation we all are in,' she concurred with a nod. 'A situation you can avoid if you downright refuse to acquiesce to the terms, Sugriv!'

'I have to adhere to the rules!' he exclaimed agitatedly. 'It is a tough situation, a dilemma we are facing,' he said, pacing the room. 'The thing to do now is to see how we're going to get out of it. I don't suppose you want this any more than I do.'

'I certainly don't want it!' Ruma lambasted.

Sugriv continued, overriding her indignation.

'But that's what the public wants from me. I don't know how I can actually prove that I am as worthy a king as Vali was. But if that's what the nobles and the people wish, I am ready to marry Tara,' he said with righteous deference.

He was struggling to convince her. Ruma smothered a gasp, slanting him a searching look. He was not thinking of her at all. She shivered. She was sorry that she was having to do this in Tara's chamber. The surroundings intimidated her, as did his words. It would have been much easier to say what she wanted to in the privacy of her own chamber—that he was hers and she could not share him with another woman. Ruma felt a surge of jealous fury.

'Why need we support and defend it?' she demanded, her voice in a note shriller.

It occurred to Sugriv at last that Ruma was not going to take it as kindly as he had supposed. 'What a question to ask! I have to! I am accountable to the court and the public,' he snapped back.

'And me?' snapped Ruma. 'I am your wife, Sugriv, and you are telling me you intend to marry your brother's wife?!' she cried, incensed.

'It's no good deceiving yourself, Ruma,' he said earnestly. 'If they have made up their mind to bring an action, nothing that anyone says will have the slightest influence.'

'Of course, you can say something. But you won't!' she charged.

'I am forced to!' he beseeched. 'I can understand you are awfully upset, Ruma. But it can't be helped. Try to understand!' he stretched out his hand and took hers. 'It's a crisis we all are in, but we shall get out of it. You know I shall never let you down.'

'You are letting me down!' she flung his hand away. 'This is most humiliating... Oh, how can you even think of marrying Tara?' she cast a bewildered glance at the other woman in the room. Tara sat pale and wan but dignified as ever, scrutinizing them closely.

Ruma looked aghast. 'If you want to, Sugriv, you can simply refuse to follow this unheard-of tradition. Tara, say something!'

'The tradition concocted by men,' Tara said steadily. 'But then, some women like you and me, Ruma, deem not to follow it.'

Ruma rounded on Sugriv, furious. 'She doesn't want to marry you either, so this tradition is a sham! It's an outrage! Which brother has married his brother's widow?'

Sugriv took an appreciable time to answer. His tone was dry. 'I will. I know that every man has his price.'

Ruma was left speechless, shock robbing her of her voice. Sugriv was saying things that she would never have expected him to say.

Tara looked on silently. She had respected Sugriv...until that moment. His reply disconcerted her; for such a clever man, it was a stupid thing to say. She was witnessing the unfolding—and the undoing—of a man and his promises to his wife.

'What price are we paying?' cried Ruma.

For a moment Sugriv was silent. Then he took Ruma's hand again and pressed it gently. 'You know, dear,' he said, 'whatever happens we must be in this together.'

She looked at him wildly. 'How can we? How can I agree that you marry Tara?' she choked.

'Well, we can't only think of ourselves in this world. But things have changed. I am more than your husband. I am Vali's brother. He is gone, and I have to take his place.'

Ruma's lips curled contemptuously. Sugriv sounded so morally righteous and he reckoned only Ruma could be fooled.

'By being Tara's husband too?' she sneered.

'I know the nobles. Nothing would make them take back their decision.'

'You forget that my father is one of the most powerful nobles!' she cried. 'He and his men won't allow it!'

'He will have to bow, too, to the need of the hour.' Sugriv said it with such conviction that Ruma felt her anger dissipate through the fear that was overwhelming her. She was becoming horribly frightened. She began to tremble.

Sugriv got up and sat down beside her with his arm round her shaking shoulders. 'Try not to upset yourself, darling. We must keep our heads.'

'I thought you loved me!'

'Of course, I love you,' he said tenderly. 'And you surely can't have any doubt of that now.'

'I do! Prove your love by refusing this...bargain!'

His face once more grew heavy and sulky.

With terror catching her breath she could barely speak. 'You are grabbing this situation as an opportunity to hide your true intention—you want Tara! You always have!'

Sugriv had the grace to blush. He found his mouth suddenly dry. 'Don't get hysterical, Ruma, I am simply doing my duty!' he remonstrated, a vein throbbing at his temple.

'No!' her voice hoarse with despair and rage, Ruma jumped to her feet. 'Who are you fooling? Are you not ashamed of yourself?' she spat venomously.

Sugriv's hand closed on her arm, the big thick fingers pinching her flesh, making her squirm.

'What matters is what is expected of us,' he heatedly said. 'I know how people will talk irreverently of us. In either case, my only chance is for you to stick with me.'

Ruma stepped back, a little flush of anger on her face. 'You keep your excuses and your lies to yourself—they don't convince me!' It was dreadful that she should love him so devotedly and yet feel such bitterness towards him. It was not possible that he understood how much he meant to her.

'Be reasonable, Ruma!'

'How can I be reasonable?! To me our love was everything and you were my whole life. It is not very pleasant to realize that, to you, it was only an...episode.'

'Of course, it wasn't an episode!' The corners of his mouth drooped peevishly. We're in a damned awkward position, and it's no time to be melodramatic.'

'To see your ugly truth, this entire situation—a melodrama, is it?' she said viciously. Oh, the pain in her heart, and the mortification! She could have screamed in agony. 'If you have no love or respect or pity for me, you could have just ordinary human decency!' She trembled in anger.

He did not speak, and once more his face wore that sullen look she despised.

Ruma refused to shed tears over him, contempt filling her eyes, as she stood dry-eyed. Though her voice was low, it was steady. 'I was ambitious myself. I was ambitious for you. I always wanted you to be king, Sugriv. But not like this.'

'You will remain my queen, Ruma. You are my wife.' His words sounded hollow even to himself.

'Your other queen, relegated to the background forever in life!'

Ruma lapsed into an angry silence. On a sudden, horrid suspicion, as sense flashed across her troubled wits, she vaguely gained an inkling into the workings of Sugriv's mind. It was like a dark and ominous landscape, hidden in the night. seen by a flash of lightning. She shuddered at what she saw. It must have seemed an age to him before Ruma spoke again. She moved slowly, her back straight.

'You want Tara,' she accused bluntly and turned towards Tara, her face hardening. 'Tara suspected this too but now you have confirmed it, Sugriv—to both her and me. She wanted me to know. She knew that you'd let me down. That's why she called me here.'

'Would you have preferred to be in the dark, Ruma?' asked Tara quietly, straightening herself, her eyes still sickeningly serene.

'You are a fool, Sugriv!' scoffed Ruma. 'Tara made me come here to make me witness what a fine husband you are. She made that move to unmask you, Sugriv. It's strange that she should have judged you so accurately. It was kind of her to expose me to such a cruel disillusion.'

His face reddened angrily as Ruma continued, a catch

in her voice. 'Tara knew that you were vain, cowardly and self-seeking. She wanted me to see it. She knew that you'd grab any opportunity to get what you wanted. The throne. The popularity. And Tara,' Ruma's voice curdled in contempt. 'That you'd sacrifice me without a pang to save your own skin, your immoral desire for her!'

His skin deepened into a mottled red. 'Ruma, you are making a pathetic scene. But if it really gives you any satisfaction to say beastly things to me, so be it.'

Ruma took no notice of his interruption. 'And now I know all that Tara has known. I know that you're callous and heartless, I know that you're selfish, I know you're a liar.' Her face was distraught with pain, 'And the tragic part is that, notwithstanding, I love you still, with all my heart.'

'Ruma—'

Ruma gave a bitter laugh. He had spoken her name in that melting, rich tone of his that came to him so naturally and meant so little.

'You won't make a fool of me any longer!'

Sugriv drew back quickly, flushing from being offended. He held her hand trying to pacify her. Ruma felt that she could not hold on to her self-control for another moment. She snatched her arm away and walked out of the room, her knees trembling a little.

Sugriv turned to see Tara looking mockingly at him.

'You orchestrated this!' he said accusingly, pointing at her.

Tara gave him a look, dulled with acute disappointment. 'I did not need to,' she replied sadly, with elaborate calm. 'You just confirmed our worst doubts.'

Sugriv chewed his underlip. He fell in his chair heavily, his fists clenched.

'We can go on arguing over this, Tara, but the crisis demands us to be seen together,' he said irascibly. 'I shall make preparations—'

'For you to be king? I *am* already the queen!' she said scornfully.

'You are being vindictive—'

'I am being honest. But then, honesty is often hurtful for the guilty.'

Sugriv again felt a hot surge of anger. He held her forearm and jerked it. 'You've got to listen to me,' he said, angrily. 'You've always thought that Vali was this wonderful man who ran around, not knowing his right hand from his left. Well, it's time you knew better. Vali wasn't all that good. He knew more about looking out for himself than I ever did. He and I worked together. He was smart. Do you know why? He had you! I wasn't so smart, that's why I am the king's minister. My brother's servant. His guard. His sentry—'

Tara smacked his face hard, the cracking sound breaking the stillness of the room, leaving angry welts on his lean cheeks.

'You couldn't protect him! What a swine you are,' she said, her face white and her eyes blazing. 'I should have expected that from you, Sugriv, you have no loyalty— neither for your brother, nor for your wife!' her lips curled contemptuously. 'And I am happy that I made you admit it, in front of Ruma that you are glad he's dead so that you can marry his wife!'

Sugriv stood very still, looking at her. He touched his face, feeling the livid impression of her fingers on his face and then suddenly shrugged, 'What the hell does it matter? Think what you like. I was foolish enough to fall for you. You're the one woman that has ever meant anything to me.

Vali's dead. Otherwise, I wouldn't have told you, but if I know you, you'll hang on to his memory until it's too late to do anything about anything. Then you'll be sorry. I'm telling you; you are hanging on to a dream. Vali was no better than—than Ravan... He was as ruthless and murderous. You well know it! His death is because of his ego and ambition. Not because of me!' he paused, exhaling forcefully. 'Whether you believe it or not, I liked him. I loved him. I respected him. But if you'd known him as well as I did, you would have hated him as much as you hate me, because you've always played for safety, and you think you like those who are safe and decent. Vali was neither—'

'He was still a better man than you!'

Her tone was thick with contempt, her face flushed with fury. And perhaps her anger was greater because in that moment of utter disillusionment, she lost all trust, all illusions about this man. She would not give in so easily.

But he was persistent. 'We'd better look sharp, if we are to make this impression of solidarity.'

She raised her cold eyes to his, 'They say there is no time like the present.'

'That is very generous of you, Tara.' His dented pride obliged him to accept her offer in his grandest manner possible. But, he could not shake the feeling that she was jeering at him.

✳

16

REAPPEARANCE

The royal hall was full of people. *What do they want to glimpse? The funeral or the coronation*, wondered Tara, sitting straight and stiff to the right of Sugriv. Sugriv looked appropriately solemn. Standing by his side was his faithful friend Hanuman, more a bodyguard these days, protecting his friend from a possible attack by Mayavi. Ruma on his left looked wretched, suffering the humiliation to which she must expose herself. Both sat like beautiful statues in the ongoing proceedings.

Tara did not know what spirit of bravado entered into her. Did Ruma's desolate face motivate her, or was it Sugriv's obsequious righteousness that prodded her like the prick of a spear? She rose from her throne set specially for her and said a thing that surprised even herself. 'I welcome you, O people of Kishkindh. It is a bitter sad moment for us, but a kingdom without a king is like a rudderless boat. Considering the situation, it is most appropriate that Sugriv,' she paused taking a deep breath, 'my brother-in-law, the brother of my brave Vali, and husband of Ruma, be named king...'

Sugriv felt himself flush with embarrassing anger, but

Tara gave a sudden smile, relief flooding her face as she turned to look at him, her eyes glistening with triumph. Tara, by smartly announcing his coronation, had publicly refused to be his queen.

'I suppose I needn't take a bridal veil now, need I?' said Tara under her breath as she sat down again on the throne.

She was watching his face and knew that her flippancy angered him.

Just then, a bellow shook the solemn silence of the hall.

Her heart froze. She knew that sound. She looked at Sugriv and he looked at her. There was just a flicker of doubt in his eyes that revealed to her that he was uneasy.

Sugriv sprang to his feet, his face deathly pale.

Tara could hardly find her voice.

Vali, she whispered, a silent scream in her mind.

The door burst open and Vali rushed in. He came to an abrupt standstill when he saw Sugriv with Ruma and Tara at the throne. Even from a distance, Tara recognized the red flecks of incoherent rage in his eyes. She saw Vali throw up his hands in mock surrender. His face went the colour of old ivory.

'It's all right, everyone, I am very much here, I am very much alive!' Vali started, his forced jocularity not concealing the repressed fury. 'I seem to be on time for this mock ceremony. So, you are now king, Sugriv?!'

Sugriv lunged forward, rushing down the steps, to greet his brother. He stood smiling stupidly, a blend of servility and horror in his eyes.

'Vali!' he shouted eagerly. 'You *are* alive!'

Tara's heart swelled with joy. Relief and amazement grabbed her, binding her to the chair. What her rational mind had kept telling her was true; Vali *was* alive.

'At last!' she cried, with a gasp of relief. Tara rose from her throne. 'Vali, you are back!' she cried with a widening smile touching her eyes, draining out the last vestige of sadness. Her heart was so full that she was afraid of bursting into tears. Only Vali, having barely heard her, had his murderous eyes still fixed on his hapless brother.

Without taking his eyes off Sugriv, Vali strode into the hall, inciting a collective gasp of astonishment echoing through the high ceiling.

Sugriv seemed paralysed, standing motionless, blinking at him without saying anything. Vali's face was a mask of undecipherable emotion. The wave of joy dissipated fast, replaced by a wave of mounting horror.

Vali is going to hurt Sugriv. Frantic to ease the situation, Tara moved quickly, stretching an imploring hand towards the enraged figure of her husband. 'Vali!'

She approached him with hasty steps, the sun in her hair, and her big, brown eyes alive with relief. 'I thought... We believed...something had happened to you!' she sighed tremulously. 'But I knew you would come back to me!'

Vali stopped in his path, looked at her, and then walked across the remaining distance to take her in his arms. She peered up at him, her eyes bewildered. He stayed like that for a long time, holding her against him, so that she couldn't move.

Tara felt something inside her melting. She clung to him, brushing her lips against his skin. She did not want this moment to end, wanting to never be out of his arms. But he suddenly yet gently pushed her away, shaking his head as if trying to clear something from his mind. He stood tall and terrifying, his white, stony face expressionless as he gazed over her head to glower at his brother.

'Yes, I am alive! No thanks to you, brother!' he growled.

Sugriv gave a start. He suddenly expelled a little hiss of breath through his teeth. He slowly straightened up and passed his hand over his sweating face.

'Vali,' he said, in a strangled voice. 'What're you talking about?' I—we—thought you were dead,' he muttered feebly, still inarticulate with disbelief.

'You were to guard the cave while I tackled Mayavi. But you blocked the cave with a boulder so that I couldn't get out!' snarled Vali.

Sugriv looked stunned at the open accusation. 'Yes, I did! But only because I thought Mayavi had killed you!' he cried, watching his incensed brother with intent, frightened eyes. 'I saw your blood oozing out of the cave...'

'That was his blood, not mine, you fool!' glowered Vali, his face contorted with vicious fury.

'But—but how was I to know?' spluttered Sugriv. 'You had told me that unlike human blood, Mayavi's blood was white as he is a Yaksha, a demi-demon. And that if I saw red blood streaming out, it would be yours and I was to assume the worst that you were dead and return to the palace...'

'You should have had some common sense, shouldn't you?' roared Vali. 'How about checking first?'

Sugriv could merely lick his lips in shock.

'You simply needed an excuse, Sugriv!' he yelled. 'You forget that Mayavi knew magic. And before he lay dying, he turned his white blood into red like mine. To fool you!' he said contemptuously. 'But I wonder why you really did leave me for dead and come back here.' He stood over him, his mouth unsmiling, his eyes granite question marks. 'For my throne? For Tara?' he asked softly, the whisper floating across the long hall, full of menace and foreboding. Tara's eyes flew wide open with shock and she looked back sharply. There was a savage note in his voice that startled her. Vali glanced across at her. When she saw the vicious glitter in his eyes, she stiffened, immobile with fear. Her own suspicions sounded gross and ominous when voiced aloud from Vali's mouth.

Sugriv inhaled sharply. A muscle in his cheek began to twitch. 'You are talking nonsense! Brother, you are back right on time...'

Vali laughed. It was a flat, mirthless noise, the nearest he ever came to showing that he was amused.

'Yes, I can see that,' he growled, and laughed again, his thick lips twisting in an unpleasant grimace. His eyes snapped fire, and his great face turned mauve with rage. He shook a quivering finger at his brother. 'You are going to be king, with my wife as queen!'

The look in his eyes chilled Tara, and she felt her throat close up in terror. Vali seemed suddenly to lose control of himself. He straightened his powerful shoulders and rushed at Sugriv. There was a look of vicious fury on his face. As he swept towards Sugriv, he kicked his legs, causing Sugriv to fall over with a thud that shook the room.

Tara heard Ruma scream and Jambavan shout in an unnaturally high-pitched voice, 'Stop, Vali!'

But Vali was past hearing or heeding anyone, as he reached down, grabbed Sugriv and jerked him to his feet. Holding Sugriv by the neck so that his toes scraped the ground, he knocked him away with a backhanded slap to his face. Sugriv cannoned into a pillar, as Vali spun him round and kicked him across the room. Another kick from Vali thudded into his ribs, sending him rolling over on the floor. He lay there, riding the pain, shivering with repressed fury.

Vali didn't stop. He pounced on his brother, pounding him with blows.

Tara realized that this was going to be a terrible fight, with Vali bent on engaging in a one-to-one duel. She shot to her feet, her mouth open in a silent scream. The distance seemed endless as she ran towards her raging husband, each of her steps in tandem with a blow he inflicted on his helpless brother.

'No, Vali, stop!' she shrieked. 'Oh, please stop. Someone, stop him!'

She looked wildly around her but no one dared to intervene, fearful of the towering rage that had overtaken Vali. Sugriv was still on his side, covering his head with his arms, trying to find a moment between the blows so that he could to get on his arms and knees and raise himself. His face was smashed in and bloodied. Vali hauled him to his feet, shoved him into a nearby pillar, put his great hand over his beaten face…and pressed. The younger brother gave a strangled scream, his head immediately going limp in a dead faint.

At that point, Tara saw Hanuman darting between Vali and Sugriv, but one blow from Vali hurled him across the marble floor. The veins in Vali's forehead bulged, and his face grew dark and threatening. He was a man gone insane.

She drew nearer, her breath ragged, her voice shaking. 'Vali, no!'

Vali's face was set in a furious, vindictive mask. He stood over Sugriv, shuddering with wrath. He lifted his great foot as if he wanted to crush him completely. But then, he drew it back.

Tara grabbed his arm with both her hands, frantically pulling him away from the unconscious Sugriv. 'Vali, you'll kill him! You wish to kill your brother?!' Her sharp voice had cut through his mad rage.

Vali fell to his knees. His fist was as bloodied as Sugriv's beaten-to-pulp face. He shivered, forcing the anger out of his body. He felt sweat running down his back. His breath was coming in great, labouring gasps.

He knelt there staring at Tara. His coal eyes were alive and flecked with red as they regarded her murderously. 'How could *you* agree to be a part of this?' he growled.

Tara watched him in silent horror, but there was a snap in her taut, firm voice to bring her husband to his senses. 'I am not part of anything! Stop this violence, that's all. We can talk this out calmly, can't we?'

From the corner of her eye, she saw Sugriv be quickly dragged away by the nimble-footed Hanuman, with Nal and Neel scurrying forward to help him carry the unconscious man.

Vali gripped her arm and spoke to her, his back to them, unaware of this swift action. 'I don't need to talk,' Vali snarled, 'I have seen it. My eyes are witness to Sugriv's deeds!'

She felt his grip on her arm tighten. Inhaling a ragged breath, dragging at her fluttering muscles, she tried to get away from him. When that seemed difficult, wrenched her arm free and raised her face at him, her eyes flashing. 'Rage has blinded you!' her voice was like a crack of whip. 'Unless you calm down, you won't see sense! Simple.'

'It's not simple!' growled Vali and he turned around to realize that Sugriv was no longer in the room. 'Where is that coward?! Where has he run off to?'

He whirled back and shook her, gripping her by her hands, the bracelet digging into her wrist. 'You little fool! You allowed him to escape—'

'Yes, from your mad wrath!' she flung back.

'I know how to treat him!' he roared, a nerve throbbing at his temple. 'You wanted to save him, didn't you? You wanted to make things difficult for me?'

'I wanted to save *you* from killing your brother! I am trying to make things easy for you,' she implored. 'You are blinded with anger; just try to see reason!'

Vali struggled for a moment to let go. His fists unclenched, slowly setting her wrist free. He glimpsed her bracelet, shook his head and eased himself slowly into a chair. He shouted at a standing guard. 'What the hell are you waiting for? Get after them, you slow-witted malingerer!'

Hearing his words, Jambavan came to life. Unsheathing his sword, he rushed across the hall and threw open the of the throne room. He heard the swish of a chariot as he stopmed out into the sunshine. He was met by other soldiers, but Hanuman's chariot was already way ahead. Hanuman didn't even seem to hear the arrows as they passed overhead.

Jambavan steadied himself against the doorway and ordered his men to fire their arrows again after the chariot. That's when a new sound startled him. A burst of arrows were shot from the departing chariot.

This is war, Tara thought wildly as she peered outside from the open door. *The two brothers are now at war*, she told herself dully.

Jambavan could no longer see the chariot, disappearing swiftly in a trail of dust. He ran back to the hall. It was empty now, the crowd having dissipated in fright at the brutal show of strength from their king and Vali and Tara having retired to their private chambers. Jambavan made his way there and found Vali sitting up, his arms still bloodied, and Tara skilfully cleaning the bloody wounds and Ruma helping Tara with the bandages.

'They got away,' he informed, his tone flat. 'Hanuman was quick to move and rescue Sugriv.'

'Clearly Hanuman is smarter than us,' Vali's tone changed ever so slightly to sarcasm.

'Welcome back, Vali,' returned Jambavan coolly. Nothing in his thick baritone revealed any pleasure. 'But instead of almost killing your brother, couldn't you simply have discussed the matter with him?'

Vali threw him a contemptuous look. 'I don't need to give excuses for my behaviour, Jambavan. Sugriv does. As should you, for handing him over my throne and my wife.'

Tara looked up from dressing his wounds and before she could open her mouth to protest, Jambavan responded, his voice tightening. 'This is clearly a misunderstanding, which can be quickly cleared up. It is a question of trust.'

'I don't trust my brother anymore!'

'All the more reason to clear this mistrust,' cut in Jambavan smoothly.

Vali gave a snort of contempt as he flexed his injured arm. His derisive tone increased Tara's trepidation. She felt that she would exacerbate the situation more by losing her calm.

Tara looked at him quickly, for his voice was strained, and she saw that his face was dully red. 'Don't talk, you are not well, Vali,' she said.

'I have to catch that coward!'

'You are not going anywhere,' she retorted hotly. She wound the bandage skilfully over a pad she had put on the deep gash. 'You can't go out like this,' she said, handling him not too delicately. A new feeling of dread and despair swamped the joy of seeing him alive. 'You can always chase your brother later,' she added steadily. 'For now, calm down and think straight.'

Tara drew away from him. After giving him a searching look, she began to gather up a bowl of water. Ruma quickly helped her in the task. Her eyes were shining with bitter mockery. They made Tara a trifle uneasy. She was not quite sure what Ruma was going through.

Tara put away her fears, concentrating on gaining some semblance of sense and peace in their situation now. But, for an instant, she was upset that the peace she had brokered had dissipated again. Now that danger was hurtling towards them, she had to stop her world from crumbling again.

She took Vali's hand and said, 'Sugriv hasn't betrayed you, Vali. Ask yourself why you would elicit such wrath and violence for some unfeasible suspicion of his alleged betrayal,' she coaxed, interring her own doubts for the sake of possible peace between the brothers. 'Or your belief that he connived to lock you in the cave. Words, not violence, could have supplied you with the answer.'

Vali shrugged his powerful shoulders. 'Answer? Sugriv is bound to deny everything—as he did right now. I don't believe him. I don't trust him anymore. He's no brother of mine!' he said quietly, but the menace of threat laced his voice. Vali was in no mood and manner to listen to anyone— not even her. And even if she did not believe the words herself, Tara knew she had to convince him likewise or all hell would break loose.

'Sugriv is your brother, Vali; he always shall be,' said Tara. 'And he is no traitor as you want yourself to believe. Believe me. Believe all the others who witnessed how hard he searched for you. We waited, Vali, for you to return. And now you are back! Is that not the best thing to happen to all of us?'

'I survived to see the worst of things! I saw losing my brother, my throne and my wife!'

Tara placed a cool hand on his shoulder, restraining him. 'Not your wife, never me!' she said fiercely. 'You are insulting me, Vali! You lost nothing; it was always yours. But you well might have lost your brother if we had not stopped you from killing him! We can well understand your anger. But it is unfounded. Seeing Sugriv on the throne, you are assuming the worst—'

'I saw my suspicions confirmed!'

Tara continued in her composed manner, as if he had not interrupted. 'Your doubts are misplaced; his loyalty is not, Vali. He was urged by the nobles to take up the throne in your prolonged absence. He accepted only because he believed you were dead. So did all of us,' she coaxed, half-truthfully—anything to broker peace. 'Someone had to rule the land!'

Suddenly he looked at her fully. His direct gaze gave her such a fright that she silently smothered a cry.

'Why did *you* accept, Tara?'

Her heart gave a sudden beat against her ribs. His eyes were still fixed on her and she could not lower hers. Tense, she tried to read his expression, but could only discern a strange watchfulness.

'I accepted for the same reason that Sugriv did,' she said expressionlessly, her hands clutched at her sides. She knew she had to be gentle. If she told Vali about her public refusal to be Sugriv's wife, she would antagonize him against his brother even further. 'We all presumed you were dead.'

'So, you were ready to be his wife?'

She started violently and felt herself go scarlet.

'Not his wife, Vali,' she corrected, her voice even. 'I

accepted it as the queen of Kishkindh. Which I am, and always will be. Nothing can take that away. Not even you, Vali.'

'Not even my death presumably,' he said. He spoke almost flippantly and when she glanced at him, she was surprised to see in his eyes a gleam of mockery. He smiled; it was a derisive grimace.

'Sugriv is gone. The traitor has fled from the palace and the kingdom, reinforcing my conviction that my brother is guilty,' said Vali tonelessly. 'And let it be that. I don't want him back. This time I might kill him with my bare hands.'

Ruma, who had been looking on from a distance walked closer and interrupted, 'Sugriv is not a traitor, you brute! Did you not see the elation on your brother's face at your return? But how could you—you were too incensed to see anything or recognize anyone! You did not give him a chance to explain, you refused to hear the truth in your blind fury. All you could do was pound him to pulp! What sort of a brother are *you*, Vali?'

She continued relentlessly, 'What was Sugriv to do but flee? He had to be helped to run away. Were it not for Hanuman...' she choked. 'Did you not notice that he did not retaliate even once—'

'Because he's guilty!' snapped Vali, his face a vicious mask again.

Ruma jumped at the aggression in his voice. Seeing that words were being rendered futile, she made a move to leave the room but not without casting him a look of unmitigated disgust.

'Wait!' said Vali.

Ruma halted, confused.

'Your husband is gone, leaving *you* here,' he grated.

'Did he have an option?' retorted Ruma, her face flushed

with fury and fear. 'I am sure your brother will come back for me!'

Vali gave a smile, an unpleasant one. 'Are you sure he'll come back, Ruma?'

Something in his voice made Tara look at him sharply. His tone chilled her.

Ruma gave him a blank look.

'What do you mean, Vali?' Tara rebuked. 'Of course Sugriv will be back. You almost killed him! Removing him from the scene was the only sensible recourse, and Hanuman must have taken him to a safe place.'

'Safe place,' Vali murmured, with an unpleasant smile, leaning back in his chair, stretching his massive legs. 'The only safe place for him is Mount Matanga, knowing full well I can't follow him there.'

The mention of Rishi Matanga's curse seemed to heighten the sense of doom.

Vali gave a hollow laugh. 'You think he will return, Tara? Ruma? Jambavan?'

His hooded eyes swept over them. 'Does he have the gall to face me? Sugriv is a spineless coward! He tried to get rid of me through subterfuge and tried to usurp my throne. And take my wife,' he said in an oddly flat and final voice.

Tara sat still, her heart thumping and her face white.

'You think wrong!' she said, keeping her voice steady with an effort. 'Give him a chance to explain—'

'Explain what, Tara? His duplicity?' he scowled. 'He might not have planned to kill me, but by not trying to save me, he left me to die. He comes back, gets my throne and vies for you! Is that not true—is that not why he propositioned you, despite Ruma being his wife?' he demanded, his voice thick with disgust.

Vali's eyes fell on Ruma. 'Ruma, how did *you* tolerate this?'

For once, Ruma stayed silent, shaking her head feebly.

'He was doing what the custom demanded,' intervened Jambavan.

Vali's eyes glittered. 'Which custom declares a man can appropriate his brother's wife?'

'It was meant to protect rights within a family,' said Jambavan discreetly. 'Customs are often conventions of convenience.'

'Especially by a king, I agree,' nodded Vali humourlessly. 'So, a man, when made king, can take his brother's wife as his own?'

'His brother's widow,' corrected Jambavan, his thick face tightening in growing displeasure.

Vali gave a scoffing laugh. 'Does a brother's death give a man the right to steal his widow?'

There was an instant's pause before Vali spoke again, the moment hanging heavily.

'And what if I were to do the same as what Sugriv did?' pondered Vali, his voice a dangerous purr, his words carrying malevolence.

Tara looked at him quickly. She thought she had heard amiss. His dark eyes were fixed on Ruma, whose face had become ashen.

'Sugriv is not dead!' exclaimed Jambavan, shocked. A man of many wise years, it took a lot to shock or shake him but what Vali just implied, left him staggering with horror and outrage.

Tara felt her heart squeeze; she knew what was coming.

'He is to me!' snapped Vali. 'He is dead to all of us here, for we know he will never dare to show his face ever again,'

Vali resumed, his eyes hooded as he inspected the stunned faces before him. 'By throwing out this traitor, I have taken back my throne. And just as he tried to appropriate Tara, I take Ruma as mine too!' he announced, his eyes gleaming with malicious fury.

Tara's face turned scarlet, then drained off all colour. Ruma looked over at Vali, gaped at Tara and then went a sickly white.

'No,' Tara whispered hoarsely.

'You can't do that; it's immoral!' said Jambavan hotly, but seeing the obduracy set on Vali's face, he went on, 'The nobles won't take this lying down. And what about Panas? Her father will revolt with his army!'

'I am taking Ruma as a prisoner, not my mistress!' returned Vali, his tone flinty. 'Except she will not reside in a dungeon but my palace, and will be looked upon with care and reverence.'

Tara smothered a gasp. She gave him a searching look, trying to find the man she had lost and found. Had he come back to her for this? Her gut churned. How much and how long had she waited to see him come back, alive and well, to be again held in his arms, to feel their strength around her...

She blinked. Her dreams dissipated, tears of disappointment shimmered in her eyes. She turned on him fiercely, 'You can't do this. Not to Ruma. Not to me!' A shudder passed through her. 'We are not some war trophies to be handed from one brother to another!'

Vali gave a crooked smile. 'Did you say the same to Sugriv? Did you and Ruma object to the travesty he orchestrated before both of you?'

'Yes, we did. But you are *not* him, Vali; you are better!'

she cried. 'And what do you know of what *we* went through? This is your fight with your brother; don't pull us into it,' she exhaled, taking a long breath.

He did not answer. She looked at him in her desperation and she could hardly restrain a cry. His face had a sort of dark pallor that suddenly terrified her. She saw in it a look of wrath and revenge. *Is it possible that he wants Ruma solely as his weapon for humiliation?*

'I shan't allow it! Don't you dare!' she stated, in a clear, crisp voice, her large, luminous eyes burning with a new fire.

'Yet I shall allow myself to do it,' he said grimly, smiling still, but his smile was set and unnatural, a shade of madness in his eyes. 'I am doing this for us, Tara. I'm doing this to get even for what he did to me, to you.'

She gave a sad shake of her head. 'I don't want your revenge, Vali. I want you,' she said simply.

Her thoughts went back to the struggle of the last few weeks. She had prayed to be granted the happiness of Vali's return, and her prayer had been answered. But now, looking at him, she could barely recognize him as the man she whose return she had prayed for. Tara, her faith shattered, looked at her husband with incomprehensible disbelief. Tears of disillusionment sprang in her eye. In that moment, love had fled, her heart seized by wrath and contempt, which her husband occasioned. She summoned the last of her courage and dignity.

'You've made up your mind to not understand, Vali!' She said. 'You are steered only by some frenzied fury. You are not you! By taking Ruma, you will be forever damned! For you, she's a means of retaliation but all will see it as a depraved conduct of lust... You are undoing all good you have done until now,' she said in a low, flat voice, feeling a despair she could not voice, the fetters which bound her to him, proving to be intolerably heavy. 'From a noble monarch, you will turn into a monster. You claim you are a victim of your brother's deviousness, but with this one action, it is he who will become the victim of your deviousness. It is *you* who will become the villain!'

Vali did not answer, his face implacable. Though his face remained impassive, the shadow of a smile once more crossed his eyes. 'Yes, I don't mind that either!' Vali barked a brittle laugh. 'But I shall let him know what it is to covet another man's wife!'

Overriding the ominous silence in the room, Vali looked up to the darkening sky. 'Sugriv, you cannot hide from me forever!' he proclaimed to his brother and to the world. 'To ensure you return and confront me some day—as any upright, honourable man should, and as you claim to be—I hold your wife captive till you come to free her. I await your return, dear brother.'

17

IN EXILE

For once, Tara wished her words would not come true. Four years since that horrific scene in the court, and public opinion remained the same. They talked carelessly about Vali. He was no longer the champion, the conqueror. It wasn't very pleasant for Tara to hear. She had to make an effort not to show how much it affected her. It embittered her listening to everything people said, no matter if she believed them or not. She knew that Vali was egotistical and vengeful, but the same people did not see the sense of betrayal he was grappling with. To them, Sugriv was the victim, and Vali the villain—the one who terrorized his brother and appropriated his brother's wife.

Yet she knew Vali was hungry for adulation. She remembered the smugness with which he had told her little stories to prove his cleverness. He was proud of his high valour and low cunning. *Was I wrong to give my heart so passionately to such a man?* She wished to distrust him as the world now did. The way he had treated her and Ruma should have opened her eyes.

She recalled how Hanuman had always held him in

disdain, even when Vali was not a king. 'He is a self-acclaimed idealist, Tara, but too arrogant and too much of an egotist for his own good and arrogant,' she remembered Hanuman once saying to her.

Tara stiffened as she noticed the presence of Ruma in her chamber.

'Forgive me for troubling you. I am afraid I have come at an inconvenient moment,' said Ruma, her eyes questioning and slightly worried.

Tara flushed, touched by her gentle tone. She forced a shadow of a smile, austere but sweet, and begged her to sit down. Ruma had spoken politely, but Tara perceived that she was instantly alert, quick to notice Tara's swollen eyes, that she had been weeping.

Ruma was startled, for she had the impression that Tara was a woman whom earthly troubles could not move. Before she could stop herself, she blurted anxiously, 'But you look frail and white and tired now and, if you allow me to say so, desperately unhappy.'

'I'm sorry you don't like my expression,' said Tara. 'The only reason I have for looking upset is that Angad is being his stubborn self and insists on going everywhere with Vali!'

Ruma's black, shining eyes rested on her and Tara knew that the former did not believe a word she said. Tara had never cared about these things as much as she pretended to.

'Then let him be. It's a father–son bond,' said Ruma, smiling. 'But it's not about Angad at all, is it?' she paused, hesitating. 'It's about Vali. And you and Vali… It's about us.' Her eyes grew watchful and Tara thought she read in them something resembling apprehension. 'We were once madly in love, but it is the disappointment that comes with love that is crushing, that kills the very love we held in her hearts.'

'That's an explanation,' Tara said lightly, regarding the other woman carefully. Ruma had always been a gorgeous woman with fine eyes. Now, her sallowish face, almost aggressively destitute of makeup, had sagged, and it was clear that she had lost the battle with the corpulence of middle age. Her fine head was sprinkled with grey hair, tightly marcelled and intricately dressed. Tara surmised that she was unwilling to accept defeat, for when she sat down, she sat very erect in a straight-backed chair with the cruel armour of feigned dignity.

'Yes, and you know it is the *right* explanation, Tara.' Recognizing the depth of meaning in her words, Tara waited for her to go on, fearful of what Ruma was about to say, for she had a pretty good idea of her shrewdness and was aware that she never hesitated to speak her mind.

'I don't think for a moment that we're still not in love with our husbands...'

Tara was startled. 'Even you?'

Ruma gave a quick nod, 'Long before you got disillusioned, Tara,' she sighed, wryly. 'I've asked myself if both of us feel the same about our husbands—do we hate to love them? I think you too have grown distant from Vali now... dislike him even. I shouldn't be surprised if you hated him because he no longer measures up against your righteous standards. In fact, I'm quite sure you're afraid of him.'

For a moment Tara looked away. She did not mean to let Ruma see that anything she said was affecting her. 'Yes,' she said slowly. 'I am not afraid for myself but of what he can inflict on others, of what he did to Sugriv. And you.'

Ruma gave her an intrusive look.

Tara caught it and flushed. 'I have a suspicion that you don't like your own husband very much either, Ruma,' she said with cool irony.

'I don't,' admitted Ruma bluntly. She smiled and there was a hint of malice in her sad eyes. 'Not after seeing what he was. He was always in love with you. And he grabbed the first chance to have you... And now, he has officially abandoned me. The coward!' she said with cold contempt. Her severe face was distorted from grief, and from the effort of restraining her tears that her gut had refused to hold back.

Tara looked away. She felt that it was indecent to peer into that struggle.

Ruma turned her frank eyes on Tara. 'But he's not here, we are. You, me. And Vali.'

Tara flinched. Ruma put ironical emphasis into their names and made them sound like the three of them were married to each other. That's what the world believed of them anyway.

Tara could not easily meet the eyes that rested on her with a detached scrutiny and with an ironical kindliness. 'No, no, it's not about him. Or me,' cried Tara, flushing to the roots of her hair. 'I wish I could do more for you, Ruma!'

Ruma gave her a bleak look. 'You have done all you could, Tara,' she said quietly. 'You have fought for me. You have supported me. You have been like a sister I never had. I know I am the reason for your discord with Vali.'

Tara coloured. She did not know what to say. Ruma put her hand out, and while Tara held it, she was conscious of those cool, thoughtful eyes that rested on her with both her personal pain and a profound understanding. 'We are nothing but their women—not wives, not mothers, not queens—just their possessions.'

Ruma's voice lost its even tone and her eyes filled with an undecipherable emotion. 'Sugriv is no saint either!' she said ferociously.

Then, Ruma gave a half-smile—that malicious, ironic look in her bright eyes and, mingled with it, a shadow of singular sadness. Circumstances and conditions had changed Ruma, now stripped of her pride and respect, but oddly clad in a cloak of mature dignity. It brought sudden tears to Tara's eyes. 'I'm so sorry, I'm so dreadfully sorry,' said Tara, 'for what Vali did to you...'

Her ready sympathy brought an edge into Ruma's voice, her eyes hardening. 'To us! What the brothers did to us!' she rounded fiercely. She struggled to control herself. 'But in an odd way, I am thankful for what Vali did!' Tara gave a start.

'You are not appalled with his actions?' she breathed in disbelief.

Ruma, unsmiling now, a reflective look on her face, shook her head. She was silent for a while, lost in thought. When at last she spoke it was to say something that startled Tara.

'No,' Ruma answered dryly. 'Vali has been kinder than what the world believes of him, than what you think of him,' she said with a slight shrug. 'You very well know that his love and respect for you will never allow him to enter my chamber. He has kept me in his palace and wants the world—and especially Sugriv—to believe the worst. He sees me as his sister-in-law; his brother's wife; his wife's friend; his son's other mother,' she paused. 'He comes to *you* every night, Tara, and that should say all,' she remarked pointedly, studying Tara, noticing her flush deepen. 'On my part, I am happier being closer to Angad, now living just across his room,' she added lightly. 'And he seems to prefer it too!'

Tara was taken aback. She looked at Ruma intently, as though she was trying to see into her innermost feelings. Ruma smiled lightly to hide her deep distress.

'By keeping me in his palace, I am seen as a part of his

harem, as his prisoner, as his plaything,' Ruma continued. 'And that's what I want Sugriv to believe too—to realize, to seethe, and to stew—that I am his brother's plaything,' she again gave that small, brittle laugh. 'It's been four years and, clearly, it has still not provoked him enough to come and take back what is his. To fight for me,' she added heavily.

Tara reddened and looked away. She could not bear Ruma's cold, steady and appraising gaze. She understood what she meant. It was a little while before she answered.

'You are being too harsh on yourself,' Tara said gently. 'And on Sugriv. He simply does not have the physical strength to fight Vali. He was almost killed, and he'll surely be killed if he attempts to confront Vali. The only way out is for Vali to make the first move and bring Sugriv back to clear the misunderstanding.'

'But Vali will not do that as he feels he's been betrayed by Sugriv! It's an impasse, Tara. We are either trophies or ransom,' Ruma responded bleakly. 'I have no hopes, no illusions now. I know who I am and where I stand,' she gave a quick lift of her shoulders. A smile wandered back into her voice. 'And I have Angad to look after. We have to raise him together, don't we, Tara?'

Tara looked at her as though she was delving into the secrets of her heart, but when she saw Ruma's anxiously appealing to her, she gave a smile. 'Yes, Angad is fortunate to have two mothers.'

This time, Ruma felt unaccountably anxious. 'Don't you ever feel jealous about that?' she asked cautiously.

'Oh no. Never,' said Tara quickly, unhesitant. 'As I said, he's lucky to have two mothers—and two fathers too. Sugriv adored him!' she said, thoughtlessly. Tara swore she could have bit her tongue for her tactlessness.

Ruma flinched. 'Come to think of it, after all what has happened, isn't it better that Sugriv and I didn't have a child together?'

Tara thought that she heard Ruma give a faint sigh. She shot a quick glance at her. A sudden thought struck her and it took her breath away. Was this what they called a broken heart that both Ruma and she suffered from?

✳

That evening, Vali came back to the palace a little earlier than usual. Tara was lying on the long chair by the open window in her chamber. It was nearly dark.

The scowling expression on Vali's face made Tara give him a second look.

'What is it?' she asked sharply.

Ever since the violent episode of his return, Vali would always talk to her quite casually, of trifling matters, as though they were formal acquaintances. He was scrupulously polite; she was stiffly formal. But throwing pretence and politeness out of their conversation for once, Vali looked decidedly troubled. 'Jatayu's dead!' he said flatly, his jaws gritted. 'Ravan killed him.'

The colour fled from her face and her heart wrenched. Vali wished he had broken the news more gently. He just put his arm around her and held her against him while she looked at him, her eyes bright with anguished tears. He felt her trembling against him.

'Why?' she said her voice a hoarse whisper.

'In the attempt to save a woman whom Ravan was kidnapping.'

He felt her stiffen against him. 'A woman? Who?' she asked with shaky breath.

'I don't know who,' he said, hunching his powerful shoulders. 'The latest I have heard from spies is that the rascal kidnapped her from the Dandak Forest. We are yet to ascertain the details, but she certainly was not a local,' said Vali. 'But I have sent my spies to investigate,' he said grimly. 'If I could, I would kill Ravan myself!' He touched her hand. 'I'll get him,' he said, quietly. 'I'll kill him for this.'

Her shoulders slumped. 'That man killed old Jatayu because he dared to save a woman from being abducted; what does it say of him?' she said forlornly. 'And on what grounds will you challenge Ravan, Vali? Isn't he your friend?'

Vali felt a hot flush rise up, her mocking words having the power to pierce him. '*Jatayu* was my friend! For him, I will confront Ravan.' He turned to leave when her next words halted him.

'Why does this shock you, Vali?' she asked, her ironic tone getting forceful.

'Don't say it, Tara,' warned Vali, his voice softly dangerous.

'You are being accused of the same,' she persisted in a low tone, unmindful of his glare. 'For all the good and the prosperity the kingdom is now enjoying because of you, the shadow of shame still lingers...'

'Public memory is short and selfish,' he shrugged his broad shoulders as was his habit when he wanted to be evasive. 'And for us, Tara, Sugriv is a forgotten chapter!'

'I am talking about Ruma—as I always do,' she said with a bite in her voice. 'Release her from this palace and treat her with the respect a sister-in-law deserves, not what Sugriv deserves!'

'She is his wife as you are mine,' said Vali with that hateful tone she loathed. 'We have gone through this over and over again.'

'Yet what Ravan does shocks you—the killing of Jatayu as well as this unfortunate woman's abduction. But you well know in your heart that what you did is no worse than what Ravan has now done. You have taken a woman without her consent. And what makes it even more disgusting is that she's your brother's wife!'

'Who says I don't have her consent?' Vali gave her a strange look. 'Does she look like an unhappy woman withheld against her will? I just met her downstairs. She was with Angad helping him with his history lessons.'

'You are only earning disrepute with this strange revenge on Sugriv!' she coaxed. 'Will taking on Ravan earn you your lost reputation? In this war between you brothers, you have lost your nobles, who have gone to Sugriv's side, particularly Panas.'

'As Ruma's father, I wouldn't *not* expect this of him!' Vali gave a wry smile.

'As Ruma's father, how could he witness his daughter's humiliation?' she retorted.

Vali looked disconcerted, then he laughed shortly, shrugging his shoulders. 'Well, this at least got him close to his son-in-law!' Tara regarded him helplessly. He frightened her now. The coal-coloured eyes were expressionless, but they were dreadful, dark and vacant.

'How many people are you going to lose over this unreasonable wrath reserved for your brother, Vali?' she said quietly. 'How much more are you going to lose? Your reputation, your honour, your family...us?' She studied Vali carefully, who stared back at her apathetically.

She sighed, defeated. 'Vali, what do you propose we should do to get through this stalemate between you brothers?'

He waited for a moment before answering. She could not see his face.

'I haven't thought about it.'

In the old days, she would carelessly say whatever came into her head. It never occurred to her to think before she spoke. But now, she was unsure of him. She felt her lips tremble and her heart beat painfully. She forced herself to speak, though she could hardly frame the words. 'Did you really want this bad blood between you and him—and how it has affected us?'

Vali regarded her with expressionless eyes. 'If I were you, I'd leave it well alone, Tara. I don't think any good will come of talking about what we should better forget.'

'But you don't forget; neither do I. I've been thinking a great deal, Vali... Won't you listen to what I have to say?'

'Certainly.'

'You think I treated you very badly. That I was unfaithful to you, Vali.'

He stood stock-still. His immobility was strangely terrifying.

'I don't know whether you'll understand what I mean. That sort of thing doesn't mean very much to a woman when it's over. I think women have never quite understood the attitude that men have,' she spoke abruptly, in a voice she would hardly have recognized as her own. 'You know what Sugriv was and you knew what he'd do. Well, you were quite right. He did what he did, the first chance he got,' she said wearily. 'I suppose I felt as guilty as he did... I know you are still angry and feel betrayed about it—'

'No, it's not about you, Tara!' Vali shook his head violently. 'It is *him*! I know you think I have been too cruel to Sugriv and, worse, to Ruma,' he said raggedly. 'And I cannot ask you to forgive me. I cannot ask you to love me as you used to love me. But couldn't we be friends? With all these people looking at me as if I am some criminal...a monster.'

'But you are not!' Tara cried. 'I know that but it hurts me more that you are painted as the demon that you are not! I have such a singular shameful feeling when I meet the courtiers and the public. I stand as accused as you! There's a silent accusation in their eyes as if...' she halted, her breath trembling.

Vali did not answer, but he did not move away. He seemed to be waiting for her to continue.

'Jambavan and the nobles keep telling me such wonderful things about you. They are proud of you, and I'm very proud of you, Vali.'

'No,' he gave a crooked smile, smiling bitterly. 'You used to, Tara, not any longer. Now you feel contempt for me, don't you?'

'Don't you know that I still love you despite all this?'

Again, he was silent. Vali stood looking at her. Her words seemed to have chiselled off a tiny bit on his stone-heart. He crossed over and pulled her gently. 'Let us not fight,' he said. 'I'm sorry for everything. I'm really sorry.'

Suddenly, she clung to him, crying, her tears not just washing away the grief of Jatayu's death but also the aftermath of the destructive strife of the brothers on all of them—Ruma, Vali, she. He held her against him. As she looked up at him with her bewildered eyes, he crushed his mouth on hers, restricting her movement, and he stayed like that for a long time.

Tara wanted to get away from him, but he was too strong. But soon, she felt her reservations melting and she wanted never to be out of his arms. She held him tight, feeling her lips bruise, but wanting him to remain like that with him.

'I don't understand you,' he said at last, pulling away from her. 'I don't know what it is that you want.'

'Nothing for myself, only for you.'

She felt him stiffen. His voice was very cold when he answered. 'I have everything...'

'Not Sugriv. You love Sugriv. You miss him.'

She felt him draw in a quick, shuddering breath. 'I cannot forgive him.'

'He will come back...' she tried to assure him, hoping to ease him of the silent sorrow he refused to show.

'No, he won't. He will never confront me,' he brushed off imperiously.

Tara shook her head in exasperation. 'He will—someday. With some help—'

'Not Ravan's, certainly! I am on my way to destroy him once and for all!'

She persisted. 'Not by himself, but through someone more powerful than you...'

Vali gave a short, sharp laugh. 'Does that person exist?'

Tara heard the question with a sinking heart. She took a long time to answer.

'What if you didn't know of his existence?'

18

RETRIBUTION

Before Vali had an opportunity to fight Ravan, he was met with a challenge from an unexpected person.

'Vali, come on out!'

A voice shouted from outside the window. It was strangely familiar.

At that point, Tara had been in her chamber, brushing her hair, while Vali had sat slightly away from her, facing her back, talking to her about something trivial—the voice caught them by surprise. Tara turned around quickly to throw Vali a bewildered look.

'Vali, that's—'

'Sugriv,' said Vali shortly, rising to his feet.

'He has come back!' She sounded both surprised and startled.

'High time he did, that coward! I know how to handle him!' started Vali, his jaw hardening.

Alarmed, Tara rose to her feet and grabbed him by the arm. 'Vali, wait. As he has come back, take this opportunity to get him home, I'll go—'

'No, you won't!' His hand snaked out to grasp her wrist,

crushing the bracelet in his grip, the beads cutting into her skin. 'Does he sound like he wants to come home? He's challenging me, Tara.'

'And isn't *that* odd?' she asked him quietly.

For a moment, Vali stood still, frowning.

'There is something wrong, Vali. Sugriv does not have the courage or the confidence to ever confront you face to face. Yet he is doing it,' she paused, letting the short silence linger. 'Why?'

Vali straightened, giving her a hard look.

'Why would a man who can never defeat you be standing at the entrance of your palace, challenging you to an open fight, which certainly means death for him. Why would he do it?' she demanded. 'This means he has help from someone, Vali. He has a secret ally or he would not return to duel you.'

Sugriv having an ally?' Vali sneered. 'No one would dare support him but for one loyal Hanuman and Panas, both of whom I can vanquish easily. That's why he has been hiding away all these years in Mount Matanga, knowing fully well he's safe from me.'

'Yet he's stepped out of his safe zone and come down here. To confront you.'

'He knows I can't resist a challenge,' said Vali.

'That's your weakness, Vali, not a claim to honour,' she retorted. 'Like every powerful person, you too have a failing—you never back down from a challenge. Your ego and anger do not allow you to.'

'I do it the old-fashioned way—man to man!' Vali lifted his heavy shoulders. 'Saves unnecessary bloodshed of armies fighting our wars. You know that, Tara.'

'But this is a war too—between you and your brother... Think about it! You like combat with powerful men. But

Sugriv is no Ravan or Mayavi or Dundubhi. Yet here he is. Think again—*why?*'

Vali frowned darkly. 'But I can't rebuff Sugriv either. I have to fight him. He is itching for a fight, and rightly so. We should have done this a long time ago and cleared things once and for all!'

'Which could have been done through a simple talk too—but you refuse to do that. You just won't listen!' she cried, desperation swelling to despair. 'You know you are powerful. You are sure you are invincible. Your greatest weapon is that boon of yours. But this very power has made you an unwilling listener. Your biggest weakness is your unreasonableness, Vali! You banished Sugriv because you were unwilling to listen to Sugriv's pleas, and instead you chose to believe the worst!' she said breathlessly.

A mask of impassiveness had come over his face again.

Tara sighed in despair. 'Things can only improve between Sugriv and you if either of you allows it. But neither of you are in a mood to reconcile. So, it's going to be a bitter fight to the end—and what will that be, Vali? You killing him? Because he is incapable of killing *you*!'

'Exactly! I don't get. Why are you scared?'

'I am scared because this will be a fight to death,' she said simply. 'And I wish neither of you to die!'

She might as well not have spoken, for he took no notice. He gave her a disparaging glance.

'You can talk to him, can't you?' she implored, her tone pleading. 'One of you has to take the high road. Why don't *you*, Vali? This might be the last chance for a reconciliation...'

'We don't want it. It's too late,' he said tightly.

'Then I shall!' she said fiercely, turning away from him. 'I shall beg him to halt this madness. Sugriv might listen to me...'

He grabbed her arm, his finger biting into her soft flesh.

'No, you will not! This is between us brothers.'

'You men, you mean,' she retorted hotly, wrenching her arm free. 'Two egotistical, ambitious, selfish men who are ready to slaughter one another!' she cried, her throat choking with desperate tears. 'You are brothers, damn it! Please, please, stop this!'

Her anguish seemed to breach his obduracy.

'I know he's no match for me, and knowing that, I shall *not* kill him.' He put down his mace and observed her reflectively. 'See, I shan't carry a weapon with me either!'

'With your strength, your bare hands are enough to kill!' she said wildly.

He shrugged his shoulders, scowling. 'I just want to teach him a lesson!'

'Haven't you done that already?' she cried in exasperation.

Tara unclenched her fists. *Does he really wish to kill his brother?* The mystery of this violent hate fascinated and horrified her. She felt a foreboding fear; she could not pin what was it about.

'Oh, why? How did the once inseparable brothers have such irreconcilable differences that they are thirsting for each other's blood?' she asked, hardly realizing that she had spoken these words out loud.

Vali exhaled slowly. He seemed to gather his thoughts from a remote distance.

'We lost trust in each other,' he said dully.

She flushed and looked away. She could not bear his cold and steady gaze. She understood what he meant. It was a little while before she answered.

'But not love,' she said softly. 'Love has the power to forgive.'

'And the strength to destroy too,' he smiled. There was a shadow of sadness in his ebony eyes.

'Whatever the threat, promise me you won't kill Sugriv,' she said in a final tone.

Vali gave a surprised look. She saw him suppress the exclamation of annoyance that came to his lips.

'Give me your promise, Vali,' she took his hands in his. 'You shall not harm Sugriv and be responsible for his death in any way. Please,' she whispered, her lips moving tremulously, her hand clutching his strong wrist.

Vali brooded for a moment. 'I will not kill him, Tara,' he said gravely. 'For you, I will not kill him. That is my promise to you.'

She gave a weak smile. 'I don't want you to be condemned as a man who murdered his brother.'

'Rather a dead man than a condemned one,' he said drolly. He straightened his tense shoulders. 'Though it's not fair of you to ask me that,' he added, narrowing his eyes.

'It is moral,' she said quietly. 'And I know you to be moral enough not to slay your brother.'

'And I shall be back in a flash, I assure you,' he laughed lightly, gripping her hand and pulling her close. 'There's nothing to fear, least of all that fool, Sugriv!'

She shook her head vehemently, her throat constricted with fear and her eyes full of unshed tears. She could not hold back the sob that choked her. He gazed at her reflectively with a deep look in his bright eyes, but mingled with it a shadow, an expression of singular tenderness. He placed his lips on her cold ones and left. She she stood, staring at his retreating back.

Come back soon, she screamed silently.

And he did—within an hour. Slightly bruised, his thick

mane dishevelled but wearing a wide grin, he approached her, trepidation dissolving into quick relief.

'I told you I'll be back quick!' he grinned. 'I beat the living daylights of my poor brother. He's worse than before. Exile seems to have blunted his combat prowess. He simply gave up and scooted off in pure terror—I hope this was the last we saw of him!' he exhaled, grimacing. 'As promised, I did not kill him, though I had an easy chance.'

Why had Sugriv provoked a fight if he was going to run off, she wondered silently, still uneasy.

'Next time, I might not be nice to him!'

'No, you can't kill your brother! Never!' she said, as she hugged him fiercely, her body limp with relief.

He placed his hands on her shaking shoulders, which calmed her immediately.

But she could not shrug off the gnawing sense of disquiet—why had Sugriv challenged his invincible brother for a win-or-die fight only to give up within minutes? Sugriv was not foolish nor was he impetuous. He must have planned something before braving Vali, whom all knew to be indestructible. Then why—why had Sugriv come back spoiling for a deathly confrontation?

*

The arrow flew straight, sizzling in the air, as it hit Vali...and she heard herself scream...

Tara's eyes flew open in horror, breaking away from a restless sleep, her heart thudding with an inexplicable fear. She turned her head to see the beautiful, sleeping form of Vali next to her, his arms holding her even in his sleep. She was safe in his arms. Then why had this sudden, strange dread filled her heart and mind? Vali looked to be at peace.

He had defeated his brother; he had won again. It was over...

She quietly got up, careful not to wake him, and walked listlessly towards the open window. She could not dislodge the heavy unease tightening around her chest. She shivered and noticed the break of dawn. The sky was clear and the early sun shed a heavenly beauty on the scene. It was difficult to imagine, on that blithe, fresh and smiling morn, that Kishkindh lay gasping, like a man whose life was being throttled out of him by a maniac's hands in the dark clutches of death.

'Why are you awake so early?' Vali drawled, his lashes fluttering up.

She bit her lip, silent. She did not wish to distress Vali. But he was sharp as always when it came to sensing her moods.

'It's over, Tara, don't worry yourself to death,' he said, briskly getting up, swinging his long legs to the floor. 'Sugriv won't trouble us anymore.'

She licked her lips. 'I checked with our spies, Vali. Angad confirmed it too,' she started convulsively, her throat dry. 'I had to know why Sugriv had dared to challenge you.' she inhaled a shaky breath. 'He is not alone; he has help.'

'Yes, his loyal Hanuman,' Vali's lips curled.

'Hanuman, whom you have consistently underestimated,' she said quietly. 'No, someone besides Hanuman, though it was Hanuman who introduced this new aid to Sugriv.'

Vali scowled. 'Who would help a loser like Sugriv?'

'Ram,' she stated.

Vali stopped short.

'Ram?' he repeated, astonished. 'The exiled prince of Ayodhya? He is helping Sugriv? And how do you know all this, Tara?'

'Though *my* spies,' she replied wryly. 'They say this Ram is in the forest right now with his brother Lakshman, in desperate search for his wife Sita. She is the one who has been kidnapped by Ravan and the woman Jatayu died saving.'

Watching his immobile face, her hands clenched again into fists. Tara tried to quell the dread deluging her.

'And Sugriv is going to help Ram fight Ravan?' Vali laughed in disbelief. 'Besides, what help can an exile offer another exile? Ram has no army to help Sugriv.'

'He doesn't need an army. He has Ram. And Ram is a one-man army, from what I have heard,' she said restlessly. 'It is clear they have met, but we don't know exactly what they have spoken about. It is also clear that Sugriv has support from Ram or he would not have risked confronting you—'

A deafening shout outside slashed the silence of the dawn, interrupting her.

'Vali! Come out and face me!'

It was that same strident voice she dreaded—Sugriv. She stared at Vali, feeling a chill run down her spine.

It was a call for death, she thought wildly. 'He is back!' she choked. She rushed up to the terrace. Even through the morning mist, she could see him, tall and lean, holding a mace in his right hand, with a long, thick garland of red flowers hanging from his neck.

'This is the last time I request a duel, Vali!' he barked, his voice floating swiftly in the silence of early dawn. 'Today, we win or die.'

'Then die!' roared Vali, swinging to his feet.

Tara turned around, grasping Vali by his arms. 'No, you won't Vali! He will kill you!'

Vali gave a scornful laugh. 'He cannot kill me, Tara, That's why he keeps coming back like bad news.'

She shook her head agitatedly. 'No, no, now I realize my folly—it's he who can kill *you*! Because Ram is helping him!'

Vali went still, stiffening. He frowned. 'Tara, no. That's not done. No warrior—not in the least an honourable prince like Ram—shall employ subterfuge in a duel. Ram is a righteous man who won't stoop to deceit. And regardless of this, I am not sure if Ram is aiding Sugriv at all—why would he interfere in a family fight? From what I have heard of Ram, he's an exemplary prince, an exemplary warrior. I would have expected him to face me himself. He's anything but a coward. It seems improbable he's supporting Sugriv.'

'He is!' she cried, tightening her grip. 'Sugriv wouldn't dare otherwise!'

'And yet Sugriv is here,' continued Vali dully. 'If Ram has agreed to help Sugriv, then so be it,' he sighed, trying to twist away from her clutching grasp. 'Let me go, Tara. Sugriv needs to be taught a lesson once and for all.'

Her mouth turned dry. 'Oh, why can't you listen to reason?!' she cried hoarsely. 'Does this daunting support from Ram not make you see the logic of all that's happening? Can't you see the danger still?'

Vali tightened his lips into a stubborn line.

'It is no wonder that this lack of rational thought has made an unexpected ally of Ram to side with Sugriv and not you!'

Vali released an unexpected smile. 'Ram has no choice, Tara. He took the help of the first person he met in the forest, and that was Sugriv!' he paused, sounding unexpectedly contrite. 'It's unfortunate that I didn't meet Ram first. And it is my misfortune that I have not helped Ram yet.'

His equanimity amazed her, driving her to despair. 'Please, Vali, make peace with Sugriv!' she moaned in appeal. 'I know it, I feel it—you will lose, you will die!'

Vali had never seen Tara so perturbed. He looked at her, his eyes composed and certain, and he held her flailing arms, trying to calm her. He felt her shaky breath on him. Pulling her against him, he tightened his arm around her. His embrace was strong and warm. She leaned into him, and he could feel her body tremble.

'These are the only moments I live for,' he said. 'It's as if the world has stood still, and only you and I are left alive.'

She was looking up at him, her eyes fevered.

'Don't leave, please' she whispered, pleading, burying her head against his chest, hearing the steady hammer of his heartbeat. Vali faced her, his hands clenching and unclenching. He gave her a tender look, followed by a smile, but his smile was a little set and unnatural. She saw an intense shade of sadness in his eyes.

'I shall be back. What are you so afraid of?' he murmured.

'That I will lose you... I just don't want you to go!' Tara cried vehemently, terror grabbing her throat.

He wouldn't do it, would he, after all that I said? He wouldn't go...

Vali gave her a bleak look. He realized that he had no choice; he would have to do this. It was not just any duel with Sugriv, it was a win-or-die combat. With an obvious effort, he pulled himself away. Looking at Tara with his familiar, kind, humorous expression, he said, 'It's not as terrifying as you are imagining, Tara. Sugriv is not much of an opponent! And neither Sugriv nor Ram are dishonest people. Ram is a righteous man who won't win by deception. Sugriv won't either. I am sure of that.'

Prying her desperate fingers from his forearm, he turned to go.

Her heart pounding, she ran to him, clinging to his arm.

'No, Tara, I have to go,' Vali said evenly, his eyes calm. 'This is my duty. This is my honour. I have to do this.'

'What false pride are you talking about? You can't mean it!' she whispered, but he shook her off. He could not allow her to touch him anymore; he would sure melt. Her eyes widened in sudden realization. 'Perhaps that is why I kept dreaming about that arrow... You and Sugriv wrestle with your bare hands or use the mace, but where did this arrow come from? Oh Vali, that arrow is meant for you! Ram is a master archer and that arrow in my dreams is meant for you!' she cried, her eyes frantic.

'Don't overreact, Tara. This is so uncharacteristic of you!' The moment these words fell out of his mouth, he felt a sudden chill of fear.

Yes, it is uncharacteristic of Tara; she is always so sensible and serene, not in the present state she is in... Should I heed her warning?

She stood in front of him, blocking his way. 'I shall not allow you to go! It's either me or him, Vali!'

The frenzied despair matched the fierce determination in her voice. It made him hesitate.

Just then, Sugriv's holler rent the air. 'Come out, Vali, come and face me, you usurper! You coward!'

Vali stepped back as if he had been hit in the face. His colour turned a waxen white.

'He is waiting for me,' he snarled.

She moved towards him, holding out her arms. 'Oh, Vali, that's a death call—oh please no, for my sake. Don't you know how much I love you?'

'Yes, my dear, I don't doubt it. And I love you more. But it's not just about love and us. We're not living just for ourselves in some paradise.'

'Kishkindh is our paradise, remember?' she asked brokenly.

He gritted his teeth. 'And we've got to make the best we can out of the circumstances that are forced upon us. You really must be reasonable.'

'How can I be reasonable when I know I am going to lose you? To me, our love is everything! You are my whole life!'

Vali cupped her ashen face in his hands.

'I'll be back before you know it,' he forced a grin.

The sparkle of the gem of his necklace blinked at her. She saw him touch it reverentially.

At the sight of the necklace, Tara instinctively knew he had made up his mind and she could do nothing. Terror-stricken, she didn't flinch or move. Despair seized her. Heavy tears rolled down her cheeks. He wanted to take her in his arms and reassure her, but looking at her defeated face, he gave her a sharp look, then reached out and patted her hand. It felt cold under his touch.

Tara moved and clung to him. 'Vali!'

'I'll be back,' he muttered hastily, pulling away. He moved his great body to the door, turned, smiled his crooked smile.

Her terrified eyes remained fixed on his broad, retreating back; would it be the last time she would see him? Would he ever return to her? The words screamed, a silent crescendo in her mind, raging in her torn heart, her lips moving in a silent prayer—*come back...*

✳

19

DEATH AND DISILLUSIONMENT

The arrow pierced Vali with a faint whooshing sound. Vali stiffened, then bent over. His arms clutched his middle. He gave a faint sigh, his knees gave way and he fell to the ground. She ran to hold him but felt the blood gushing out of him. Oh, her hands—the blood, hot and sticky to her touch...

Tara gave a start, her eyes widening in horror, to find unchecked tears flowing down her drenched cheeks. *Why was she crying?*

Vali, she cried silently, oh Vali, where was he?

A heavy scuffle of footsteps behind her warned her of what was to come. She didn't ask if he was dead. She knew he was. She flushed faintly, and then her face became white, as if the blood had shrunk away from her entire body. A shiver passed through her.

'My Queen, it is about Vali... He is dying... He has taken down by an arrow,' said a voice.

She turned around slowly, felt herself turn hot and then cold, and her heart missed a beat. Jambavan was there; one look at his distraught eyes, she sensed a cold feeling around her heart. She had never felt so shattered before. She knew he would never have come to her chamber unless he had nowhere else to go.

'Who killed him?' she asked, her fists clenched.

'Vali lies fatally injured by Ram's arrow,' informed Jambavan, his voice firmer.

'It was Vali and Sugriv fighting a wrestling duel. Where was Ram?'

She didn't sound angry, but just as if she were thinking aloud in a dazed, bewildered way.

'Hiding in the bushes,' replied Jambavan tersely.

She recoiled. 'From where he shot the arrow at Vali when he was grappling with Sugriv?' she struggled away, her heart on fire.

'Yes, at his heart...' his voice thickened with anguish and Jambavan struggled to control himself. 'The news has spread panic in Kishkindh and the Vanaras have been seen fleeing the city in terror—'

Shocked, she flew to her feet. 'That has to be stopped!'

He threw her a desperate look. 'Only you can halt the ensuing chaos after a king's death.'

Quickly, Tara composed herself, wading off the engulfing wave of grief. She would have to be there for her people. She would have to take a hard decision forthwith. She gathered the folds of her skirt and her composure, and headed purposefully towards the terrace. Below, people were running helter-skelter in utter panic but at the sight of their queen in the open balcony, they halted in their tracks, looking up at her for assurance. Her mouth dry, her face pale, she swallowed convulsively.

'The King is dying,' she announced colourlessly, her clear, crisp voice carrying across the sea of people down below. A fervid murmur went up in the crowds. 'But that does not mean you are orphaned. You are safe. Vali would want his brother Sugriv to be your king.'

'Ram killed Vali! Now he'll kill us!' cried a voice in the crowd.

Her throat constricted. 'No, he won't. Ram killed Vali to make Sugriv your king. He has no wish to cause you any harm, hence, there is no reason to flee. Your lives are in no danger, and there is no cause to flee in fear. Accept Sugriv as the new king.'

She was met by a shroud of silence and then the gathering broke into a loud applause. 'Long live Queen Tara! Long live the King.'

Tara joined her palms in acknowledgement and bowed to the people. As she turned, the nobles stiffened slightly, their eyes on her, waiting for instructions. Her pale, pinched face told them nothing, but her brown eyes were hard as she said, 'Tell the army to stand down. There will be no attack on Sugriv or Ram.' She heard a loud intake of breath behind her.

'You announced your husband's death even as he lies dying in the field!' breathed Jambavan in shock. 'By doing that, you have saved the kingdom!'

Tara detected relief in Jambavan's voice. 'We had a double crisis on our hands—the scared public and the angry nobles. They want to crown Angad as king and trounce Sugriv. You avoided a rebellion if not a civil war!' he exclaimed, unable to hide the admiration in his voice. Even as her husband lay dying, Tara had attended to the public and not to her grief. She had taken a quick decision, possibly detrimental to her as a widow and her orphaned son but her first thought was for Kishkindh and its people.

Looking at Tara now, Jambavan realized just how far she had come. The sway she had over the people—what a power she had become! He valued her rise to such heights where he could be of real use to her.

Tara stopped pacing and fixed at him her cold, hard eyes.

'Get the chariot, Jambavan. I want to be there at once where Vali lies injured.'

'You can't!' he gasped. 'We will bring Vali here...'

Again, she shook her head. 'Vali is dying and nothing matters anymore. I have to see him!'

No sooner had the chariot arrived, she hurriedly got in, her bleeding heart racing faster than the galloping horses. She barely waited for the chariot to halt as she rushed down the steps, running across the field, over rubble and bramble, into the forest, her breath coming in short gasps, her mind filled with one name—*Vali*...

And then she saw him. Her breath halted at the sight. He was as she had dreaded all though these excruciating moments—his massive frame, still, in a pool of fast-spreading blood, with an arrow deep in his chest. There were others—Sugriv and two young men, as well as Angad who had just arrived at the scene. But her eyes were only on Vali, gripped by the sight him lying on his back on the uneven ground. Her breath whistled through her tight mouth and she was trembling so violently she could scarcely stand. She swayed and slowly sank to her knees, her shaking hands gathering him close, placing his head on her lap.

With a shaking hand, she touched his face. It was warm. A little trickle of blood ran from his mouth and down his chin. His thick dark silky hair hid most of his face. She saw his fingers move, then slowly close into fists, then open again.

She gently pushed aside a thick lock of hair from his face. His eyes were closed, but at the touch of her fingers, he opened them and they looked at each other.

Vali tried to say something; his beautiful lips moved.

'Tara,' he sighed, his lips twitching in a weak smile, 'I should have listened to you.'

'I won't leave you,' she choked. 'Ever. I am here.'

Futile words, but she couldn't think of anything else to say.

He shut his beautiful eyes to open them with a ragged sigh. 'Forgive Sugriv; forgive me, Tara.'

Feebly, he tugged at his neck to pull down the dazzling necklace, his hands stretching weakly towards an ashen-faced Sugriv standing behind Tara. 'Keep it, Sugriv. Now this is yours... It's over. I shall blame you no more... Look after Angad as a son, a prince. And listen to Tara. Seek her advice,' he gasped, his fingers opening and closing convulsively, his muscles twitching.

Coughing blood, Vali turned to a sobbing Angad, 'Sugriv was always your father... Now your king,' he whispered. Vali gritted his teeth and tried to move but fell back. He closed his eyes and held onto her hand, crushing the bracelet in his hard grip, feeling himself sliding off the edge of the earth.

'Tara,' he whispered thickly.

She pulled him closer to her heart. 'Hear me, Vali. We are together.'

He moved his head slightly, then his face stiffened. Tara felt a shudder run through the great body. She could no longer support his head, and it tilted inertly away on her lap. He suddenly gave a jerk. A dry gasping sound came from his throat. He tried once more to say something, but his expression suddenly went blank. He was still.

Tara shut her eyes, embracing the silence in the woods like a shroud. Neel came forward, then bent low and gently drew out the arrow from Vali's chest. Blood gushed out, still warm. Tara startled and knelt forward, looking down at Vali's inert body for a stretched moment, her face expressionless, her eyes dark. She didn't move; she said nothing. Her stiff face made Sugriv nervous. He wished she would cry or something. Anything would be better than sitting there with that set face and eyes that looked like holes in a white sculpture.

Aware of the strained silence stretching between them, Hanuman stepped forward and tried to console her. 'Vali has died a warrior's death and has found his place in Heaven,' he said gently. 'Let us not lament but commemorate this man. His son will be crowned king in due course and we shall then rejoice!' He felt her trembling, her shoulders drooping. 'Let us now think of performing Vali's obsequies—'

Tara gave a slow shake of her head. 'I care for nothing now,' she said forlornly. 'Angad cannot sit on the throne; it's unsafe! Let Sugriv become king after all that he did to get what he wanted.' There was a catch in her voice. 'Sugriv can do the obsequies too; Vali would wish it so,' she turned savagely on Sugriv. She looked at him at last, with pent-up loathing for him in her eyes. 'You couldn't kill him after all,' she said dully. 'Ram did that for you!'

Sugriv clenched his fists, his pale face tightening.

'Where is he?' Tara cried.

The sudden viciousness in her voice jolted him and he threw a furtive look at the tall, dark man standing opposite him. Her eyes followed Sugriv's frantic ones, and she continued in a flat, toneless voice. 'This is Ram, I presume—the man who helped you kill your brother.'

Ram regarded her with hesitation. She stared back at him, without any trace of anger, just bottomless sorrow in her large, luminous eyes. She picked up the bloody arrow

Neel had extracted from Vali's chest and held it out to Ram, her arms stretched.

'With this weapon with which you killed my Vali, kill me too, O, brave prince. Be assured, it won't be sin, but a merit of uniting husband and wife... It may well cleanse the sin of your treacherous slaying of Vali.'

Even Ram could not evade the raw agony burning in her eyes. Her stillness was strangely menacing. It gave him the feeling of a wild beast prepared to spring.

'Since when have warriors fought from behind trees? From when did archers shoot at the unarmed? Since when have princes fought other people's family battles?' she asked, her voice rasping, dripping ice. 'O brave Ram, that you could string your decisive arrow on a helpless man, that you could kill an innocent, who was not your opponent, who was not a rival in any way shall surely add glory to you and your righteous honour. That you could attack a man as he wrestled with another just speaks so wonderfully of you, O Prince of Ayodhya!'

Ram's face twitched, his jaw tightened. The other young man standing to his side was more vocal. 'How dare you speak in this manner to my brother?' he barked, and only the restraining hand Ram placed on his shoulder, seemed to rein him in.

'And you must be the loyal brother Lakshman... So unlike *this* brother!' she scoffed nastily, her eyes swivelling back to Sugriv. 'I dare to say what I said because it is the truth. A shameful truth! I dare, Lakshman, because your brother killed my husband dishonestly,' she stated evenly, grief tearing at her sundered heart, 'without motive, or rivalry, or purpose. Vali was murdered by deceit, O great Princes!'

Lakshman turned red in discomfiture.

Frenzied rage drove Tara to glower at Sugriv weeping disconsolately at his brother's side. 'Don't shed false tears to impress the world, Sugriv! You used another man to help kill your brother, the wimp that you are!'

The hum of conversation petered out, and all eyes turned to Sugriv in a silence that seemed to pile up around him like a drift. She looked at him with open loathing in her eyes. 'You were his brother and you betrayed his trust—his and mine!' she grated, her voice low but rasping in passion. She was beyond fury, the dead expression in her eyes alarming. 'Were it not for your devious designs, Sugriv, this wouldn't have happened. I warned Vali about Ram, but he wouldn't believe me. He believed in both of you—that both of you were too honourable to even consider such a dastardly crime. He was too decent to die like that!' she waved her hand over his body. 'That's the way people like *you* should die!' her voice broke, grief choking her. 'You robbed him of a hero's death he deserved, instead killing him by treachery. Both of you are cowards. And you call yourselves brave, righteous warriors!'

Lakshman made a movement but Ram restrained him.

'Amma, please be calm!' a weeping Angad took her hand in his.

Sugriv put his hand gently on the young boy's shoulder, but he threw it off so violently that Sugriv stepped back, startled.

Lakshman's eyes flashed. 'What sort of a hero was he?' he asked. 'What kind of an honour that he fatally attacked his younger brother, a brother physically weaker than him? That he exiled him, took his brother's wife!'

'Stop!' commanded Tara, her voice striking like a whiplash. 'Is that the sob story Sugriv fed you?' she said scornfully. 'I know Vali did no such thing! You have killed him; don't assassinate his character. Vali never touched Ruma, not even in his thoughts. That is something I cannot say about Sugriv, now, can I?' she threw Sugriv a scathing look before turning her sorrowful eyes on Ram. 'If this is the moral argument for punishing my husband, how is Sugriv not accused of the same crime?'

She expected some reaction from Ram, but his unruffled and apparent indifference to what she had said cut the ground from under her feet.

Finally, Ram's clear voice cut the thick silence. 'Sugriv asked you to be his queen with courtesy and as custom demanded,' Ram said gravely. 'Vali did not. He appropriated his brother's wife in the name of revenge...'

Tara stood still, her heart thumping and her face white.

'Sugriv did the same in the name of tradition,' lashed Tara. 'He is the one touched by covetous thought, not my Vali.'

Sugriv paled, frowned and opened his mouth to say something. But the next second he changed his mind and bit his lip.

'Vali stole his kingdom,' Ram reminded her sternly.

'It was never his to be stolen!' retorted Tara.

Ram continued, 'Vali was a tyrant. He was the older brother and should have behaved as such. The younger brother should be treated like a son. Even if Sugriv made a mistake, Vali should have forgiven him, as an elder brother should—'

'And as a younger brother, Sugriv should have given his older brother and his sister-in-law the respect and loyalty he promised. That was his duty,' sneered Tara, her voice thick with sarcasm.

'Vali threw Sugriv out when he could very well have killed him. But he did not—he could have never killed his brother—not even today!' she disdained, her voice rasping. 'Vali had promised me that! What was his crime that he merited such a terrible death? Or was it the power of Indra's necklace that made you not confront Vali yourself but hide in the bushes to hunt him down like one would a defenceless animal?' she said scathingly. The muscles either side of Ram's jaw stood out suddenly.

'And even if you believe that Vali committed a crime against Sugriv and Ruma, what right do *you* have to kill Vali? He was not your enemy; he had not harmed you. Then why did you offer to kill an innocent man?' she demanded, her voice shaking. 'If you wanted to kill him, why did you not engage in a direct battle with Vali?'

'Tara, you should know better. You are the lady of the jungle. Does the hunter intimate his prey of his presence? For the hunting king, his priority is to kill the deer, come what may,' Ram stated.

Tara smiled suddenly; it wasn't a pleasant smile.

'No, that's not the rule of the jungle. That's man's law. In the jungle, an animal kills another only when hungry. What was *your* motive?'

The snap in her voice told Ram that nothing he could say would make any difference to her. He wanted to console her but controlled himself.

Rage grabbed her throat. 'You did what came your way—you were so desperate to get your wife back that you agreed to do the unthinkable! Vali would have helped you in getting Sita, had you asked. Ravan could have listened to Vali. They were allies. And if Ravan had not heeded his plea, Vali, the honourable man that he was, would have fought for you too against Ravan and defeated him. No conspiracy; completely transparent. *That* is the difference between Vali and Sugriv!'

Sugriv broke in desperately. 'Tara, *I* am your perpetrator, not Ram! Ram's slaying of Vali has a special significance. After he was shot down by this arrow, Vali argued with Ram on why he had to kill him in a cowardly way. Ram explained to him. Vali was convinced he erred. Ram is not just the exiled prince of Ayodhya, he is the Vishvarupa—world's benefactor. Everything was pre-ordained according to *kaal* and karma,' continued Sugriv, helplessly. 'Ram generously granted him moksha. Vali died a content man, Tara. Eventually convinced, Vali even advised Angad to stand by me and assist us in Ram's divine task.'

Tara seemed paralyzed. She knelt there, gently easing Vali's head from her lap onto the ground, his lifeless hand still slack in her long fingers. She drew in a sharp breath. Only her eyes were alive and they regarded Sugriv murderously.

'You have a righteous explanation for everything, you hypocrite!' she cut in contemptuously. 'Vali may have asked for forgiveness; he may have forgiven you,' Tara's voice trailed, 'but *I* won't!' she said softly, and Sugriv felt a prickle of fear.

Tara suddenly expelled a little hiss of breath through her lips and let Vali's hand slip out of her fingers. She stood up slowly and passed her hand over her pale, damp face. 'While I can come around to accept Vali's death as his punishment for seizing Ruma and exiling you, can both of you be acquitted for *your* crime?'

Sugriv stiffened. His eyes shifted away from Tara's accusing ones. Lakshman scowled and moved uneasily. Ram's face was immobile. His serene eyes met her stormy ones. She turned her eyes away from Ram and caught Sugriv's gaze again.

'You committed a dishonourable deed, Ram—more dishonourable than the death you bestowed upon Vali!

Because you killed Vali while hiding behind a tree, because you shot an arrow on an unarmed, vulnerable person, may you also be killed the same way—helpless and defenceless.'

A gasp of horror rippled through the group.

'Tara, no,' begged Sugriv.

Ram gravely shook his head. He bowed. 'Yes, so be it. I will be blessed that it shall be Vali who will slay me—but in our next birth.'

Tara was past listening, a blistering rage clawing at her throat.

'You killed Vali to search for Sita. In your desperation to search for your lost wife, you killed an innocent man—my Vali—separating him from me forever. May you suffer the same grief of losing your partner... You will find Sita now, but will lose her again forever as she returns to Mother Earth!'

'Stop it, Tara!' shouted Sugriv. 'You have gone mad!'

'Yes, mad with grief, mad with pain, mad with fury!' she cried, tears coursing down her pale cheeks. 'All because of *you* and this man who you used to get back at your brother!'

She turned upon the silent Ram. 'Oh Ram, did you not see that you were a mere weapon in this senseless battle of the brothers? I have heard you are a wise person, a sensible man—could you not have knocked some sense into them?'

Ram stood stock-still, his head bowed. Something in his silent surrender to her ominous tirade made her pause, her anger slowly draining out. She abruptly stepped back as the realization hit her in the face. Her colour turned a waxen white. She had uttered portentous words of doom. Her hands flew to her mouth, her eyes stricken. 'No, no, I take back my terrible words... Oh, what did I do?'

'Those were the words of a grieving wife,' said Ram gently.

'But you are a grieving man too, desperate to get back your wife,' she whispered brokenly. 'Oh, what have I done!' she cried, aghast, her hands to her mouth, the horror of her words dawning upon her. 'You're not even upset with me,' she said, a catch in her voice. 'Are you—some kind of saint?'

And as she said those words, looking into his calm eyes, it dawned on her. Sugriv's earlier words rushed into her brain, and she knew Ram was no ordinary man.

Sugriv turned to her, speechless, his face ashen, his hands shaking.

'You have cursed Ram!' he muttered, his hands covering his face. 'And it's because of me. I brought all this upon us...'

Tara straightened her shaking shoulders, leaned forward, raking Sugriv with loathing.

'Yes, *you* did. *You*, not Ram. You did this, Sugriv,' she repeated dully. 'And I shall suffer for it. So shall Ram and Sita—and all of us, because of *you*!'

Wiping her tears, she turned to Vali, looking down at his ashen face, into his, sightless eyes. Even so, he looked radiantly handsome, his thick hair spread like a glorious mane—like a lion in the jungle.

She turned to Sugriv, hate simmering through her tears. 'You're not going to get away,' she said softly, her voice controlled. 'I knew all along you'd threaten our happiness, but you'll pay for it from this day on. Let's see how long you can run away from your conscience, your guilt!'

Sugriv heard the hate in her voice and he lifted his lean shoulders in a gesture of resignation. *Let her hate me!* He was sick of hiding, running away, being too frightened to speak. He had loved and lost Tara. The irony was that he had lost her by making her lose Vali.

Tara gathered herself together. No one could describe

the scorn of her expression or the contemptuous hatred she put into her words.

'You and your love, Sugriv—or was it plain desire?' she disparaged, her lips twisting. 'How destructive was it! You hurt him, you hurt me, you hurt Ruma...and Angad. Oh, you have destroyed us!'

With a choked cry, Tara ran from them, stumbling blindly towards the waiting chariot. She gave a groan of horror and felt herself falling. Her mind cried out for Vali.

Angad gave an agonized yell and sprang to her, lifting her up. She felt two strong hands gripping her shaking shoulders. Angad was standing in front of her. She looked up, frantically into his tortured eyes. He raised her to her feet and, partly dragging her, partly carrying her, got her into the chariot with Hanuman's assistance. She was moaning, almost insensible. Angad put his arms around her.

'It's all right, Amma,' he said. 'I'm here.'

Something in his voice made her look at him in her haze of grief: her boy had become a man.

20

THE NEW KING

She seemed to be carried in a palanquin, dressed in bridal finery. She felt a swaying motion as the bearers marched with a long, uneven stride. She entered the city of Kishkindh that was changed, so vast and yet dim, where the crowd thronged about her with curious eyes as it tried to snatch a glimpse of the queen-bride. Then, as she passed the memorial temple, she heard the echo of mocking laughter. She turned. It was Sugriv... But then Vali came towards her and took her in his arms, lifting her out of the palanquin. She tried to tell him it was all a mistake. She felt his kisses on her mouth and she wept with joy... And then there was an abrupt, hoarse cry from Sugriv and they were separated—between them, the heaving mass of Vanaras, dark and bare, hurrying silently, pushing them away from each other...as they bore a dead body. Vali's...

Tara blinked, her grief closing down on her. She stared unseeingly at the empty room. Last week had been the day of Vali's funeral. This week was Sugriv's coronation. But before that, their wedding. She shut her eyes against the prick of the unshed tears.

She heard a knock at her door. Tara straightened herself

in the chair. She saw Hanuman standing at the threshold of the doorway of the hall.

He paused, wary. The change in her appearance was extraordinary. This was no longer the broken woman who had cursed Ram in her grief or the fiery widow who had accused Sugriv of treachery. The assured astuteness that was ingrained in her personality and that he had witnessed in the royal court was back, her face composed, her eyes clear and clever as always.

Hanuman knew he had to be frank and firm.

'It is about the coronation,' he started.

'Yes, that I gathered. I am waiting for the others to arrive. Did Jambavan send you, Hanuman?' she smiled wryly. 'He knows you are one of the few whose opinions I respect, something I did not have the last few years.'

'I was never far,' he said solemnly.

A flurry made them turn towards the interruption. *Sugriv*. Tara lifted her head and stared at Sugriv, her brown eyes shuttered. She hadn't seen him after Vali's funeral.

'Where is Panas?' Tara asked.

'He is showing Ram our army,' he replied shortly.

The arrival of Jambavan came as a relief and set the tone of the remaining meeting.

'By announcing Sugriv as king, Angad becomes the crown prince,' started Hanuman.

Tara gave a faint nod. 'I did it to halt the panic on the streets. The news of Vali dying was enough for the people to flee the city.'

Jambavan's mouth tightened. 'We have gone through a tragedy. But the past is past us; we can't undo it. What we can control is the now—and ourselves. You are the queen, the mother of a prince,' he added astutely. 'Angad is the heir; unlike last time, he is sixteen now and old enough to be king.'

She sat motionless, her hands clasped. 'No, let Sugriv be king. There are nobles picking sides—Vali's or Sugriv's. I want to end this bickering once and for all!'

Sugriv, like Hanuman, maintained a diplomatic silence.

Her voice dipped low but firm. 'Besides, I shall not fall into that trap of announcing Angad as king and be accused of the throne being successional.'

'It *is* successional—through you, as we are a matrilineal clan,' reminded Jambavan.

'Then as Angad becomes king through me, I don't need to marry Sugriv at all.'

She saw Sugriv straighten up. He looked at her, his eyes confused.

'We have discussed this before. The people expect us to marry, Tara,' he maintained gruffly.

Tara looked up, 'I will,' she said steadily, but both the men could detect the ripple of emotion under the tranquillity. 'Oh, I will!'

'Vali won't come back; I can't have more violence. Let there be peace...' she paused intensely, her eyes critical. 'At any cost. And if it takes me marrying Sugriv, I shall do it.'

Jambavan's face was now set, and his eyes flickered. 'Then you have to lead too—as Queen of Kishkindh, the queen of a kingless kingdom.'

'Yes, I am ready to be Sugriv's queen,' she reiterated strongly, clenching her fists; she could not escape the world she had been running away from.

Sugriv felt his face began to glisten with sweat, his eyes widening slightly in disbelief.

'You say it with a fundamental distaste,' Jambavan said

admonishingly. 'Whatever the disagreements, both of you have to keep a united front.'

She held his disapproving eyes with her unwavering gaze. 'I am taking this decision, however much repugnant, so as to keep a unified façade. I shan't allow emotion to come in the way of duty,' she said stiltedly. 'I did it once and permitted myself to lose reason... I uttered the unspeakable, which I shall regret all my life.'

'Lord Ram understands,' intervened Hanuman, observing her distress.

She shook her head agitatedly. 'But I don't!' she said, the words spilling out of her mouth. 'It shouldn't have happened... Ram was a desperate man, lost and frantic for his wife, and yet I cursed him!'

In palpable silence, Jambavan looked over at Tara, who sat as if turned to stone, her fingers wringing in quiet agitation, her eyes enormous. There was an expression of self-loathing and remorse on her face that made him feel sorry for her.

'Don't be too hard on yourself; it was meant to be,' he said cryptically.

'Lord Ram is above all this and wishes to fulfil his promise to Sugriv at the earliest,' added Hanuman.

'Yes, so that Sugriv may fulfil *his* promise, and with the Vanaras' help, Ram may proceed in his search for Sita,' she said, rubbing her jaw. 'From now on, we will be fighting someone else's war.'

Jambavan shook his head of full hair burnished copper. 'Let us look past the past. Now we can only look forward.' His eyes narrowed in close scrutiny.

She crossed her arms, stating firmly. 'The wedding will be a small formality.'

'I will be queen. I will be wife—in name only. But not more,' she stressed, throwing Sugriv a meaningful look. 'I hope I am clearing all doubts and misgivings.'

Sugriv gave a perceptible start. 'But if we are to be married, we need to keep this antagonism less obvious. We need to have a truce...'

'For truce, we need trust.'

The quiet finality in her firm voice left him shaken.

Sugriv stood still, staring out of the window while he thought.

'And I don't have your trust anymore,' he admitted tiredly. 'Not yours. Not Ruma's. Not even Angad's... That is why he threw me out.'

'Let's not repeat ourselves over and over again,' she said, her voice smooth. 'It's our obligation to live with the consequences now.'

He shot her down, in sudden frustration. 'No! If you call yourself fair, Tara, how could you allow how Vali treated me?' He leaned forward, his fists tightly clenched till his knuckles turned white. 'I wasn't his servant. I was his brother. His partner. We created an empire together. I may have been in the shadows but it was my life's work too. Vali had no right to recklessly throw me out and expect my blind loyalty.'

Her voice dripped contempt. 'You were never partners, Sugriv. Vali valued you because you were his younger brother. He loved you. He wanted and needed your friendship. But you betrayed him to get back at him!' she spat, her voice low and husky. 'But for all your mutual hostility, I could have never dreamed that it would cost me my husband's life.'

'You never dreamed that I would have the courage to defy him!' snapped Sugriv.

Tara stiffened. 'Cowards prefer to insist on their own courage.' She gave a weary shrug.

'Anyway, I want to see the end of this,' she said. 'You don't think I want to stay out of it now that Vali's gone, do you? I don't wish to go through the old arguments again. I shall remain Queen of Kishkindh but I would not want to humiliate Ruma more than what she already endured...'

'Not after what Vali did to her!' Sugriv scoffed.

Tara started to say something and then stopped, biting her lip.

'Yes, Sugriv,' she said quietly, a few moments later. 'But his intentions were far more honest than yours.'

There was complete silence in the chamber, thick with suspicion and hostility. The other two men watched Tara and Sugriv, not moving, aware of the escalating tension between them.

Tara looked up at Jambavan, her eyes suddenly trusting. 'I presume everyone agrees with me. The power and position I now have will remain, as it was when I was Vali's queen,' she asserted. Her imperiously spoken words made Sugriv suddenly feel like a servile servant who answers to instructions.

Jambavan again nodded his approval. She was, like him, a shrewd diplomat, he thought. All she needed was a little backing to support the decision she so subtly mandated.

'I cannot find any fault in your argument,' Jambavan said mildly. 'And I am sure your brother-in-law, Sugriv, as the new king will agree to these terms to maintain peace and harmony in this kingdom.'

Again, Sugriv nodded briefly.

'Now that's decided, let us move to more pressing matters,' she said crisply.

Looking ahead, planning, making decisions, taking chances, moving forward or withdrawing—this was now part of her life.

'We have to be careful with the nobles. There's a rift between them, forcing them to take sides. We must minimize this as far as possible.' Tara paused to think, throwing Sugriv a direct stare while Jambavan waited, confident she would solve any problem. 'Besides the warring nobles, all the tribes, clans and settlers must feel reassured. They must accept both of us—Sugriv and I—as part of the royal family whose interest it is to keep Kishkindh first. And no one else.'

Sugriv narrowed his eyes. 'You mean some resent the presence of Ram here?'

'Yes, for what it portends. They fear he will take over the kingdom through you.'

Sugriv shifted uneasily.

Tara continued, her tone crisp and efficient, 'I am sure you will convince them otherwise, Sugriv. But first things first—the coronation is to be held for the people to know they are not bereaved, that they have a king again. And a queen.'

His face set, Sugriv motioned to Hanuman, 'Hanuman will be overseeing the coronation formalities. That should be all for now?' His eyes moved to her. 'I shall confirm to all that you are ready for the coronation. And the wedding.'

Tara wondered how she could keep a straight face even as the world was crumbling around her. She gave a brief nod, unable to speak.

Looking at Sugriv as he walked out briskly with Hanuman, Jambavan decided this immature man was no competition for this no-nonsense woman. A woman so much wiser than him had to be the right choice for Kishkindh.

'Don't let Sugriv rush you. He has a lot of support now

that Vali is dead. The stage must be set before he goes into action... I don't have to tell you that,' Jambavan said.

She stared fixedly at him.

'No man rushes me.'

He paused, then went on, 'And Angad? I have heard he is disgruntled and collecting support with the courtiers...'

'He said he will agree to whatever I decide,' she said firmly. 'He is ready to give up the throne for now and serve Sugriv instead.'

Jambavan shook his head. 'Angad does not trust Sugriv anymore. In fact, Angad wishes to stay back in Kishkindh and not join in the search for Sita. He has his supporters who are revolting against Sugriv right now, unknown to him.'

Tara inhaled a sharp breath.

'This was unknown to me too,' she said, her tone cold and hard, suddenly realizing what Jambavan had been doing all along. 'Now I know everything.'

'There's more,' remarked the older man. 'Hanuman, sniffing trouble from Angad and regarding his intentions to establish a separate kingdom, has warned Angad of the consequence.'

Her face puckered, and she looked away from Jambavan. 'I owe Hanuman a lot; I should thank him,' she sighed unhappily. 'Angad is impressionable. He is angry and hasn't had time to grieve. He needs to feel assured that Sugriv and Ruma love him unconditionally and that Sugriv will never cause him any harm.'

'But Angad can harm Sugriv. This is where your marriage to Sugriv will be useful. It is the best way to keep peace, not just in Kishkindh but between the two men as well.'

She threw him a troubled look. 'But Sugriv worries me too.'

'He is fickle,' Jambavan nodded. 'He works best under a leader. Right now, he's obligated to Ram. He has to pay Ram back, but does not realize what such a big responsibility and the power that comes with it really mean. But he is important to us—'

'Solely because he is Vali's brother,' she flatly said.

'And a capable policy-maker,' reminded Jambavan. 'You know the sway you have over him; you mustn't neglect him.'

'I know how to use him,' she said tersely.

Both fell silent for a few minutes. On a rational level, Jambavan was aware that Tara was a clever tactician, an expert in statecraft. She had the intelligence to anticipate coming events.

'Our priority right now is to ensure that there is peace in the kingdom,' she said, 'between nobles and between Angad and Sugriv. Considering Sugriv has Ram and Lakshman as his ready army, it is all the more important that my son does not antagonize Sugriv.'

Even if it means marrying the man you distrust most, thought Jambavan as he lifted his bushy eyebrows. 'You are a dutiful woman.'

Tara had saved the day. Yet again. Jambavan had always been impressed by Tara. Even now, at his age, when he no longer bothered with niceties, he had always been aware of her innate wisdom, her calmness and her efficiency. With this woman, he told himself, Kishkindh couldn't go wrong. If Tara continued to be queen, the kingdom was safe. She was the queen he wanted, whom he would vouch for. She was the queen the kingdom needed.

*

On the wedding day, Sugriv scarcely recognized Tara as a bride—this tall, severe-looking woman with her dead eyes, her hair put up in an austere style. She was wrapped in ivory white and gold silk. He was quick to notice she had not removed Vali's bracelet, which jangled with the single bulky gold bangle she wore. She looked immaculate, efficient and remote. In all his impassioned dreams over the years, he had imagined this moment in several ways but never had he thought it would be this—so sterile.

As she stood aside, Sugriv, a little dazed by this unexpected transformation, walked into the palace's temple, where the wedding rites were to be performed. Without hurrying, she came up the steps leading to the temple and went past him without looking at him, stationing herself discreetly near the priest. He felt a surge of exasperated rage rush through him, and he had to restrain himself from jumping to his feet and going after her. She was like an iceberg now, he thought. Nothing moved her.

Ruma was conspicuous by her absence. Nothing Sugriv said could make her attend the ceremony.

'Ruma is a sensible woman,' Tara had said softly but he had heard the hard undertone. 'It is not every day that a woman gets to see her husband marry the wife of the brother he murdered.'

Her words had lanced through him like white-hot fire. His jaw had clenched. He had pursed his lips, unable to retort. The viciousness in her voice had shocked him.

The wedding ceremony had been kept small but symbolic, meant for him to gain social approval. Not Angad's, though.

Before the ceremony could start, Angad made his disapproval open.

'Chikappa, you have been like a father to me, and

Chikamma my mother. I have always believed that I was extraordinarily fortunate to have two fathers and two mothers. But now...' his voice shook, coming out in an angry rasp. 'You kill my father for reasons I can fairly understand, but now...this? This marriage to my mother? She is your sister-in-law, Chikappa!' Angad leaned forward, sweat beads on his forehead, his teeth bared. 'You should have treated her like a mother, not...oh, I cannot word the pain you have wrought on us, Chikappa—on me, on Amma and on Chikamma. Is she even here? Do you care?'

Alarmed, Sugriv put an arm on Angad's shoulder in quick assurance. 'It is a political marriage, Angad! Your mother is doing this for you! It is her attempt to secure your future and that of the kingdom. We have to be together now... It is not what you think it is!'

'What a legitimate pretext you have, Chikappa!' snarled Angad and for a terrifying moment, Sugriv was reminded of Vali. Wanting to shout at him, but controlling his voice with an effort, Angad flung his uncle's arm away in open disgust.

Sugriv drew back, exasperated.

'You can fool everyone, but not me!' Angad cried, his face contorted in anguish. 'I am the crown prince and I owe you my political loyalty. As does my mother,' he gritted his teeth, giving Tara a painful glance, his eyes flashing. 'But I am no longer your son and you are no longer my father, Chikappa. My father died the day you killed him. And with that, both my fathers passed away. I am now merely your subject.'

Choking with emotions, Angad stared at Sugriv, a red mist of rage before his eyes. Not trusting his temper anymore, he turned and walked away from the temple.

Knowing it would be useless to try to persuade Angad, Sugriv kept a straight face and continued with the rites. Tara looked away from him, her posture stiff yet dignified—even in hate, he thought drearily. The mother and son had both publicly put him and their relationship in place; Tara was just performing a political duty, as would Angad.

The marriage was followed by the coronation ceremony; she had to suffer through it that same day. The hall was indeed crammed with the most eager, enthusiastic crowd Tara had ever seen. The fireworks flared noisily outside, lighting up over hordes of people—sailors, tradesmen, labourers, hunters. Inside the coronation hall, in a semi-circle the nobilities of the kingdom sat like immortal gods, righteous to the backbone. Tara looked around with apprehension but tried to calm herself with the thought that they were her people and she had no cause to falter before them.

Tara was sitting on Sugriv's right, not relinquishing her position of power as the queen of the land. Ruma, to his left, wore the haughty look she was famous for, reserved especially for her husband. Tara threw a worried glance at Ruma, who turned her face away to stare unseeingly at the gathering crowds in the hall. The jubilation had no effect on either Ruma, or her—both were mourning, weeping inside with a smile on their lips. Ruma finally turned to look at Tara; she returned the look, her eyes expressionless. The two women then looked down the hall, wooden and bitter in their loss. They said nothing.

Their impassive faces made Sugriv nervous. He glanced to his right—he wished Tara would smile. Anything would be better than sitting there with that set face and dead eyes. She looked like a ghost, not his bride, nor his queen. It took away from the delight of having both princes of Ayodhya—Ram and Lakshman—attend his coronation ceremony.

Tara could hardly believe her eyes still. The genuine

respect Sugriv was accorded by the two princes of Ayodhya, as they came up to Sugriv to congratulate him on the coronation, confounded her. Knowing his limited intellectual capacity and physical prowess, she was astounded that the world should think of him as an uncommonly clever, brave man. The ceremony, mercifully, was short and simple, with the presence of Ram and Lakshman giving it all the validation it needed.

It was time for Sugriv to address the hall. He rose to his feet and began his speech. Ruma leaned over towards Tara and whispered, 'Sugriv is a mere figurehead of a king from now on, Tara. You are the true power of Kishkindh; everyone knows and respects that. Besides, it is mostly Jambavan and Hanuman with whom Ram and Lakshman confer with. They should know that most of the pearls of wisdom they acquire are from your brain.'

Surprised by the unexpected praise, Tara regarded Ruma quizzically.

'It could be jealousy on my part, but I always expected to hear something to your disadvantage ever since you became Vali's queen,' said Ruma with unexpected candour. 'But, on the contrary, everything seemed to proceed very satisfactorily and you had all the qualities needed to be the queen of Kishkindh—aptitude for politics, keenness in making deals and treaties, common sense, concern for the people. Sugriv was almost scared of the power and popularity you wielded. It worried him endlessly. Perhaps I was prejudiced too because I was ambitious for Sugriv. But you *are* cleverer than Sugriv—and even Vali. You occupied yourself with ideas that none of us could conceive; your mind was ever engaged in the smallest and the minutest of issues. Sugriv was only interested in policy-making, Vali in warfare. It was extraordinary that every one but you should so highly estimate your intelligence, Tara. You deserve the throne, and I know it will be you who will truly rule Kishkindh,' said Ruma with unleashed vehemence, the colour high on her pale cheeks.

By then Sugriv had finished his speech and had sat down between them. Then, in unison, the audience broke into thunderous applause. It was no perfunctory clapping of hands; they rose as one and shouted and yelled with enthusiasm.

'Long live Vali! Long live Sugriv! Long live Queen Tara!' cried a voice. The air was filled with robust shouts and cheers. Everyone in the hall was in a frenzy of jubilation. Jambavan warmly took Ram's hand and held them in quiet reverence, bowing deeply.

Hanuman was at Ram's side, and he cheered loudly, 'Hail Shree Ram!'

And the crowd burst into loud applause all over again. The scene may well be described as one of unparalleled enthusiasm. Shouts of 'Hail Shree Ram!' rent the air.

'Ram is the hero. Not you, Sugriv...not us,' Tara murmured to Sugriv, bending her head close to his. 'Through Ram, you have gained all you aspired for—the kingship, the kingdom, the throne, the crown. You got back your wife...and me.'

The smile died on his lips and she gave him a glance that lacked in amenity.

'Ram did what he promised.' She was looking at him, her hand clutching the arm of the throne tightly, her eyes triumphant. 'Now it's *your* turn, Sugriv.'

Sugriv sat still, staring. The enormity of her words weighed upon him, as the audience opened its mighty mouth and roared, then burst again into 'Hail Shree Ram!'

21

THE SAVIOUR

The wind had stiffened and great, swollen clouds had come up from the west, blotting out the clear sky, the stars and the moon. Tara had glanced at these clouds floating over the mouth of the river. A few large drops began to fall.

There was merciful silence in the chamber. It was as empty as her heart, grief-gnawed, with her memories marauding silently. She was sitting alone, trying to relax against the din. But suddenly, over the raucous ring of drunken revelry, she heard a clap of thunder. The clouds roared and burst, ruthless and sultry, like finally unleashed fury. The downpour was breathtaking, as it always was at this time of the year. The rain fell in torrents, thick and fast, and showed no sign of ceasing. The steady rain held a melancholy note as if dousing the sounds of cheer.

Against the crashing rain, she heard—and felt—an unfamiliar sound: the sound of the palace door shaking.

'Who is that at the palace door?' she asked sharply, her voice echoing in the large, lonely chamber.

The guard outside her chamber gave an imperceptible nod and ran off to investigate. He returned within a moment, his face no longer bland, his eyes troubled.

'It is that younger prince from Ayodhya, my Queen. He just kicked down the city gate and has approached the palace. He is threatening to destroy Kishkindh.'

She did not need to hear more; she could guess why, as she jumped to her feet. *Lakshman is here to remind Sugriv of his unfulfilled promise*, she thought with dismay.

After the wedding and coronation festivities, Ram had retreated to the Pravarshan mountains, with the hope that Sugriv would start his search for Sita. But despite Hanuman's pleas and her reprimands, Sugriv, in his mood of extended revelry, had clearly ignored his agreement with Ram. Hanuman and she had been anxious for days. Ultimately, an impatient, restless Ram must have sent the more aggressive Lakshman to pay Kishkindh a visit and do the needful. From the state of things described to her and what she had just heard, he was in a murderous rage. The day of reckoning had arrived, with Sugriv lying in inebriated bliss. Tara, on the other hand, was very brisk and alert.

'Where is Sugriv?' she asked the guard.

The guard stood silent.

His silence spoke volumes. Sugriv must be in his harem, drunk to the gills, she presumed, her lips pursed in frustration. There was a loud, ringing noise—it was the sound of Lakshman twanging his bow string. Tara's heart sank from the sound that filled the palace, heralding fear and dread to all of Kishkindh.

Sugriv's personal guard rushed into her chamber as she was wondering what to do next.

'I have a message from the King, O Queen Tara. He implores you to go meet Prince Lakshman in person.'

'Where is Hanuman?' she asked severely.

'On his way to meet you, O Lady.'

Before her anxiety could boil over, the sight of Hanuman at the doorway gave her quick solace. 'We need to stop Lakshman.'

'*You* need to meet him,' he returned calmly.

Tara did not know what to say, momentarily speechless.

'Why not you, Hanuman? You are the right person. They like you, respect you. And you could calm him down with your smart words.'

Hanuman shook his head. 'I am just a messenger; you are the Queen, the head. And Lakshman is in no mood for hollow assurances from an envoy. My mere presence might trigger violence in him. But not with you—'

'Because I am a woman?'

'Because you are the Queen. More importantly, you are a master diplomat. And yes, for all his fire and fury, Lakshman is known to be courteous towards women and shall not confront you with violence.'

Tara gave a short bark of laughter. 'Try telling Ravan's nose-less sister that!'

'Lakshman loped off Surpanakha's nose only because she was going to attack Sita—as was his duty!' Hanuman retorted with uncharacteristic vehemence. 'His responsibility was to protect Ram and Sita, and however much he may be condemned for this act, Surpanakha got what she deserved. Rebuffed by the men, she was going to harm an innocent woman.'

Tara's eyes widened as she stared at him. 'Hark, you are quite their new loyalist!'

Hanuman, she knew, was a very loyal person, the gentlest of men, his humility as deep as his inner strength—assets he failed to realize himself. His unparalleled devotion towards

Sugriv—and now Ram—and his unconditional love made him not just the most faithful friend but the most trusted and intelligent ally. That he had preferred Sugriv over Vali was probably one of the reasons for Vali's downfall and one of her genuine regrets. It was now Ram whom he was so devoted to. That would change a lot of things, particularly for Sugriv, she frowned, looking at him thoughtfully.

Hanuman nodded, his mouth tightening. 'Are you doubting me?'

'No, never,' she said swiftly. 'You are the most loyal friend one would be fortunate to have. It was Vali's misfortune that you were not his.'

'Vali had *you*,' he said evocatively. 'You have a way with words. In your demeanour, in the knowledge of the world and in speech, you are unparalleled; your mere authority will halt Lakshman in his tracks. After that, I am confident you will do the needful to calm him down with your usual sagacity.' Taken aback by his unexpected commendations, Tara hesitated for just a moment before she turned around and strode out of the chamber with a quick nod, down the meandering corridor and through the courtyard, hoping to stop Lakshman before he met a drunk, insensible Sugriv.

She glimpsed an approaching figure in the drenched darkness: Lakshman marched in finely, with angry, abrupt movements—very upright, a scowl on his sullen face.

'Where is Sugriv?' barked Lakshman, uncaringly discourteous.

He stood towering, facing her, the rain coursing down his hard, bleak face. With his tall, spare form and his great eyes flashing, he was an impressive figure. His sincerity was obvious in the fire of his gestures and in his deep, ringing voice.

She forced her lips to work into a small smile and greeted him, her hands folded. She looked down at her steady hands, and a slight colour rose to her cheeks. Her mind trembled a little. She did not trust herself to speak, but she had to.

'Welcome to Kishkindh,' she said sedately. 'But certainly not in this way.'

Lakshman detected the note of disapproval in her placid voice. He hid his surprise. He had intended confronting Sugriv, not this royal widow of the man whose death they were all responsible for. The Queen stood elegantly in front of him. He watched her unhurried movements, graceful and fluid, like a tiger watches his prey. Standing under the alcove, with the mist of the rain drenching her face, she commanded a compelling presence, exuding a magnetic aura, and yet he couldn't not be intrigued by her serenity and by the way she was looking directly at him without any sign of fear or diffidence.

He fixed his angry eyes on her, her remote composure confusing him.

'I have not come to play nice. That ungrateful Sugriv made a promise he has not kept,' he roared. 'And I'll thrash him for that!'

She bit her lip to hide a smile; she would have relished witnessing such an event. Instead, she moulded her voice into a plea. 'He has delayed, I agree. But there is surely a reason for it.'

Lakshman burst into a long, passionate tirade; his fury, Tara noticed, had a savage eloquence. Around them, the pitiless rain fell—fell steadily, with a fierce malignity that was all too human.

'Ruin awaits him! It's been months since Ram crowned Sugriv king, handing him Kishkindh's, wealth and throne, and yet Sugriv has not bothered to reciprocate the gesture. That makes us wonder if Sugriv intends to keep his promise at all. He was to trace and find Sita with his army of Vanaras and his sources. He has not even bothered to keep us informed. Where is he?' demanded Lakshman harshly.

'With his wife Ruma,' she said.

She regarded him solidly, her chin up, her golden brown eyes gleaming.

Lakshman glowered, 'He's enjoying himself here while Ram is fretting and fearing that—'

Tara gave a gentle shake of her head. 'Lakshman, please understand. After enduring months of fear, poverty and persecution, Sugriv is now able to enjoy the pleasures and the prosperity Ram has secured for him,' she started, noticing a slight softening of expression at the mention of Ram. She continued, her tone low and persuasive, 'I agree that this success has gone to his head, and Sugriv has lost his senses to drink and revelry. I know his fault. But please try to forgive him, for it is only the superior who knows the foolishness of the inferior. Do not be harsh in judging Sugriv's surrender to temptations of the flesh, especially after his long trials and privations. But I can assure you, he has never lost sight of his debt or his duty to you. He has already issued orders for mobilizing the Vanara warriors from all quarters. By the end of this week, they will all be here. Then the search for Sita and the war against Ravan will begin in earnest. Have no doubts. And now, pray come in and see the King.'

Lakshman flushed, his face darkening. 'Fine words to save Sugriv! He hasn't even started with the search!'

Tara remained still, her eyes looking directly into his. Her unblinking, stare had the power to make him look away.

As she said nothing, disconcerted, Lakshman went on, 'Ram did so much for Sugriv, and Sugriv has not returned the favour. He has the temerity to barricade the city knowing full well that we might start an offensive attack. I had to crash down the city gate and—'

'We know, Lakshman, that you single-handedly have the anger and armoury to destroy Sugriv and our kingdom,' she interposed smoothly. Her collected composure rankled him. She was cool, undisturbed by his fury.

He moved restlessly, glaring. 'I don't wish for violence but I shall not tolerate Sugriv breaking his vow to Ram. He has to be punished...' he paused, his tawny eyes flicked contemptuously towards one lit palace window, 'as he hides himself from me and enjoys sensual pleasures, while Ram suffers alone, wondering whether he placed trust in a worthless man.'

She looked at the falling rain and then at him.

'I can well understand your agitation,' she said soothingly, her voice dulcet, 'which prompted you to arrive at the inner chambers of the palace to seek Sugriv out.'

'He's a spineless debauch!' he retorted, his face livid, 'who directs you, his Queen, to placate me with her "fine words"!'

He turned his stormy eyes on her, and his voice trembled with contempt against the thundering torrent. The storm was beginning to get on his nerves, fuelling his fury. It was not like the soft Ayodhya rain that dropped gently on the earth; it was unmerciful and terrible. He felt the the malignancy of the primitive powers of nature in the droplets. Her crisp voice cut through his thoughts.

'Do my "fine words" ring false? They are honest words, a desperate plea,' she said. 'Yes, Sugriv is scared to face you, but it would take a truly brave man to stand up against you, Lakshman, especially in your current mood,' she said, her lips relaxing in a thin smile.

Lakshman exhaled slowly. He was becoming baffled by this woman. Was she playing him?

'I agree that Sugriv erred,' she nodded, her voice soothing and acquiescent. 'He wasted time celebrating and carousing, but then, remember, he has been away from his wife for the last two years,' she paused, her voice stoic. 'You of all people should know what separation from a wife means, what agony it is...'

The muscles either side of Lakshman's jaw stood out suddenly. His eyes darkened in sudden pain. *Urmila*! The imprinted image of his Mila's serene face surfaced before his stinging eyes. Tara caught a glimpse of the fleeting anguish in his eyes, and it struck her that his arrogant expression had changed. His eyes had a haunted look. She gave him a slanting glance. There was a long pause of silence while Tara shrewdly studied Lakshman's ashen face. Her eyes were demure now, and her tone persuasive.

'Sugriv is not you, Lakshman,' she continued, her voice clear against the lashing rains. Standing stiff, Lakshman nodded wordlessly.

On firmer ground, Tara proceeded with assuring grace. 'He has his reasons for the delay. But starting a search for Sita in this torrential rainy month is next to impossible, especially in these parts of the forest. Look at the rain!' she exclaimed, spreading her hands, pointing to the rain that crashed down on the ground outside with fury. 'We need to wait for the rains to dwindle to venture out for an extensive search. It would be foolish to waste time and men, scouring in this storm and wet wilderness.'

'Since the day he has been crowned, there has been no communication from Sugriv's side,' remarked Lakshman, his voice relatively temperate now. 'He went back on his word—

simple. That's treachery, and I don't like traitors.'

Tara winced. *Treachery. Traitor.* The words she had used for Sugriv herself, but she could not let Sugriv be at this volatile man's mercy. She nodded in quick agreement.

'Again, my apologies,' she said in that quiet, controlled voice that seem to have an unusual calming effect on everyone. 'Hanuman or I should have informed you, but the rains kept adjourning our plans. I understand your ire, Lakshman,' she sighed, knowing each time she personally addressed him, the angry man mollified significantly. 'But you need to understand that however strong a king is, he needs an ally. Ram needs Sugriv as an ally at this juncture.'

Lakshman's face was now set, and his eyes gleamed intensely.

'I am in agreement with what you say, but till now, Sugriv has not lived up to his role and responsibility as an ally!' he sneered.

'He will, I assure you,' she said. 'We have it all laid out. Only an army of the intrepid Vanaras who know the jungles like the back of their hands will be able to locate Sita through the labyrinth of thick woods, mountains, rivers and caverns that is Dandak.

'Ram needs a powerful army to fight a powerful foe. Sugriv, as promised, has summoned all his commanders and troops to the capital. Besides, you will need the wise counsel of Hanuman and Jambavan as well as the skills of our engineer Nal, personally groomed by his divine architect father, Vishwakarma, is a master of construction—be it houses, palaces, army camps, bridges and towers. Bridges are his specialty—over any waters—be it rivers, lakes, bays or even the sea—'

'Sea?' Lakshman lifted his eyebrows.

'Nal has been blessed with a gift to make stones float!' she explained, noticing the intent expression on his face. She had managed to catch his attention, distracting him suitably from his rage. 'Interestingly, it was a curse, which he and his friend Neel turned into a gift. They were mischievous kids who had the habit of flinging anything and everything into the water. Once they dropped idols of gods and the *kamandalu*—the holy water pot—belonging to Sage Suthikshna into a well. Sage Suthikshna, furious, cursed that whatever they throw in the water will not sink but float. I guess they turned the curse around and transformed it into a gift, and that's why they became engineers!' she smiled. 'You will surely need them on this mission. Besides, Neel is a ferocious fighter as well as an expert in finding the shortest routes. He can help in actively searching for Sita—*if* she's still in the forest.'

Lakshman was quick to notice the note in her tone. 'She is not? You know where she is?' he exclaimed.

'I can have an informed guess,' Tara ventured tentatively. 'Ravan is sure to not retain her in the forest. He was said to be seen carrying Sita southwards—that means, almost certainly, he is sure to have headed back home to Lanka, the safest place for him.'

Listen to her, Lakshman recalled Vali's dying words. He nodded slowly, his eyes filling with mounting admiration for the woman in front of him, small but defiant, grave and graceful in her mourning.

'Also, my father Sushen can be of huge help as a healer.'

'The royal physician is aged,' stated Lakshman. 'Will he be ready to accompany us on this long and arduous journey?' he added, looking doubtful.

'He's a veteran doctor, a warrior in his own right. He knows the tradition of Patanjali to treat any patient, irrespective of age, colour and clan, and can render medical assistance irrespective of political, racial or religious affiliations.'

Lakshman perked up, his eyes showing interest.

'And there will be the injured soldiers to be treated,' he nodded slowly. 'You are a healer too, aren't you?'

Tara looked at him, feeling a prickle of excitement at the plans. She smiled pleasantly. 'I can join in,' she offered quickly.

Lakshman vigorously shook his head. 'No, you are the Queen of Kishkindh. You should be here as head of state, looking after your land and people.'

She made a little gesture of appeasement with her hand. 'Agreed, someone has to be here. But Hanuman will be able to provide further details—he is devoted to Ram,' she observed shrewdly.

'Possibly because Sugriv is mostly absent,' remarked Lakshman dryly.

'Be assured, Sugriv will see to it that all is in control. It is just that we did not wish to start in this stormy season.'

Lakshman straightened his shoulders and made an impatient gesture to leave. 'I shall let Ram know forthwith.'

Regarding him thoughtfully and noticing his subsided fury, Tara gave a slim smile. 'Let's settle this right now before you inform Ram. I give *my* word to start the search for Sita immediately, irrespective of the rains,' she said, her tone sharpening.

Lakshman was the sort of man who always acted first and thought later. He found himself listening to her. He sighed. 'When would that be?' he demanded, his eyes narrowing. 'When?'

He uttered the last word with a passion of indignation.

'Within a fortnight,' she said mildly. 'Does that convince you?'

Lakshman stared. There was something imperious and positively impressive in the triumphant assurance of this woman's manner. She too looked at him in turn. The probing stare made him feel uncomfortable.

Her eyes were direct and hard as she said, 'Do you agree or do you still wish to rage?'

'I have no choice but to believe you,' he admitted grudgingly. 'If the plans are laid out as you claim, then I shall return with Ram next week—as I have faith solely in *your* word,' he returned curtly, bowing low. He gave her a knowing look. He had an impression that she was weaving a net around him, carefully, systematically and suddenly. When everything was ready, she would pull the strings tight.

'You *will* find Sita, and that is an assurance from a grieving woman.' Tara's golden-brown eyes lit up suddenly and her voice grew mellow and soft. 'Ram will return with Sita to Ayodhya, I promise. We in Kishkindh never turn out a guest in need. Never.'

For the first time since he could remember, Lakshman felt embarrassed, sweat beads breaking out on his forehead. He had come here to destroy Kishkindh all in righteous wrath, but the way this conversation had been manoeuvred left him suddenly drained of all his frustrations. He bowed again. He knew that this was no ordinary woman and that his anger was a blunted weapon. He was shrewd enough to know that he had been manipulated to giving more time for Sita's search to start.

Lustrous as the moon, dressed in white and gold, she looked every inch the royal widow, unruffled yet decisive. Lakshman saw Tara in a new light and his lips twisted in a sad smile.

'You remind me of my mother,' he said abruptly. 'Just as elegant, with sadness tingeing her calm eyes; just as wise, making decisions, guiding people, quietly and firmly.'

He was surprised to see colour rise to her cheeks.

'Mother!' she murmured. 'I *am* old!' she said with a chuckle. 'Your mother Queen Sumitra is known for her quiet wisdom. Your father took her advice.'

'Just as Vali took yours,' said Lakshman and immediately regretted his impetuous words.

'When he needed it the most, he didn't,' she said tonelessly, her eyes suddenly dulled in pain. She gave a wan smile. 'But yes, I am a mother too—Angad's. Have you met him?'

'Briefly,' he said shortly, recalling the young boy's outburst at his mother's wedding.

'I guess he will be joining you with his uncle in your quest. He wants to. He does not wish to remain here and mourn for his father any longer. He is restless and is eager to help Ram.'

'If I had known this, I could have saved myself some embarrassment over my abominable behaviour today,' said Lakshman, with an unexpected smile. It transformed him, wiping his perpetual scowl away.

Masking her astonishment, she said gravely, 'I hope I have saved my kingdom from your wrath. We are at your mercy. You brothers have the power to destroy us.' There was no bitter diffidence but a certain resigned tolerance that did not diminish her defiant dignity.

Lakshman had the grace to look contrite. 'It is my turn to apologize. Please forgive my manners and pardon me for abusing Sugriv,' he said huskily, his face flushing. 'It is only because of you that I got to realize that there was more to this than what I believed. It was a shortcoming on my part, which you opened my eyes to. Through your timely intervention, the crisis has been averted.'

She appeared quite at ease.

'Also, you needlessly not worry. Ram and I shall never harm Kishkindh or your son—never. He is the crown prince, and no harm will come to him. And that's my promise to you,' he nodded, his voice softened. 'Your political wisdom and diplomatic acumen are legendary. But I also see a fearful mother desperate to save her son and empire. And that is why it is you, and not Sugriv, who is here talking me out of my temper.'

She was surprised at this unexpected perspicacity; she had assumed him to be an impetuous man of vitriolic mood.

She did not smile, but her eyes were kindly. 'I want Angad to do what's right. And I hope you shall guide him.'

Lakshman, vexed with himself because he had been uncivil to her, looked anxious. 'That would be my honour.'

She bowed. 'Gratitude. Teach him what you would to your son.'

'I don't have one,' he said simply. 'Yet.'

His stark sadness was not lost to her. Was he missing his wife like she missed Vali?

'Then let Angad be a learning step for you,' she said with a gentle smile.

Lakshman, bemused, made no answer. He looked around instead. It had stopped raining during the course of their conversation. Across the bay, he saw nestling among the trees the huts of the village he had not noticed when he had entered Kishkindh in his ungovernable fury.

'It has finally ceased raining,' he exclaimed. 'I have never seen such rains before! They are enough to make anyone jumpy,' he continued in visible amazement. 'Doesn't it ever stop in this place?'

Her lips outlined a smile. 'It goes on pretty steadily in the rainy season. You see, it's the shape of the bay and the river against the hills—it seems to attract the rain from all over!'

He nodded and his face brightened.

'The view stays as dramatic when it stops raining,' she told him.

Slowly, sunlight flooded the courtyard, sternly dispersing the black clouds.

'Even Nature seems to concur with our agreement,' Lakshman observed. 'And on this conclusive note, I take my leave,' Lakshman said bowing to Tara. He turned to leave, but hesitated. He gave Tara a long, searching look.

'You know that one cannot find peace solely in work; neither in grief nor in all the happiness of the world; neither in some haven nor in a shrine; but only in one's soul,' he paused. 'As my brother Ram would say, that peace comes after forgiveness.'

Tara startled, but Lakshman passed swiftly out of the courtyard, into the drenched sunshine.

22

WAR AND PEACE

That peace comes after forgiveness.

The words rang in her ears, as she made her way to Sugriv's chamber. Tara suddenly felt warm. She was paler than ever, tired, but her eyes shone with an extraordinary fire. It seemed as though she were filled with an overwhelming triumph.

'Fear not, Sugriv. Lakshman has left,' she called out as she entered Sugriv's private chamber. Her voice was low, the words compacted under the weight of contempt. Sugriv, raised his aching head from the pillow and straightened up. Surprised to be directly addressed, he had a timid man's resentment at being forced out into the open.

'What did Lakshman say?' he countered belligerently. Sugriv was now sitting straight, his head resting on the bedpost, his face swollen and creased with overindulgence of alcohol. He looked washed out. Ruma was absent. At the sight of Tara, the last vestiges of intoxication left him, and he felt wan and nervous.

'It has been decided between us that the mission of searching for Sita starts next week—in earnest.'

'And how do you plan to do it?' he sneered.

'By using our own people—the army of Vanaras *you* promised Ram,' she returned serenely, but there was a dangerous purr in her voice. 'Your neglect notwithstanding, my spies have been scouting around for months. We have a fair idea where Sita may be.'

'Where?' he demanded, his mind suddenly alert.

'I could have divulged it to Lakshman right away but was deliberately vague,' she mentioned pointedly. 'But to get you back into their good graces, you may disclose this to them yourself once the brothers arrive here.'

Sugriv was confounded that Tara had the information he needed and was willing to give him credit for it even though contempt for him was palpable.

Sugriv, knowing so little, had been convinced that there was little to know in the first place, believing that he knew everything. Smug in the assumption that he held all the power, he had failed to realize his own ignorance.

'Please tell me, where is Sita?' he repeated hoarsely.

'Most likely in Lanka.'

He gave a start.

'But that, of course, not very difficult to deduce knowing Ravan is said to have gone south in his chariot. The problem is where exactly in Lanka Sita is. That you will need to find out. Considering what a self-respecting woman Queen Mandodari is, she won't allow Ravan to bring Sita in her home, though the palace should be the safest place to guard Sita,' she observed, and with a reflective pause, added. 'No wife likes another woman sharing her husband. Or vice versa.'

Sugriv detected the ironic note in her voice. He flushed red and made an inarticulate sound. 'I can't talk to Ram in riddles. I have to give him information that is sound and sure.'

Tara shook her head. 'Then be part of the search party, Sugriv. Be there for Ram instead of wasting yourself,' she insisted, her piercing glance on the spilled liquor on the floor.

Blinking, Sugriv grimaced, 'How will we reach Lanka, though?'

'To reach Lanka you have to cross the sea...' she hinted, wondering if she should divulge more and exert her influence to spare herself and him the humiliation of Ram's ridicule

Sugriv gave a slow nod of agreement.

'But how?' she persisted. 'We don't have ships. Unless we build them, but that's too time-consuming.'

'What do we do?' Sugriv cried in rising frustration.

'You will have to use your Vanara force—call each and every tribe, clan, family. It is now our collective war, not just of Ram against Ravan. Gather your army and use them, not just as warriors, but as builders—either to build ships, or build a bridge.'

There was a short silence, and Sugriv collapsed into a mockguffaw. 'Both are ludicrous ideas!'

Tara ignored his interruption. 'Building ships would have been easy if we had the right kind of wood to build them. But we would create another crisis by cutting down so many trees and deforesting our own jungle. Besides we have no time. That leaves us no option but to choose the other alternative—building a bridge.'

'Across the sea to? To Lanka?' His voice rose in incredulous disbelief.

She regarded him with her serene brown eyes. 'Yes. There's no other option.' Her placid confidence intrigued him.

He heard himself mumble. *Yes.*

She made an impatient movement. 'You need to be more assertive if you want to convince them. After all, it is *you* who accepted the arrangement with Ram, so it is up to *you* to deliver the results!' There was a quiet urgency in her firm voice. 'Ram handed you Kishkindh *and* Ruma, but you have neither won nor wooed back either... Where *is* Ruma?'

Sugriv remained silent for a moment. He stared across the room at the sun's rays that cast dancing shadows on the ceiling. He hesitated, then speaking rapidly as if to force out the words, said, 'She's gone. Gone from my palace, from my life,' he said dully. 'She says she prefers to remain in the quarters Vali had stationed her in—in your palace.'

It was then that Tara realized how distraught Ruma must be. She checked the angry sarcasm that constantly rose to her tongue in Sugriv's presence. She treasured in her heart the wrath and scorn that Sugriv occasioned. But, strangely, seeing his plight, vengeance did not seem as sweet. Sugriv stripped off his dignity and hope, of his cloak and crown—in his nakedness he was a pitiable figure.

'Sugriv, you are a survivor. You survived so long by milking your skills of playing a victim. I advise you to exploit it to gain public sympathy...and Ram's forgiveness.'

Sugriv was listening keenly to each word but his mind was reeling. 'Should I play victim even if tarnishes Vali's good name?' he said incredulously.

She smiled thinly. 'You have already done it. Vali was an idealist; you are an opportunist. It's people like you who prosper in the world,' she said cynically. 'Answering your question—yes, Vali will be damned forever—' she felt a lump in her throat, '—but never for me. He lives in my heart, my mind, my decisions.'

Sugriv's face began to glisten with sweat. 'Why are you

doing this for me?' he demanded, bewildered with her open generosity of ideas and advice.

She still had the placid expression, but the brown eyes came alive. 'Sugriv, it is not for you! It's never been about you. I am doing this for *our* survival. For Kishkindh. Because of you, Sugriv, we are at their mercy! *You* gambled us—Vali, me, the family, the people and Kishkindh!' she lashed out. 'With your single decision, you are going to make my people and my land suffer. You have dragged them into a needless war that is not theirs to fight and a death that is as certain and pointless! Do you realize how many Vanaras will be killed because of your selfish, solitary wish to destroy Vali?'

She leaned forward, glaring at him, and her large, questioning eyes seemed to pierce into his soul.

He gave a sudden gasp. He burst into a torrent of confused supplication and the tears of remorse coursed down his sallow cheeks.

'No, stop it! You've defeated me, Tara! I got the throne but I lost everything, everyone—you, Ruma, Angad! I shall do whatever you say...'

'I am helping you as much as I can, Sugriv,' she said curtly, shocked at his impassioned despair. His tortured eyes, flecked red with anguish, went to her tired face, then back down to his folded hands.

'Save me, Tara, just as you just saved Kishkindh! You saved me from Lakshman just now. You saved Kishkindh from his wrath and destruction!' he cried. 'Save me, Tara, save me from you,' he repeated. 'Save my soul!'

She gave him a hopeless look. 'Only you can save yourself. It is your war from now on...you and your conscience!'

'And your forgiveness, Tara! Can you not ever forgive me?'

The desperation in his voice made her go stock-still. Her immobility was strangely vulnerable.

'It's dreadful, isn't it, living in guilt?' she said dully. 'It is a slow death!'

He threw her a despairing look.

She continued lifelessly. 'It makes everything else seem so horribly trivial. I blamed you for my misfortune but I am to blame too.' She ignored his frantic protest, her eyes empty. 'This hate, I can't live with it anymore. Vali doesn't seem human anymore. When I see him in my mind, I can't remember him fondly, I see only blood and hate...'

She could not hold back the sob that choked her.

'All the love has gone, and now I have nothing but hate in me, Sugriv!' she cried and looked away. She could not bear his pleading eyes, which saw no flaw in her. 'Because each time I see you, I can feel only anger, hate, rage, resentment... Oh, I am terrible! I cannot forgive you, I cannot forgive myself for what I have become this... mess of hate and anger!'

Sugriv stiffened at the raw pain in her voice, remorse clutching at his heart.

'It's me, Tara, not you... I guess I turned you into the embittered soul that you are now,' he inhaled shakily. In the light of the lamp, Tara saw he had gone white, his eyes sunk in the sockets.

'I don't know whether you'll understand what I mean to say,' he started slowly. 'That sort of thing might not mean very much when it's over. I think you have never quite understood what I had to endure.' He spoke abruptly, in a voice he would have hardly recognized as his own. 'Vali knew...' he whispered wretchedly, 'that you could never love me back. He won, Tara. He knew he had won. Not just you, but in every possible way he left me defeated...' he sighed. 'As you are doing now. You are proving that Vali was a worthy man, and in your eyes, I am this worthless creature, his unworthy brother. I suppose I shouldn't have been taken in by my hurt pride, my sense of injustice. But can I ask you to forgive me? Can I ask you to like me as you used to like me?' he said, his voice going up a note, with frantic hope. 'Couldn't we be friends as we once were? With all these people laying their trust in us—'

'But can I trust you, Sugriv? Can I ever?' Her voice was hollow.

He winced and sat down. He stared into her unhappy eyes.

'Am I worth your hate?' he sighed in a flat, tired voice. 'I feel this more so after knowing what you did with Lakshman today. Your resilience and wisdom, your self-sacrifice is remarkable. But seeing your anger and your hate, I can't help being affected by it. It is absurd and disproportionate to distress yourself because a foolish man like me has betrayed your trust. I'm much too worthless and insignificant for you to give me this importance. These people and their hopes are far above me. I am unimportant; I am inconsequential.'

Tara did not answer, but she did not move away; she seemed to be waiting for him to continue.

'We too are at war, Tara. You and me. Can we not end it? I surrender! I beseech you, I implore you. I need you, Tara... I need you to forgive me!'

She clenched her fists, feeling the beads of Vali's bracelet strain against her skin.

'You used to not be like this—cold and unfeeling—yet you feel contempt for me. Don't waste it on me.'

She could not trust herself to speak.

'I don't understand you,' he blurted. 'I don't know what it is you want... But I only want you to be a little less unhappy.'

He felt her blanch. Her voice was very cold when she answered.

'I am beyond being unhappy. I have a great deal too much to do to think of grief anymore.'

'That is because you resent Vali is dead and I am alive!' he drew in a painful breath. 'I know I failed you, Tara.'

'It does not matter anymore. Don't fail your kingdom or, the promise you have given to Ram, Sugriv,' she said, suddenly feeling drained.

She did not trust him. The wound of this betrayal was deep. He, on the other hand, vaguely realized that this was the hardest of all wounds to heal. And right now, the strongest emotion he invoked in her was that of pity.

'If you can't forgive me, don't shame me further with your charity... Tara, I'm so sorry, I'm so dreadfully sorry!' he wept openly.

Tara stood very still and the faint rays of the sun made the pallor of her impassive face startling.

Through his tears, Sugriv knew that there was only one thing he could do for Tara now.

'I plead you to forgive me—not because I am worthy of it—not for my sake any more, but for your own,' he said with a ragged breath.

But will she ever forgive me, he wondered, regarding her hard, expressionless face through his tears. Now that the incredible had overwhelmed his consciousness and he had realized that Tara's forgiveness meant the most to him, Sugriv had only one thought, and that was to make her life easier for her by sucking out from her soul the rancour that poisoned it. If he was to die in the coming war, if he could die at peace, it seemed to him that he would die being at peace with himself. He thought now not of himself at all, but only of her.

'Tara, let me be honest just this once. I've been foolish and wicked and hateful. I've been punished terribly—in my mad desire for you, I lost both you and my brother. I gained a crown but I lost everything—even the last vestige of respect! I'm determined to save myself from further hell... Oh Tara, I beseech you to pardon me,' he rasped, his hands folded in a desperate grip, bowing low to slowly sink to his knees. 'I'm so desperately sorry for the wrong I did to you. I regret it so bitterly.'

She still said nothing. She did not seem to hear him at all.

He felt obliged to insist. It seemed to him that her soul was a fluttering moth and its wings were heavy with hatred.

'Oh, my precious, my dear Tara! If you ever liked me—I know you respected me once, and what I did to you was hateful—I beg you to forgive me. Once I am gone from here, I would have no chance to show my repentance. Have mercy on me! I beseech you,' he said, his voice trembling.

She turned and looked at him slowly. Her face was white and set, but the sight of him grovelling at her feet, his eyes tormented, his haggard face as tortured as his soul, made her heart heavy. A lump rose in her throat.

His raw remorse brought gave rise to a sob in her throat. That weak and handsome face was distorted by grief and by the effort in restraining his tears. Tara looked away.

'Tara?' he whispered. 'Please, Tara!'

Has hate made me so heartless? A shadow passed over her wan, hard face. It was less than a movement, and yet it gave the effect of a terrifying convulsion.

Then something heart-wrenching occurred—Sugriv saw two tears run slowly down Tara's pale cheeks. Two little drops that flowed silently, silently towards the dark, eternal sea of darkness, into all that she had seen and suffered... He stopped. He looked at her, breathless, waiting passionately for a reply. He saw that she tried to speak.

'Is it not pitiful that we, in this world of so much pain, should thus torture ourselves?' Tara said under her breath. The tears were now streaming down her pale cheeks.

Sugriv burst into a paroxysm of remorse and relief, burying his face in his hands, his tears seeping through his quivering fingers.

'If desire corrupted your mind, Sugriv, it was anger that corrupted Vali's,' she heard herself say in a resigned voice. 'You say he enjoyed your discomfiture, but it was your forbidden desire that drove him to his irrational anger and turned him into a man he was not, instead of a brother he should have been, replacing all the love and affection with distrust and hate...'

She hesitated. Then speaking slowly, as if to comprehend the words herself, she said, 'I know this now. That Vali became a victim of his own unreasonable fury. He nursed his wrath, the wounds open and festering, making Vali depraved, just as desire did for you. Truly *kama* and *krodh* did you both in,' she whispered huskily, her throat constricting. 'Desire and anger are said to be root of human evil, creating monsters out of man.'

Tara stopped her hot flow of words, pondered long and intently, watching the weeping man, and she thought of herself and Vali, and this man who loved her so strangely. *Vali is dead*, she thought with a soft sob. But through her grief, she found that there was no longer left in her heart any anger against this distraught man who was openly crying at her feet.

Out of their tragedy, she gathered the courage for a desperate resolution. Something seemed to twist her heart, and suddenly she felt exultation, a sense of wonderful freedom... She moved forward slowly, her legs leaden but a skip in her heart. She placed a trembling hand on Sugriv's bowed head, still shaking with tears and remorse.

'You seek forgiveness, Sugriv? I need it myself,' she sighed, lightly touching the bracelet on her right wrist, 'for me to go forward, for us to go forward. We both need it to survive... Forgiveness is too lofty a word, but it is humbling. If you want my forgiveness, I give it, Sugriv. I do forgive you... But what about the regret I feel? I am ashamed for what I did to you and I seek your forgiveness too... Please?'

Sugriv raised a tearful face, his eyes glistening with hope. He caught her hands and buried his face in them. 'Yes, Tara, yes. Release me of this torture!'

She gave a sad shake of her head. 'I have... But I think your path of redemption is only through your humble service to Ram, as mine is to Kishkindh,' she murmured, her eyes misty. 'Kishkindh was our vision. Vali's and mine. Let me, with hope, fulfil our dream...'

The past is finished; let me bury my past, my hate, my anger, she prayed, moving her lips. She was a healer and she hoped with all her heart that she had healed herself; that she had cleansed herself from the corrosive hate and fury and had learnt compassion and tolerance. She could not know what the future held for her, but she felt in herself the strength to accept whatever was to come.

She shook her head and slowly smiled through her tears, feeling the shuddering sorrow Sugriv was grappling with. 'I'm not downhearted, Sugriv. I cannot rage, I cannot resent anymore... If life is about endurance and tolerance, then it's best to endure and tolerate with a smile than a tear,' she sighed, her breath quavering.

To be here in Kishkindh, Tara breathed in a long, content sigh, as the sun shone on them. She divined a scene of such breath-taking loveliness that, briefly, the anguish in her heart was assuaged, all doubts dispelled. All human tribulation seemed to reduce to dust. The sun scattered the mist, and she saw across the ageless river the path of love and loss she had suffered. There was another path, she dimly discerned, that they were to follow—the path that led to peace.

She smiled firmly.

'All I have now is hope and courage. For both of us.'

Epilogue
TARA'S CURSE

He sat down on the grass, leaning his back against the broad-trunked tree, stretching out his legs. *The time has come*. He smiled and closed his tired eyes.

The forest air was still settling into silence—

But for the rustle of a shooting arrow.

Krishna felt a cold swish of air as something hit him. His body arched in agony, his hands clawed at the soft earth and his breath dispelled in a throbbing sigh. The cold ball of pain began to uncoil inside him, rising in his throat, spilling out in a calm, knowing smile. He closed his eyes. *The time has come...*

He opened his eyes and his groping hands closed over the arrow. His hand held it and it seemed to be draining the life out of him. He knew the fatal arrow had a prophetic significance.

Krishna forced a smile through the crashing waves of agonizing pain; those were the frenzied words of a weeping Gandhari heaped on to him at the death of her hundred sons in the battlefield of Kurukshetra. Deaths, she held him morally responsible for.

Through the haze of pain, he saw the figure of a man emerge through the slender trees. It was the hunter whose arrow had hit him.

Krishna's bloodless lips outlined into an eloquent smile. *It's Vali!*

Across the silence of the forest came a faint scraping noise of his footsteps as the hunter slowly approached the prostrate man, blood running down his leg.

'I am Jara!' he cried, his voice trembling with horror and consternation. 'My arrow—' he blurted incoherently, staring at the arrow in puzzlement. It was the one he had made from the piece of metal he had found in a fish, sharp and pointed.

'—was as doomed as me,' Krishna smiled through his pain. 'As cursed,' he gasped.

'It was not meant for you… I am sorry!' Jara cried fearfully, falling at Krishna's feet, imploring for mercy.

Krishna shook his head, grimacing in pain.

'You are Vali,' he whispered, the crashing pain in his impaled foot filled him with a certain peace. 'It is not your fault,' he muttered softly in his kind voice.

He could hear distant words coursing through his numbed mind. *Because you killed Vali while hiding behind a tree, because you shot an arrow on an unarmed, vulnerable person, may you also be killed the same way—helpless and defenceless.*

'Tara's curse.' Krishna smiled as he rolled over on his side, his fingers opening and closing convulsively, his muscles twitching, blood smothering his throat.

'I didn't mean to kill you! Let me help you…' Jara stammered, petrified, his hands clutching Krishna's in bewilderment. They were cold and limp.

'I was waiting for you, Jara,' said Krishna with difficulty, moving his head slightly, his lips stiffening. 'The laws of karma have to be respected,' he gave a short laugh.

Smiling gently, Krishna exhaled his last breath.